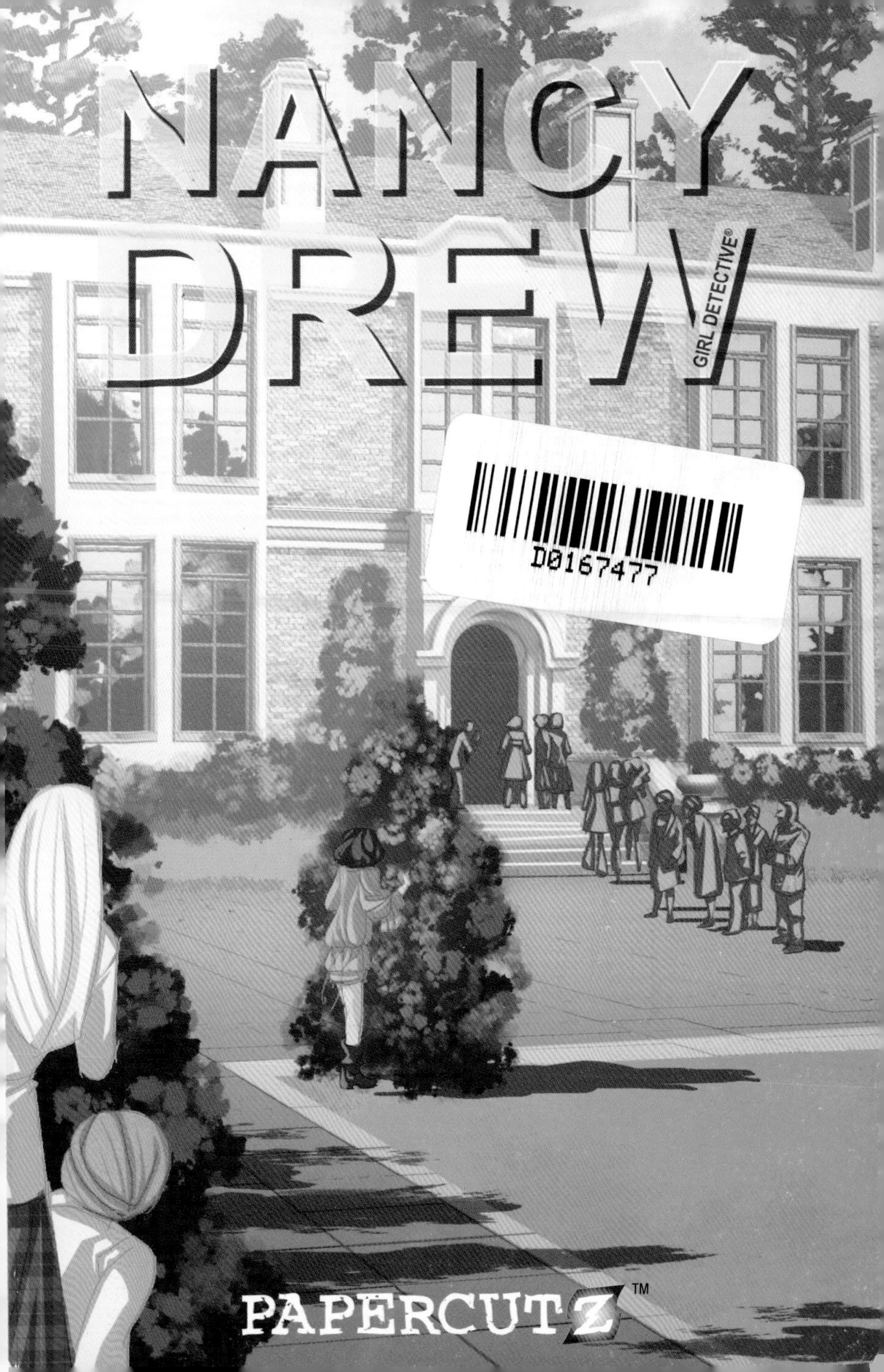
NANCY DREW
GIRL DETECTIVE®
PAPERCUTZ™

#1 "The Demon of River Heights"

#2 "Writ In Stone"

#3 "The Haunted Dollhouse"

#4 "The Girl Who Wasn't There"

#5 "The Fake Heir"

#6 "Mr. Cheeters Is Missing"

#7 "The Charmed Bracelet"

#8 "Global Warning"

#9 "Ghost In The Machinery"

#10 "The Disorient-ed Express"

#11 "Monkey Wrench Blues"

#12 "Dress Reversal"

#13 "Doggone Town"

#14 "Sleight of Dan"

#15 "Tiger Counter"

#16 "What Goes Up..."

#17 "Night of the Living Chatchke"

#18 "City Under the Basement"

#19 "Cliffhanger"

#20 "High School Musical Mystery"

NANCY DREW

GIRL DETECTIVE®

#20 *High School Musical Mystery Part One*

STEFAN PETRUCHA & SARAH KINNEY • Writers
SHO MURASE • Artist
with 3D CG elements and color by CARLOS JOSE GUZMAN
Based on the series by
CAROLYN KEENE

New York

High School Musical Mystery Part One
STEFAN PETRUCHA & SARAH KINNEY – Writers
SHO MURASE – Artist
with 3D CG elements and color by CARLOS JOSE GUZMAN
BRYAN SENKA – Letterer
JUNTO CREATIVE – Production
MICHAEL PETRANEK - Editorial Assistant
JIM SALICRUP
Editor-in-Chief

ISBN: 978-1-59707-178-9 paperback edition
ISBN: 978-1-59707-179-6 hardcover edition

Printed in China.
March 2010 by New Era Printing LTD.
Trend Centre, 29-31 Cheung Lee St.
Rm. 1101-1103, 11/F
Chaiwan, Hong Kong

Distributed by Macmillan.

10   9   8   7   6   5   4   3   2   1

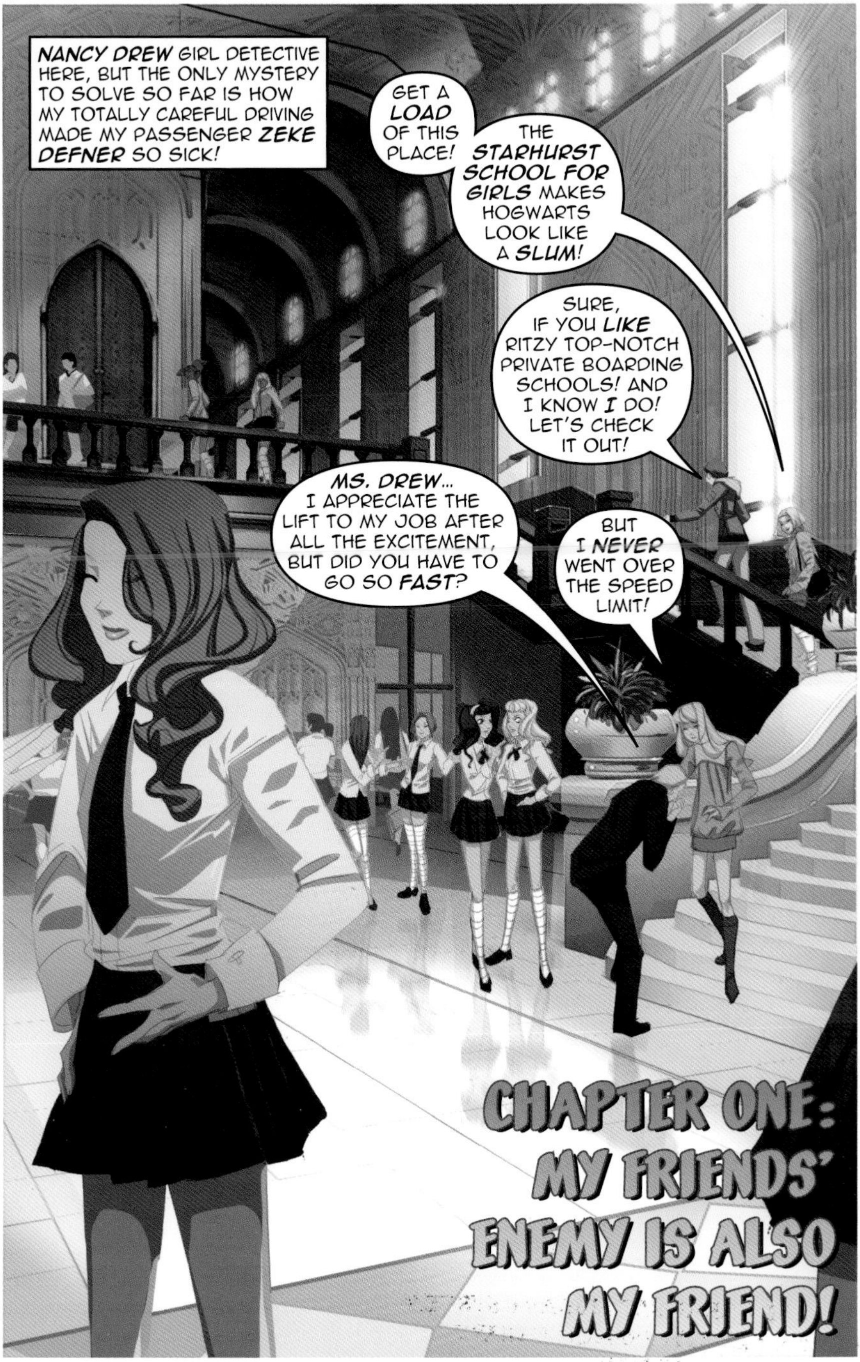
NANCY DREW GIRL DETECTIVE HERE, BUT THE ONLY MYSTERY TO SOLVE SO FAR IS HOW MY TOTALLY CAREFUL DRIVING MADE MY PASSENGER ZEKE DEFNER SO SICK!
GET A LOAD OF THIS PLACE!
THE STARHURST SCHOOL FOR GIRLS MAKES HOGWARTS LOOK LIKE A SLUM!
SURE, IF YOU LIKE RITZY TOP-NOTCH PRIVATE BOARDING SCHOOLS! AND I KNOW I DO! LET'S CHECK IT OUT!
MS. DREW... I APPRECIATE THE LIFT TO MY JOB AFTER ALL THE EXCITEMENT, BUT DID YOU HAVE TO GO SO FAST?
BUT I NEVER WENT OVER THE SPEED LIMIT!
CHAPTER ONE: MY FRIENDS' ENEMY IS ALSO MY FRIEND!

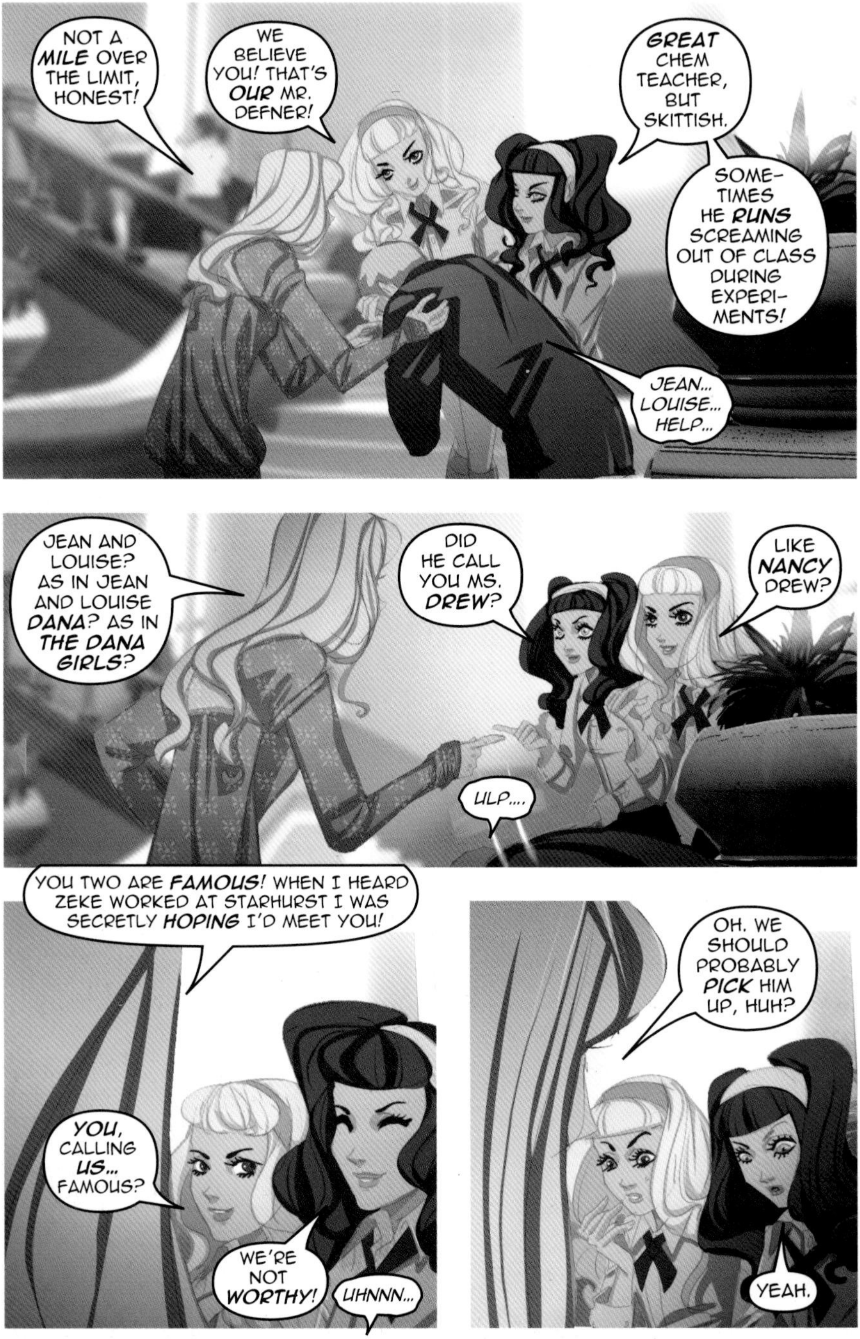
NOT A MILE OVER THE LIMIT, HONEST!
WE BELIEVE YOU! THAT'S OUR MR. DEFNER!
GREAT CHEM TEACHER, BUT SKITTISH.
SOME-TIMES HE RUNS SCREAMING OUT OF CLASS DURING EXPERI-MENTS!
JEAN... LOUISE... HELP...
JEAN AND LOUISE? AS IN JEAN AND LOUISE DANA? AS IN THE DANA GIRLS?
DID HE CALL YOU MS. DREW?
LIKE NANCY DREW?
ULP....
YOU TWO ARE FAMOUS! WHEN I HEARD ZEKE WORKED AT STARHURST I WAS SECRETLY HOPING I'D MEET YOU!
YOU, CALLING US... FAMOUS?
WE'RE NOT WORTHY!
UHNNN...
OH. WE SHOULD PROBABLY PICK HIM UP, HUH?
YEAH.

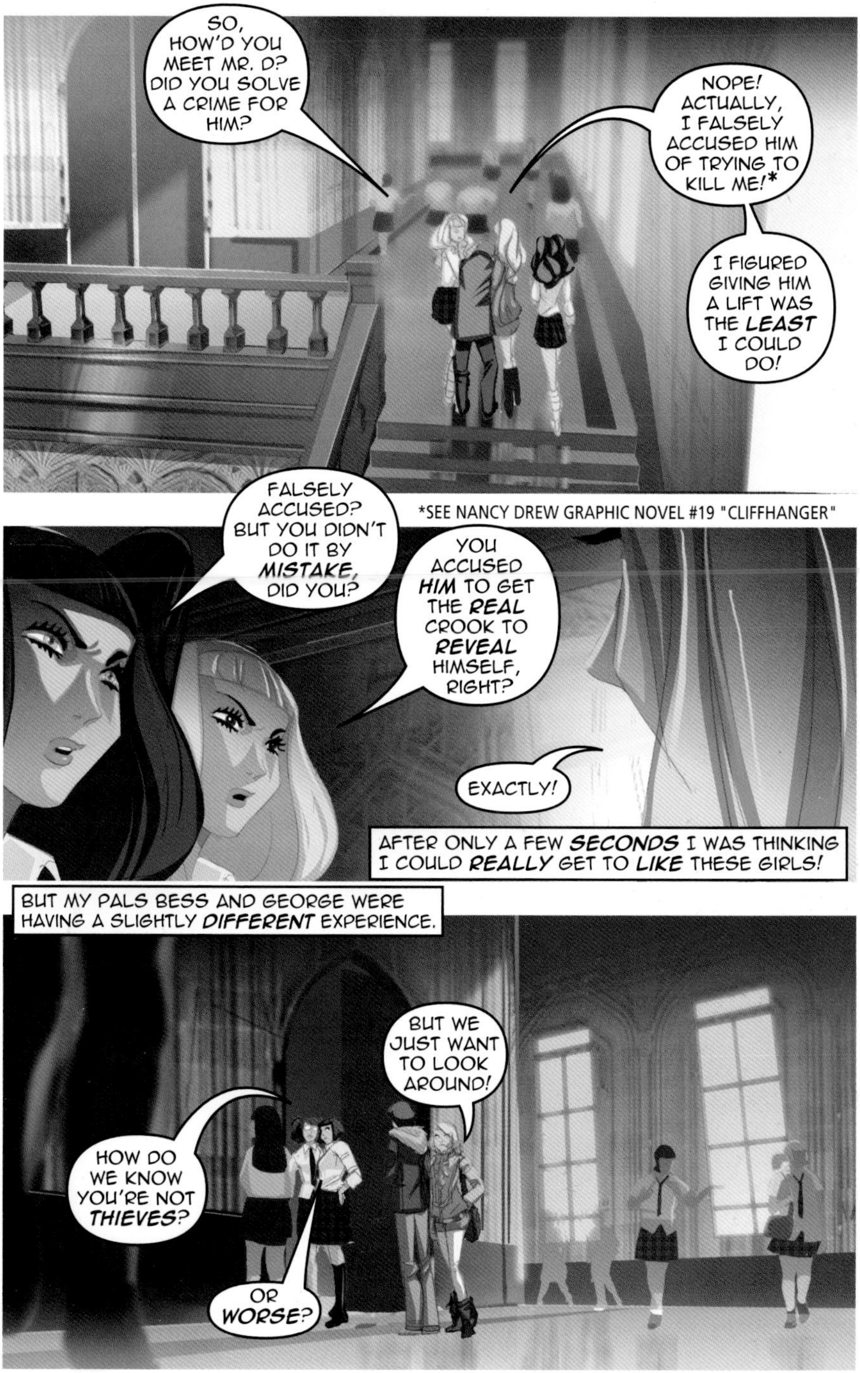
SO, HOW'D YOU MEET MR. D? DID YOU SOLVE A CRIME FOR HIM?
NOPE! ACTUALLY, I FALSELY ACCUSED HIM OF TRYING TO KILL ME!*
I FIGURED GIVING HIM A LIFT WAS THE LEAST I COULD DO!
*SEE NANCY DREW GRAPHIC NOVEL #19 "CLIFFHANGER"
FALSELY ACCUSED? BUT YOU DIDN'T DO IT BY MISTAKE, DID YOU?
YOU ACCUSED HIM TO GET THE REAL CROOK TO REVEAL HIMSELF, RIGHT?
EXACTLY!
AFTER ONLY A FEW SECONDS I WAS THINKING I COULD REALLY GET TO LIKE THESE GIRLS!
BUT MY PALS BESS AND GEORGE WERE HAVING A SLIGHTLY DIFFERENT EXPERIENCE.
BUT WE JUST WANT TO LOOK AROUND!
HOW DO WE KNOW YOU'RE NOT THIEVES?
OR WORSE?

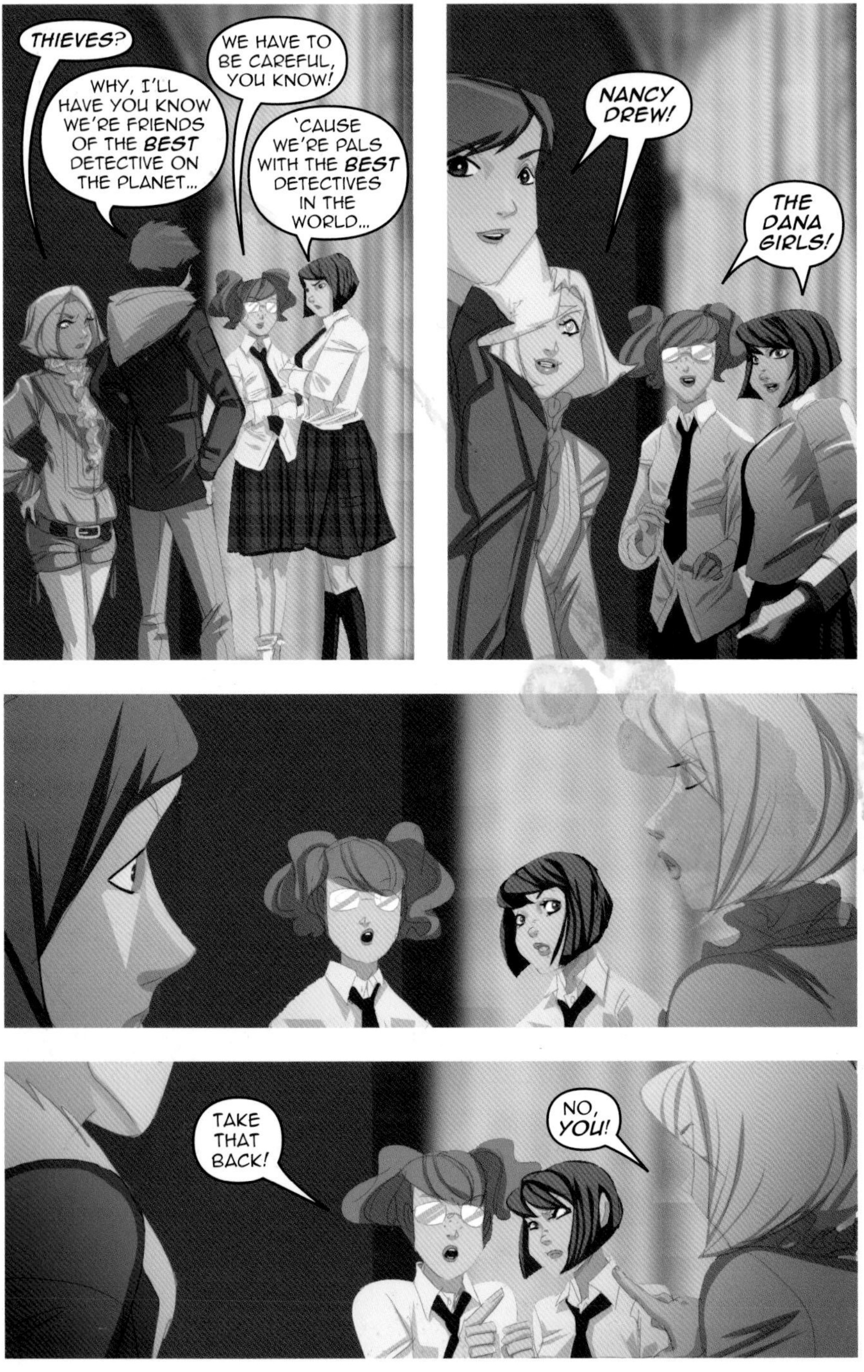
THIEVES?
WHY, I'LL HAVE YOU KNOW WE'RE FRIENDS OF THE BEST DETECTIVE ON THE PLANET...
WE HAVE TO BE CAREFUL, YOU KNOW!
'CAUSE WE'RE PALS WITH THE BEST DETECTIVES IN THE WORLD...
NANCY DREW!
THE DANA GIRLS!
TAKE THAT BACK!
NO, YOU!

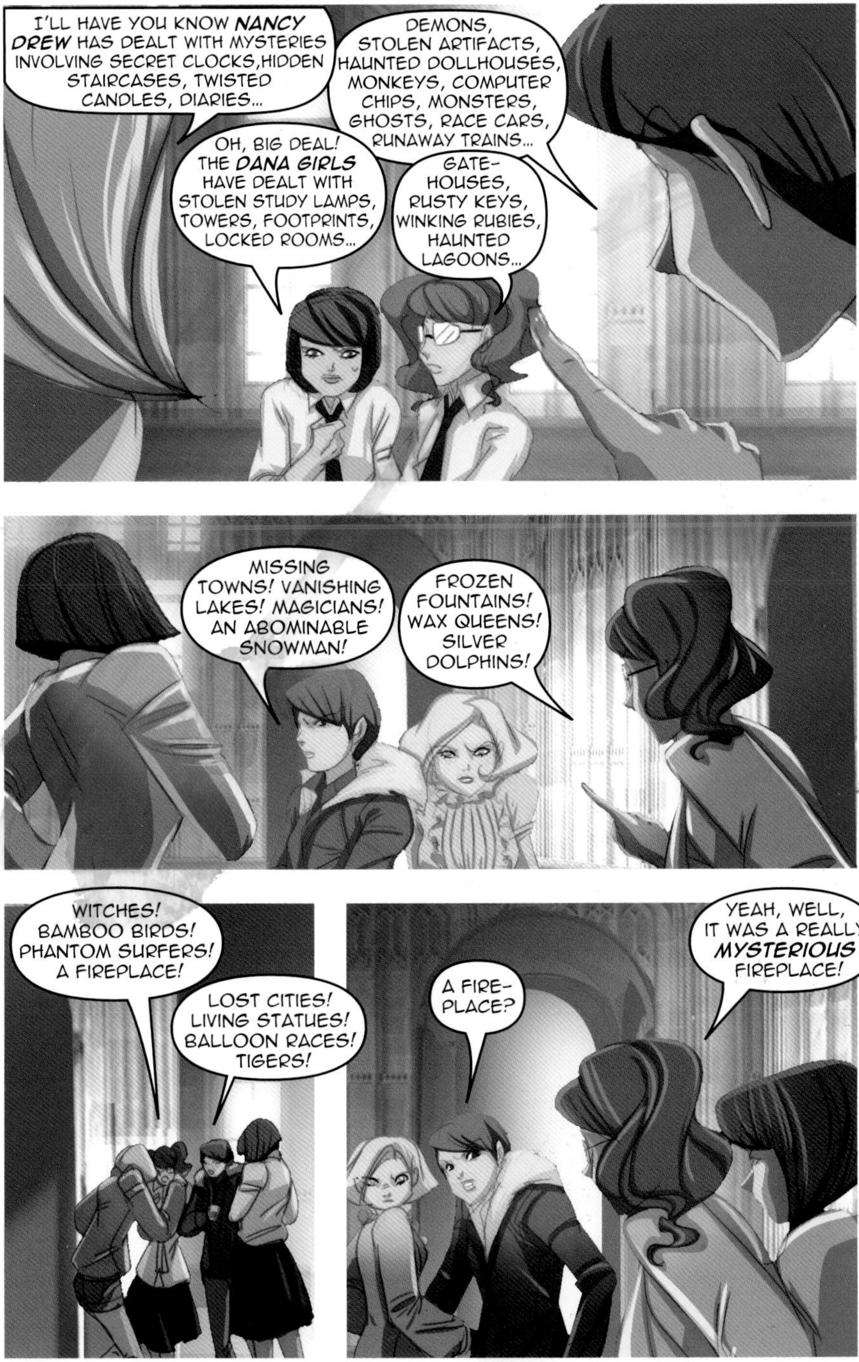
I'LL HAVE YOU KNOW NANCY DREW HAS DEALT WITH MYSTERIES INVOLVING SECRET CLOCKS, HIDDEN STAIRCASES, TWISTED CANDLES, DIARIES...
DEMONS, STOLEN ARTIFACTS, HAUNTED DOLLHOUSES, MONKEYS, COMPUTER CHIPS, MONSTERS, GHOSTS, RACE CARS, RUNAWAY TRAINS...
OH, BIG DEAL! THE DANA GIRLS HAVE DEALT WITH STOLEN STUDY LAMPS, TOWERS, FOOTPRINTS, LOCKED ROOMS...
GATE-HOUSES, RUSTY KEYS, WINKING RUBIES, HAUNTED LAGOONS...
MISSING TOWNS! VANISHING LAKES! MAGICIANS! AN ABOMINABLE SNOWMAN!
FROZEN FOUNTAINS! WAX QUEENS! SILVER DOLPHINS!
WITCHES! BAMBOO BIRDS! PHANTOM SURFERS! A FIREPLACE!
LOST CITIES! LIVING STATUES! BALLOON RACES! TIGERS!
A FIRE-PLACE?
YEAH, WELL, IT WAS A REALLY MYSTERIOUS FIREPLACE!

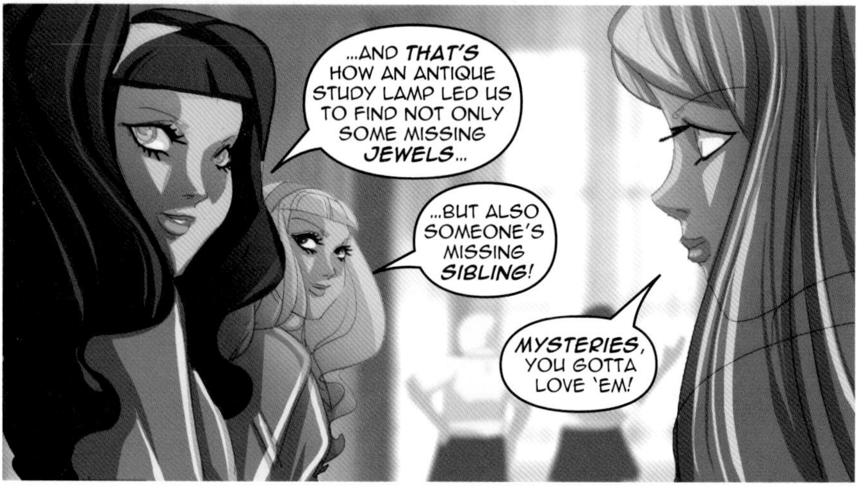
...AND THAT'S HOW AN ANTIQUE STUDY LAMP LED US TO FIND NOT ONLY SOME MISSING JEWELS...
...BUT ALSO SOMEONE'S MISSING SIBLING!
MYSTERIES, YOU GOTTA LOVE 'EM!

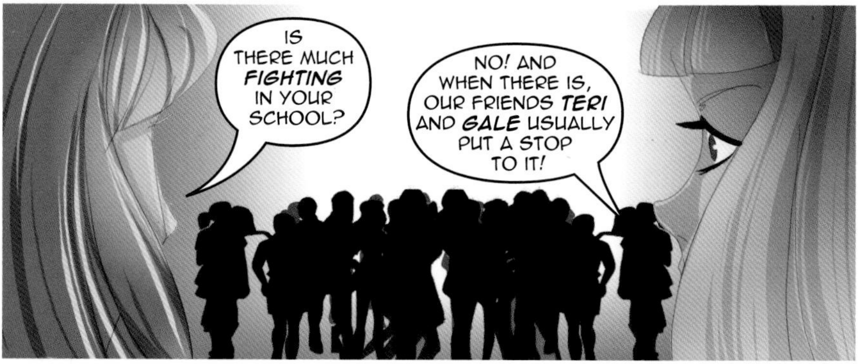
IS THERE MUCH FIGHTING IN YOUR SCHOOL?
NO! AND WHEN THERE IS, OUR FRIENDS TERI AND GALE USUALLY PUT A STOP TO IT!

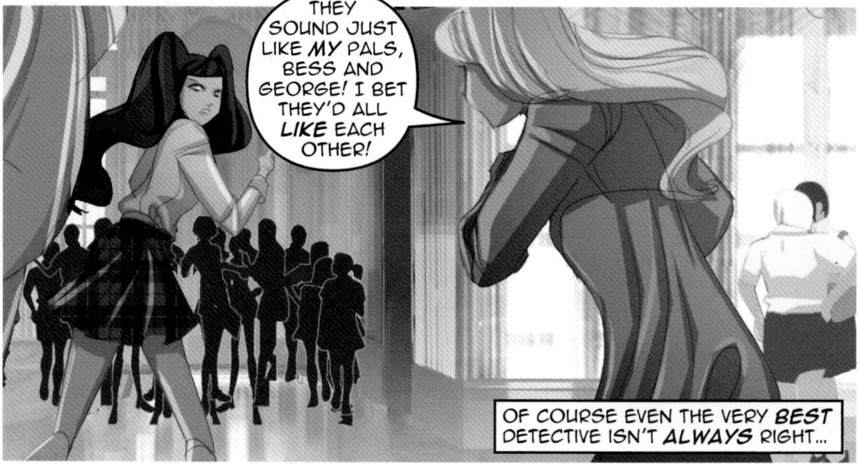
THEY SOUND JUST LIKE MY PALS, BESS AND GEORGE! I BET THEY'D ALL LIKE EACH OTHER!
OF COURSE EVEN THE VERY BEST DETECTIVE ISN'T ALWAYS RIGHT...

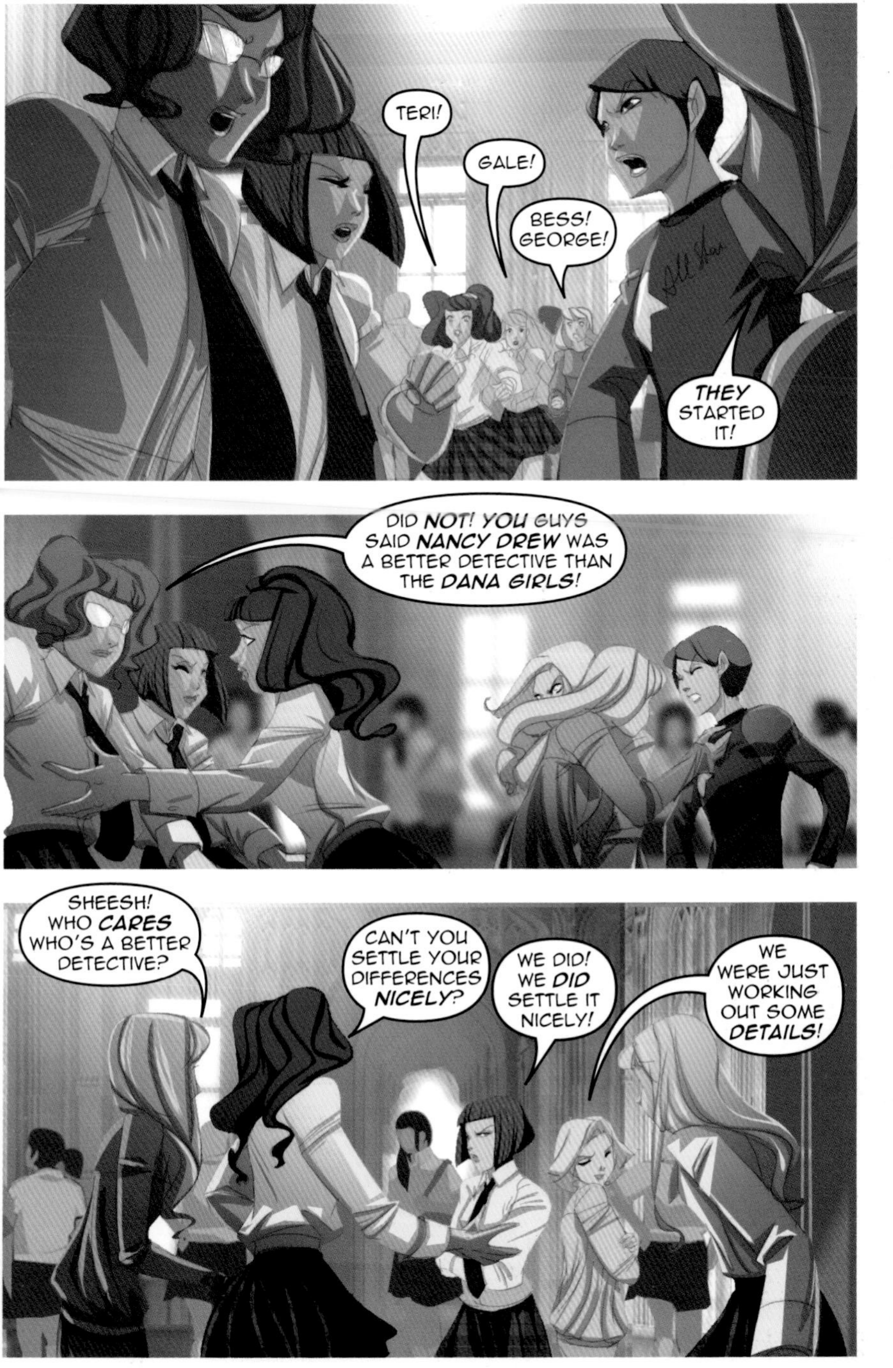
TERI!
GALE!
BESS! GEORGE!
THEY STARTED IT!
DID NOT! YOU GUYS SAID NANCY DREW WAS A BETTER DETECTIVE THAN THE DANA GIRLS!
SHEESH! WHO CARES WHO'S A BETTER DETECTIVE?
CAN'T YOU SETTLE YOUR DIFFERENCES NICELY?
WE DID! WE DID SETTLE IT NICELY!
WE WERE JUST WORKING OUT SOME DETAILS!

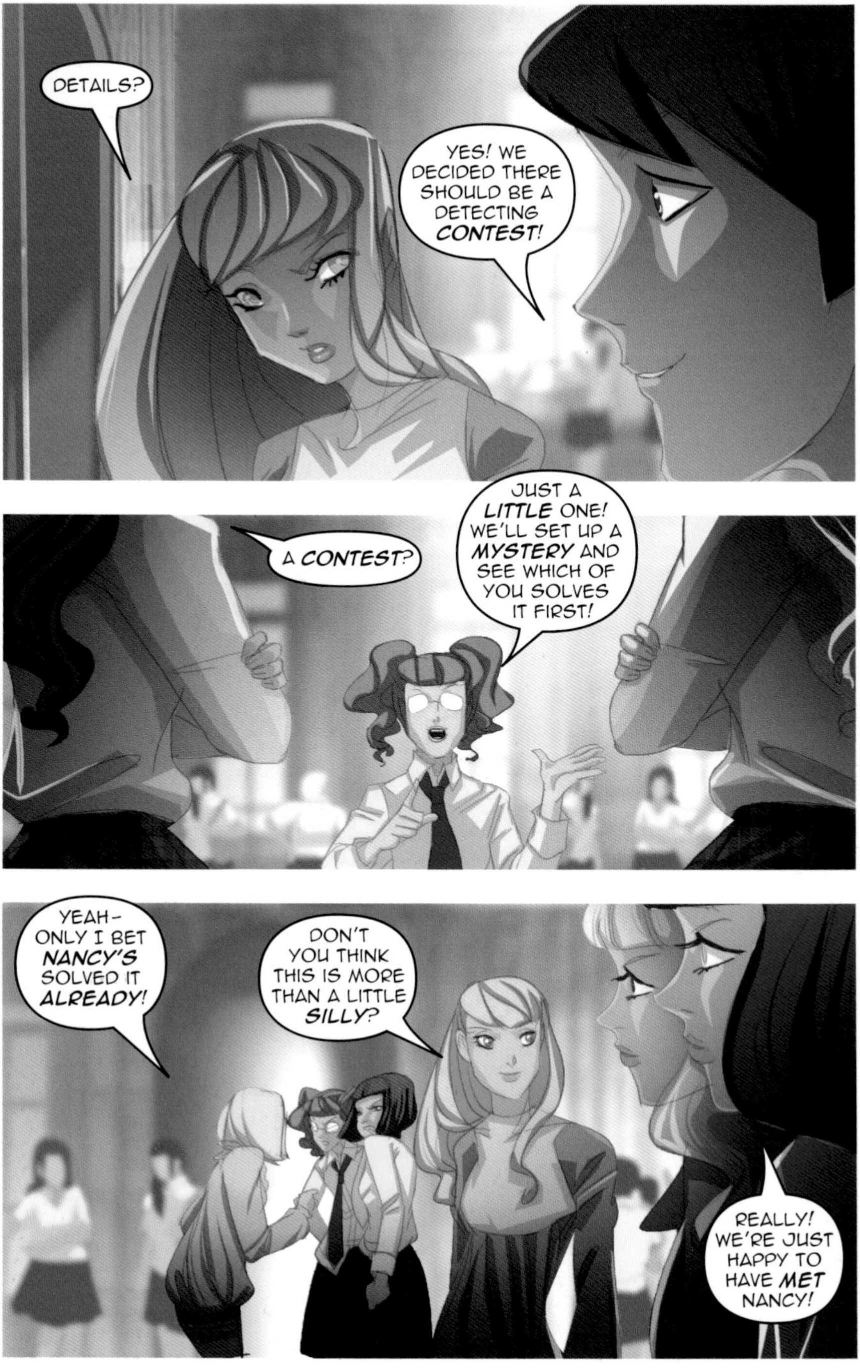
DETAILS?
YES! WE DECIDED THERE SHOULD BE A DETECTING CONTEST!
A CONTEST?
JUST A LITTLE ONE! WE'LL SET UP A MYSTERY AND SEE WHICH OF YOU SOLVES IT FIRST!
YEAH- ONLY I BET NANCY'S SOLVED IT ALREADY!
DON'T YOU THINK THIS IS MORE THAN A LITTLE SILLY?
REALLY! WE'RE JUST HAPPY TO HAVE MET NANCY!

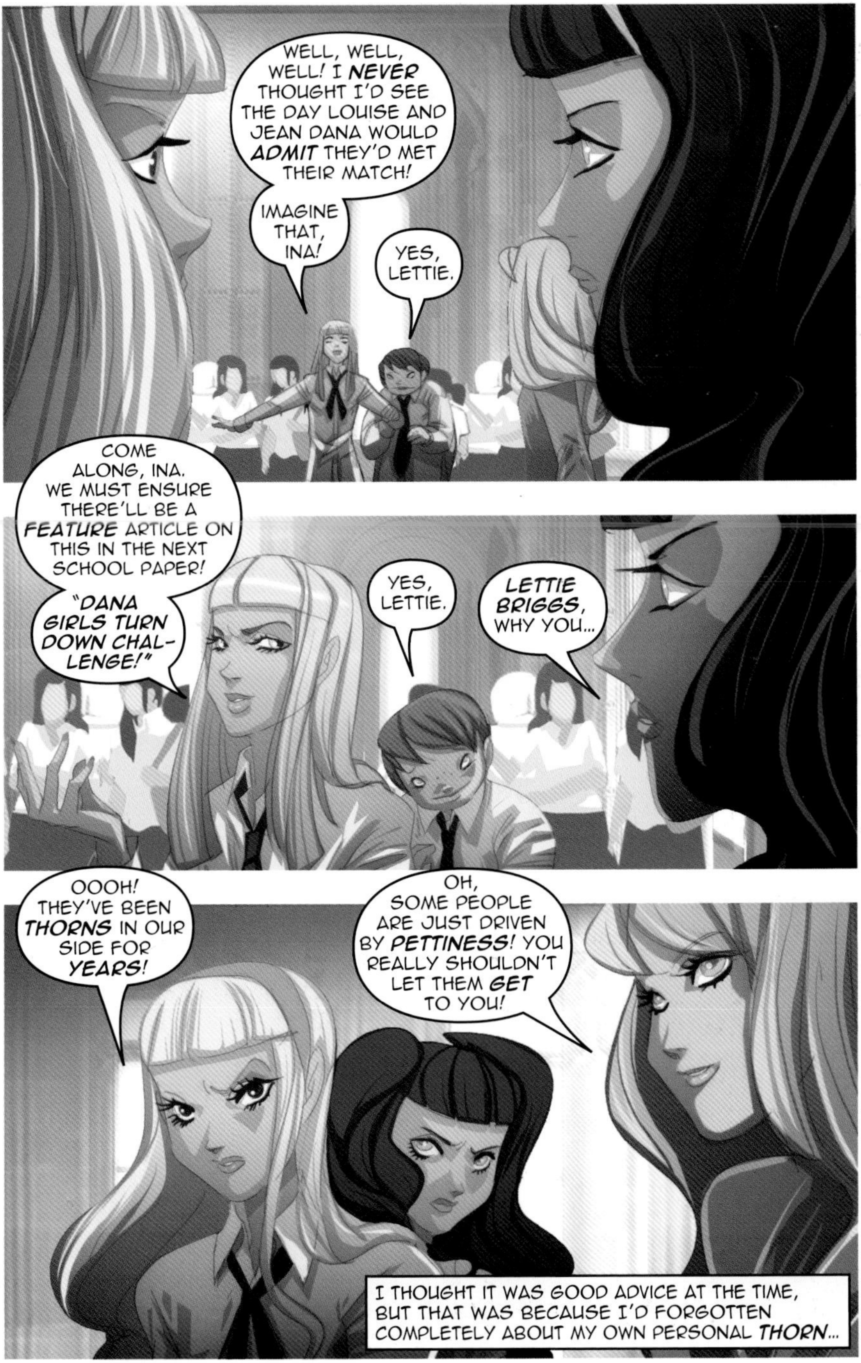
WELL, WELL, WELL! I NEVER THOUGHT I'D SEE THE DAY LOUISE AND JEAN DANA WOULD ADMIT THEY'D MET THEIR MATCH!
IMAGINE THAT, INA!
YES, LETTIE.
COME ALONG, INA. WE MUST ENSURE THERE'LL BE A FEATURE ARTICLE ON THIS IN THE NEXT SCHOOL PAPER!
"DANA GIRLS TURN DOWN CHAL-LENGE!"
YES, LETTIE.
LETTIE BRIGGS, WHY YOU...
OOOH! THEY'VE BEEN THORNS IN OUR SIDE FOR YEARS!
OH, SOME PEOPLE ARE JUST DRIVEN BY PETTINESS! YOU REALLY SHOULDN'T LET THEM GET TO YOU!
I THOUGHT IT WAS GOOD ADVICE AT THE TIME, BUT THAT WAS BECAUSE I'D FORGOTTEN COMPLETELY ABOUT MY OWN PERSONAL THORN...

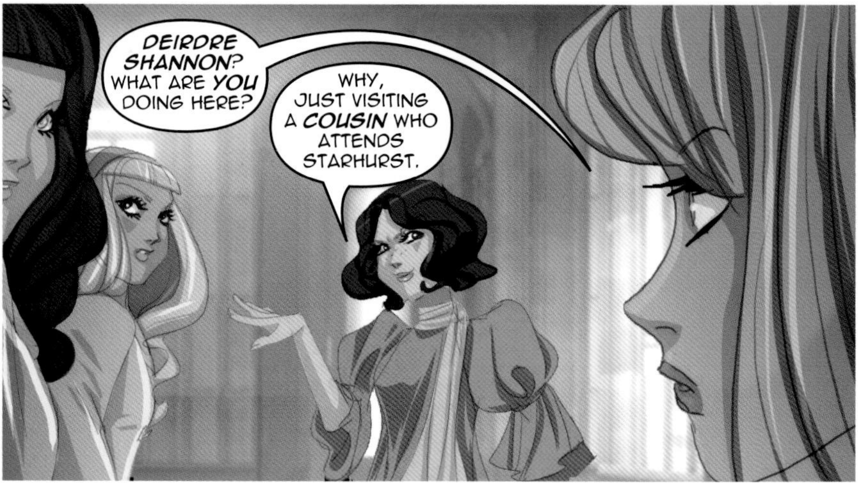
DEIRDRE SHANNON? WHAT ARE YOU DOING HERE?
WHY, JUST VISITING A COUSIN WHO ATTENDS STARHURST.

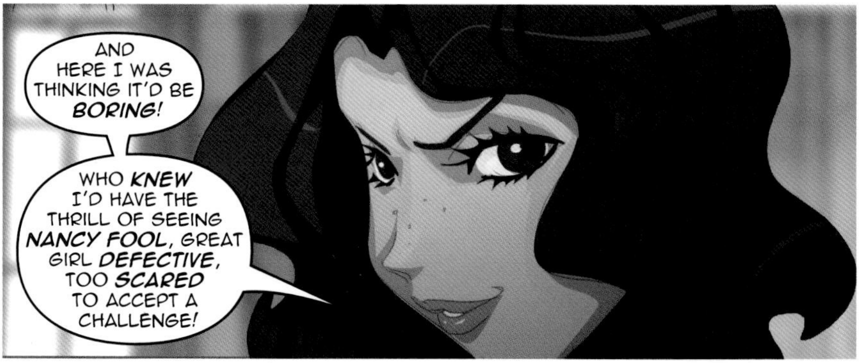
AND HERE I WAS THINKING IT'D BE BORING!
WHO KNEW I'D HAVE THE THRILL OF SEEING NANCY FOOL, GREAT GIRL DEFECTIVE, TOO SCARED TO ACCEPT A CHALLENGE!

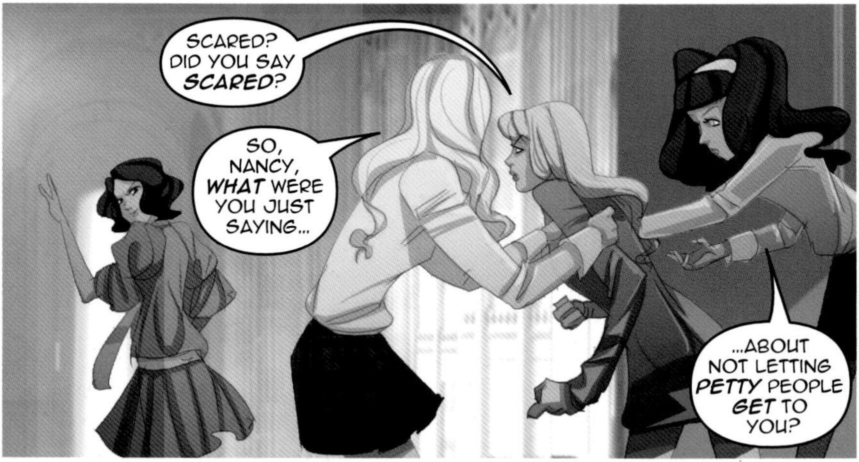
SCARED? DID YOU SAY SCARED?
SO, NANCY, WHAT WERE YOU JUST SAYING...
...ABOUT NOT LETTING PETTY PEOPLE GET TO YOU?

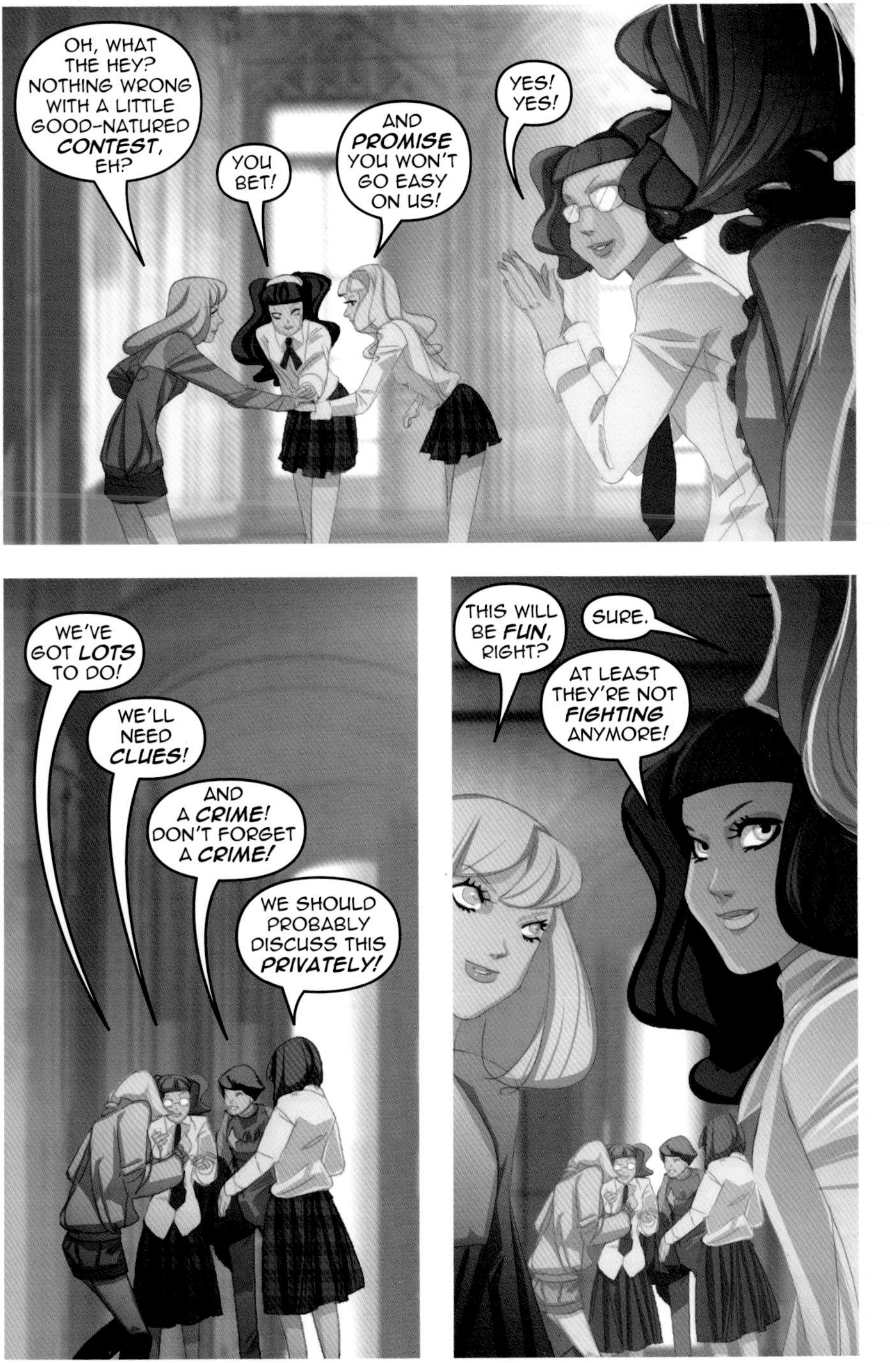
OH, WHAT THE HEY? NOTHING WRONG WITH A LITTLE GOOD-NATURED *CONTEST*, EH?
YOU BET!
AND *PROMISE* YOU WON'T GO EASY ON US!
YES! YES!
WE'VE GOT *LOTS* TO DO!
WE'LL NEED *CLUES*!
AND A *CRIME*! DON'T FORGET A *CRIME*!
WE SHOULD PROBABLY DISCUSS THIS *PRIVATELY*!
THIS WILL BE *FUN*, RIGHT?
SURE.
AT LEAST THEY'RE NOT *FIGHTING* ANYMORE!

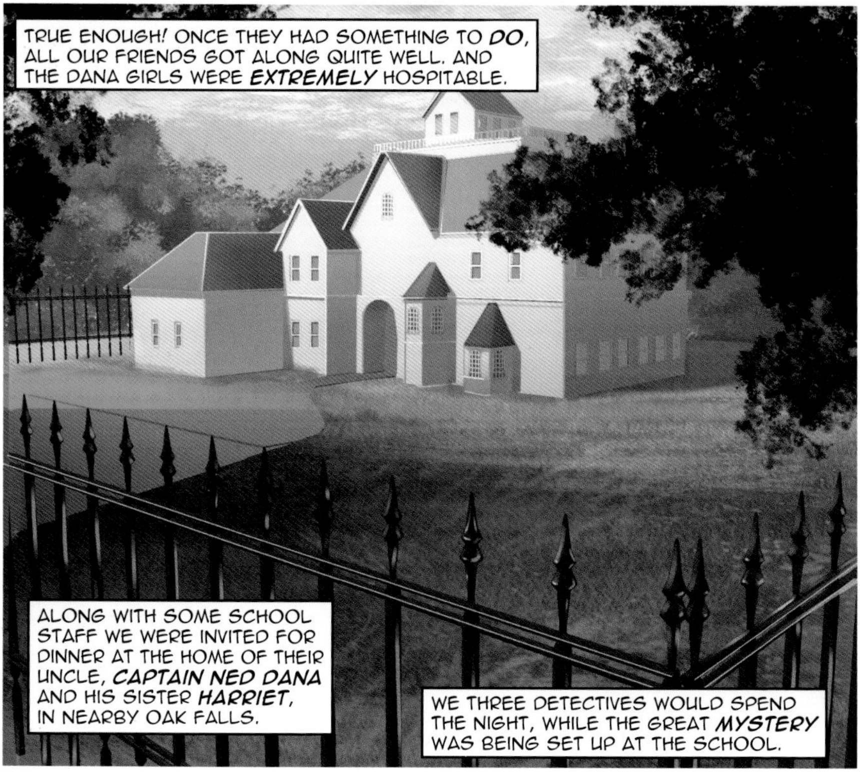
TRUE ENOUGH! ONCE THEY HAD SOMETHING TO DO, ALL OUR FRIENDS GOT ALONG QUITE WELL. AND THE DANA GIRLS WERE EXTREMELY HOSPITABLE.
ALONG WITH SOME SCHOOL STAFF WE WERE INVITED FOR DINNER AT THE HOME OF THEIR UNCLE, CAPTAIN NED DANA AND HIS SISTER HARRIET, IN NEARBY OAK FALLS.
WE THREE DETECTIVES WOULD SPEND THE NIGHT, WHILE THE GREAT MYSTERY WAS BEING SET UP AT THE SCHOOL.

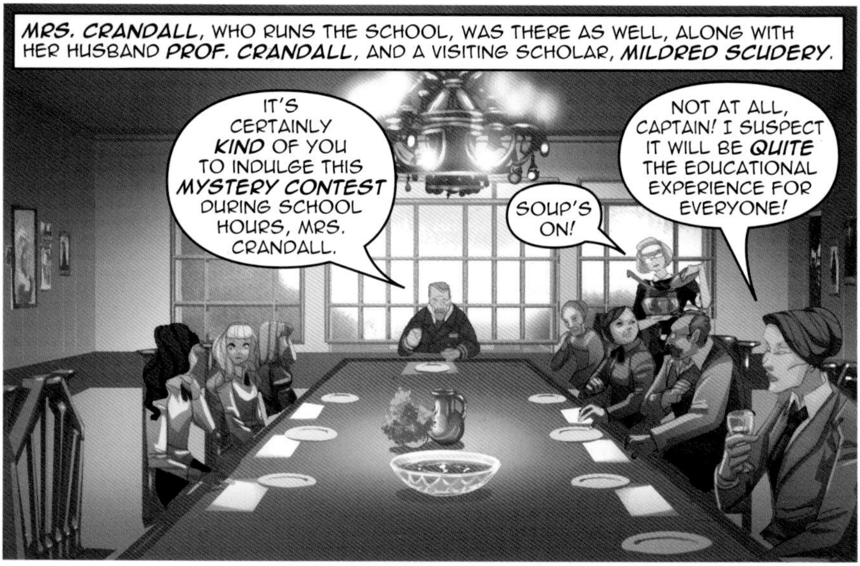
MRS. CRANDALL, WHO RUNS THE SCHOOL, WAS THERE AS WELL, ALONG WITH HER HUSBAND PROF. CRANDALL, AND A VISITING SCHOLAR, MILDRED SCUDERY.
IT'S CERTAINLY KIND OF YOU TO INDULGE THIS MYSTERY CONTEST DURING SCHOOL HOURS, MRS. CRANDALL.
SOUP'S ON!
NOT AT ALL, CAPTAIN! I SUSPECT IT WILL BE QUITE THE EDUCATIONAL EXPERIENCE FOR EVERYONE!

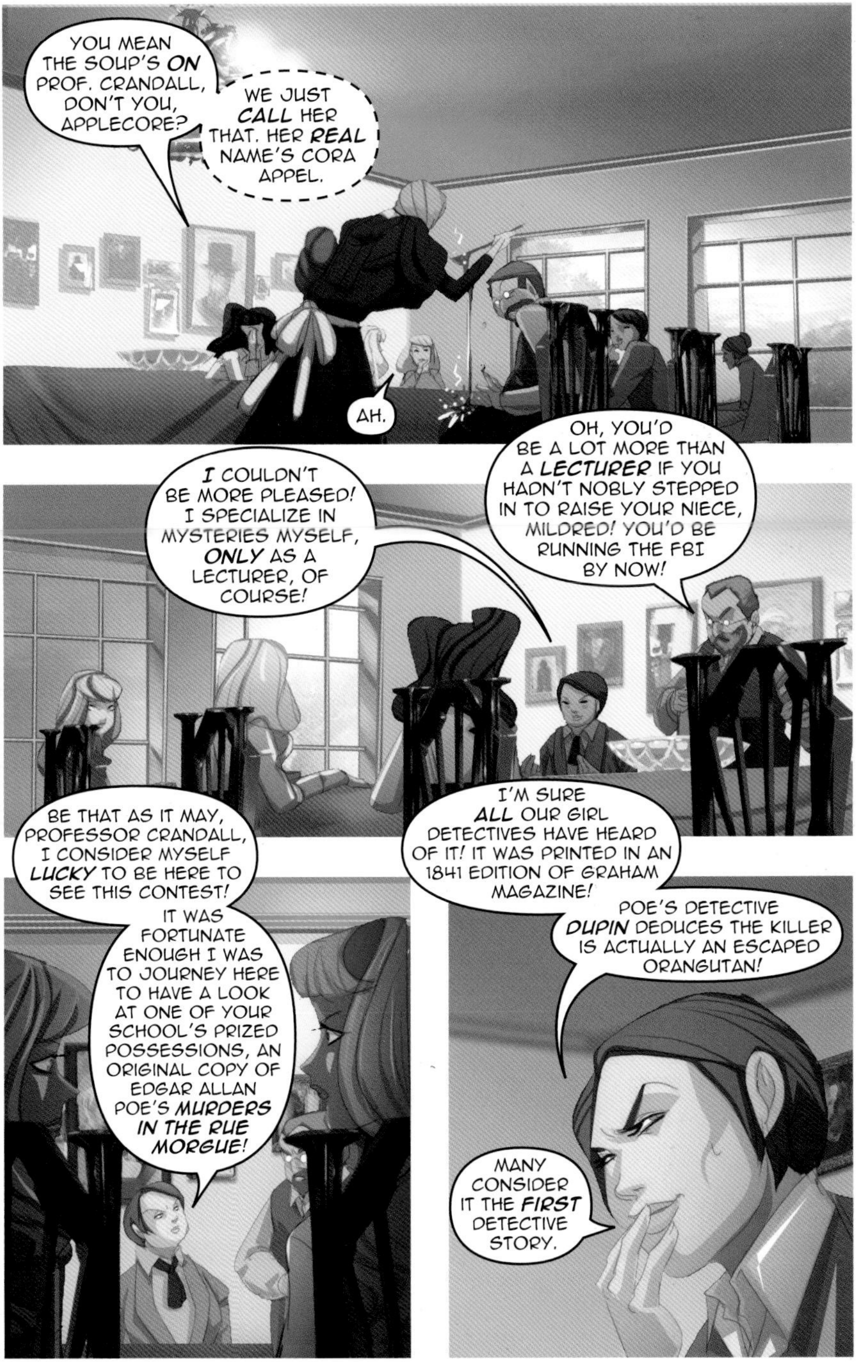
YOU MEAN THE SOUP'S ON PROF. CRANDALL, DON'T YOU, APPLECORE?
WE JUST CALL HER THAT. HER REAL NAME'S CORA APPEL.
AH.
I COULDN'T BE MORE PLEASED! I SPECIALIZE IN MYSTERIES MYSELF, ONLY AS A LECTURER, OF COURSE!
OH, YOU'D BE A LOT MORE THAN A LECTURER IF YOU HADN'T NOBLY STEPPED IN TO RAISE YOUR NIECE, MILDRED! YOU'D BE RUNNING THE FBI BY NOW!
BE THAT AS IT MAY, PROFESSOR CRANDALL, I CONSIDER MYSELF LUCKY TO BE HERE TO SEE THIS CONTEST!
IT WAS FORTUNATE ENOUGH I WAS TO JOURNEY HERE TO HAVE A LOOK AT ONE OF YOUR SCHOOL'S PRIZED POSSESSIONS, AN ORIGINAL COPY OF EDGAR ALLAN POE'S MURDERS IN THE RUE MORGUE!
I'M SURE ALL OUR GIRL DETECTIVES HAVE HEARD OF IT! IT WAS PRINTED IN AN 1841 EDITION OF GRAHAM MAGAZINE!
POE'S DETECTIVE DUPIN DEDUCES THE KILLER IS ACTUALLY AN ESCAPED ORANGUTAN!
MANY CONSIDER IT THE FIRST DETECTIVE STORY.

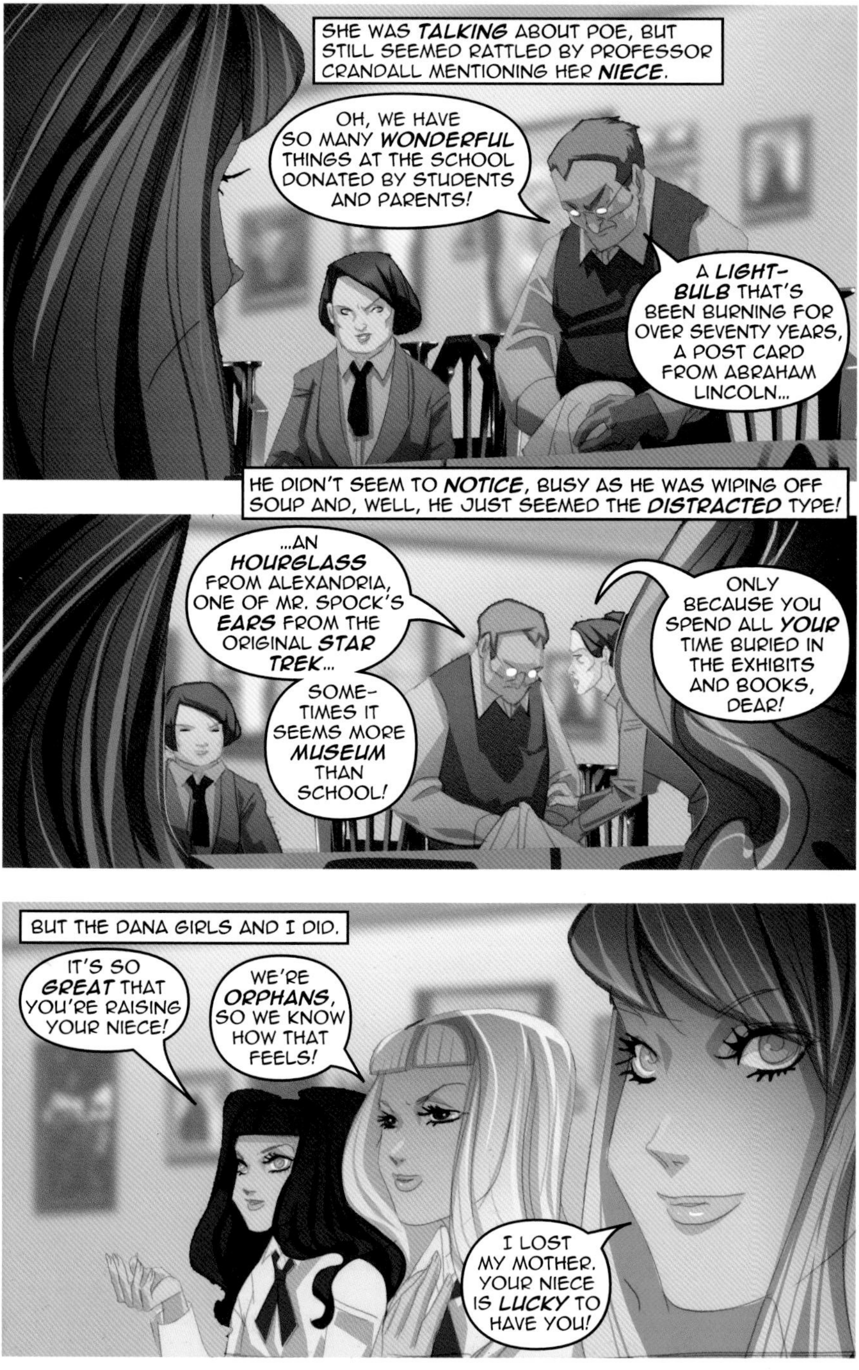

SHE WAS TALKING ABOUT POE, BUT STILL SEEMED RATTLED BY PROFESSOR CRANDALL MENTIONING HER NIECE.
OH, WE HAVE SO MANY WONDERFUL THINGS AT THE SCHOOL DONATED BY STUDENTS AND PARENTS!
A LIGHT-BULB THAT'S BEEN BURNING FOR OVER SEVENTY YEARS, A POST CARD FROM ABRAHAM LINCOLN...
HE DIDN'T SEEM TO NOTICE, BUSY AS HE WAS WIPING OFF SOUP AND, WELL, HE JUST SEEMED THE DISTRACTED TYPE!
...AN HOURGLASS FROM ALEXANDRIA, ONE OF MR. SPOCK'S EARS FROM THE ORIGINAL STAR TREK...
SOME-TIMES IT SEEMS MORE MUSEUM THAN SCHOOL!
ONLY BECAUSE YOU SPEND ALL YOUR TIME BURIED IN THE EXHIBITS AND BOOKS, DEAR!
BUT THE DANA GIRLS AND I DID.
IT'S SO GREAT THAT YOU'RE RAISING YOUR NIECE!
WE'RE ORPHANS, SO WE KNOW HOW THAT FEELS!
I LOST MY MOTHER. YOUR NIECE IS LUCKY TO HAVE YOU!

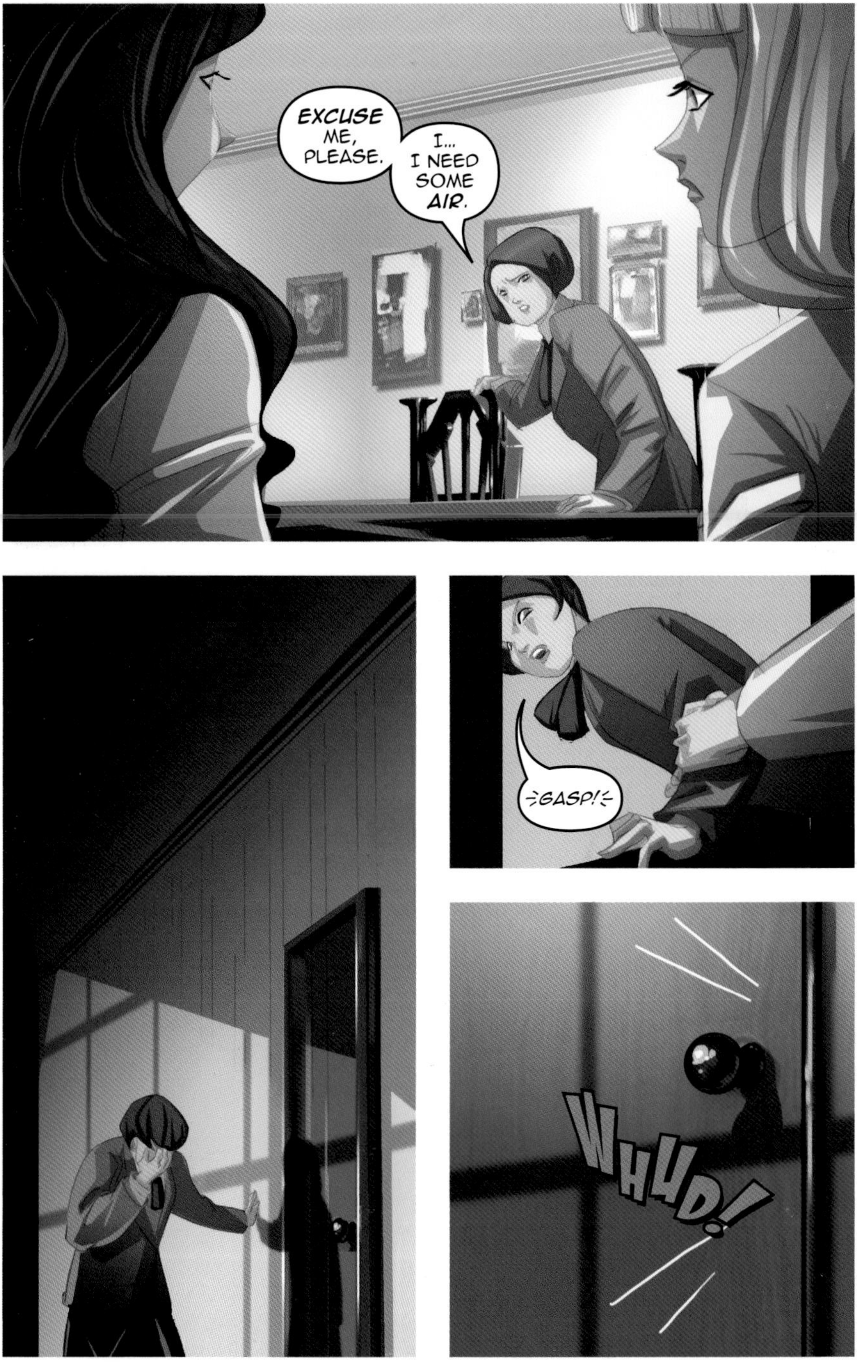
EXCUSE ME, PLEASE.
I... I NEED SOME AIR.
GASP!
WHUD!

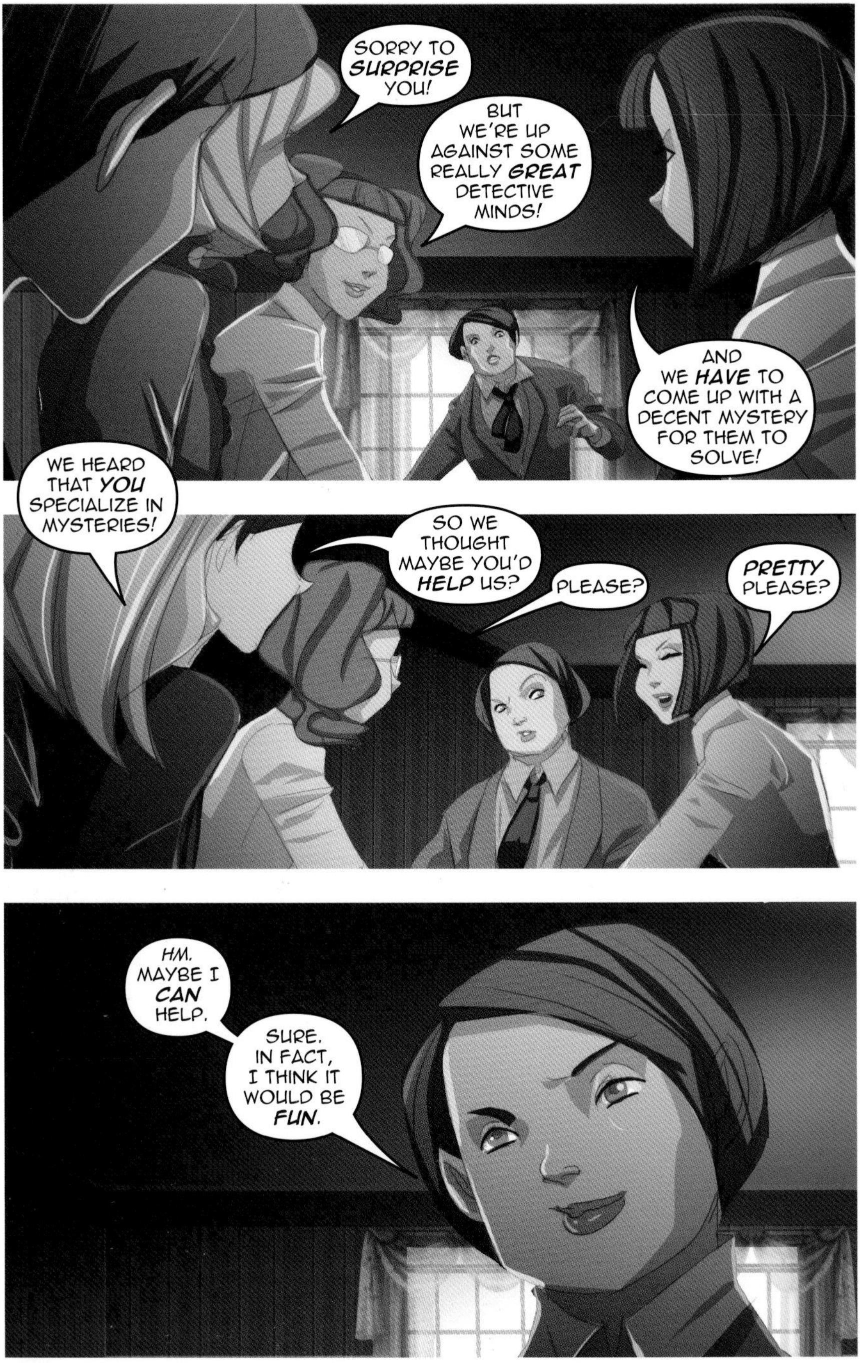
SORRY TO **SURPRISE** YOU!
BUT WE'RE UP AGAINST SOME REALLY **GREAT** DETECTIVE MINDS!
AND WE **HAVE** TO COME UP WITH A DECENT MYSTERY FOR THEM TO SOLVE!
WE HEARD THAT **YOU** SPECIALIZE IN MYSTERIES!
SO WE THOUGHT MAYBE YOU'D **HELP** US?
PLEASE?
PRETTY PLEASE?
HM. MAYBE I **CAN** HELP.
SURE. IN FACT, I THINK IT WOULD BE **FUN**.

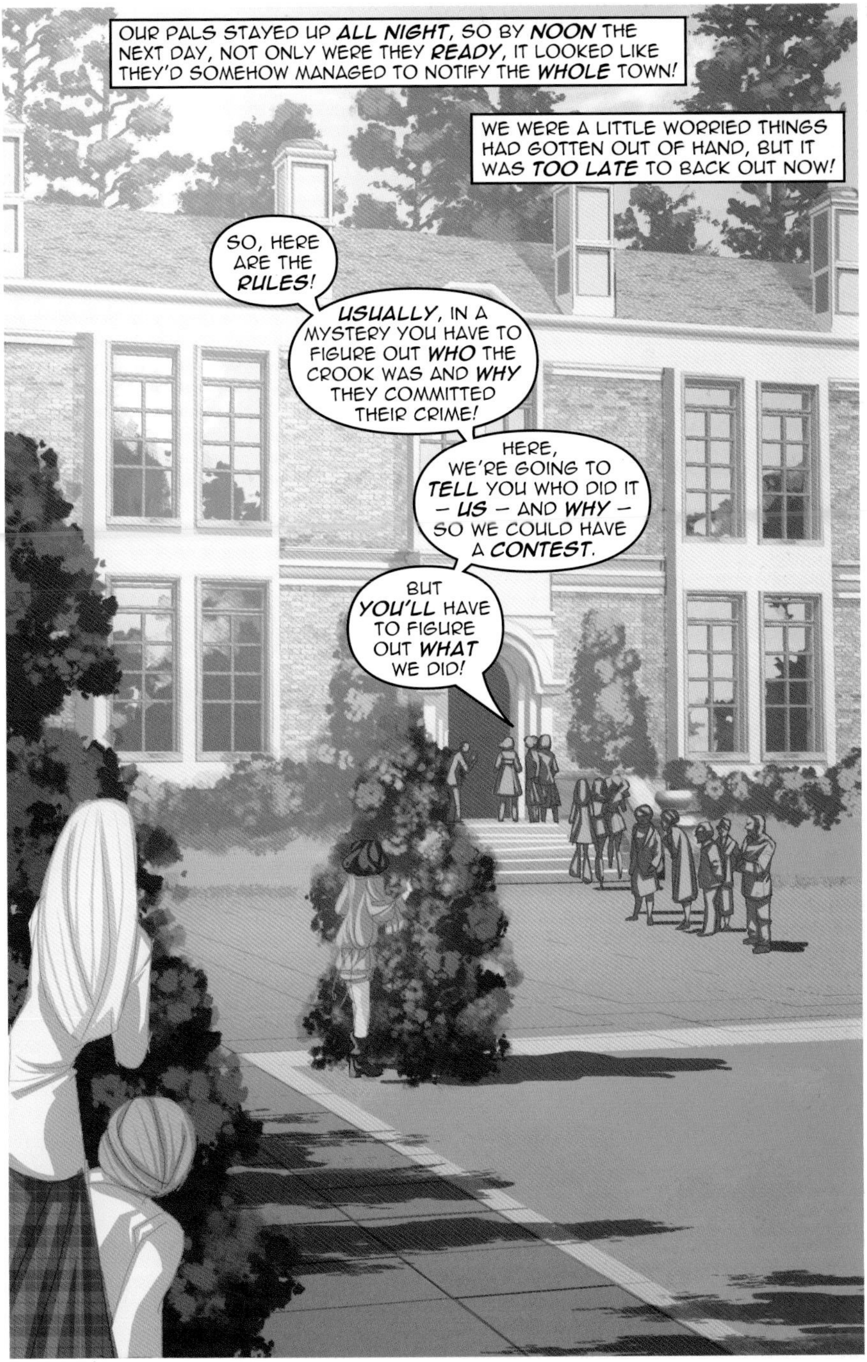
OUR PALS STAYED UP ALL NIGHT, SO BY NOON THE NEXT DAY, NOT ONLY WERE THEY READY, IT LOOKED LIKE THEY'D SOMEHOW MANAGED TO NOTIFY THE WHOLE TOWN!
WE WERE A LITTLE WORRIED THINGS HAD GOTTEN OUT OF HAND, BUT IT WAS TOO LATE TO BACK OUT NOW!
SO, HERE ARE THE RULES!
USUALLY, IN A MYSTERY YOU HAVE TO FIGURE OUT WHO THE CROOK WAS AND WHY THEY COMMITTED THEIR CRIME!
HERE, WE'RE GOING TO TELL YOU WHO DID IT – US – AND WHY – SO WE COULD HAVE A CONTEST.
BUT YOU'LL HAVE TO FIGURE OUT WHAT WE DID!

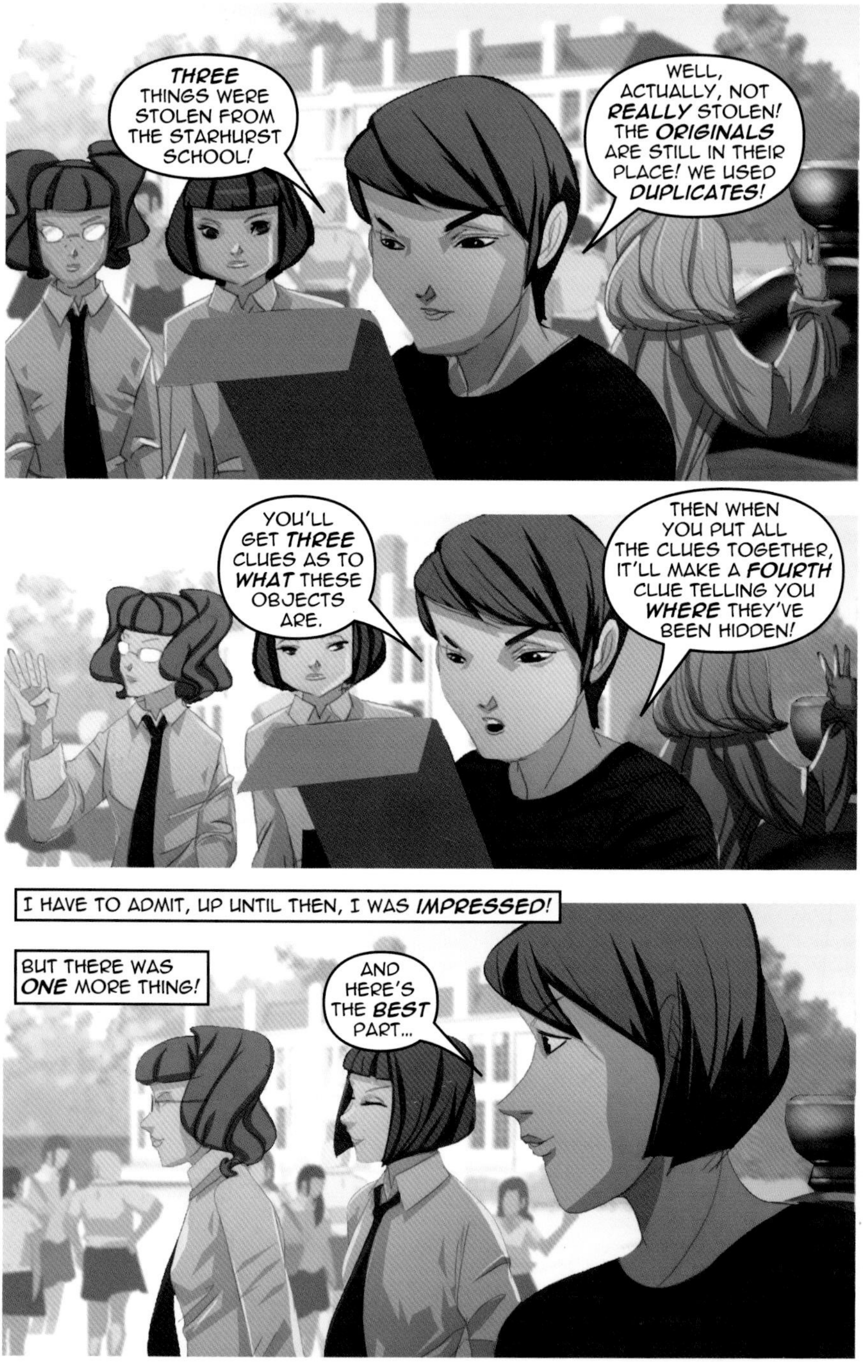
THREE THINGS WERE STOLEN FROM THE STARHURST SCHOOL!
WELL, ACTUALLY, NOT REALLY STOLEN! THE ORIGINALS ARE STILL IN THEIR PLACE! WE USED DUPLICATES!
YOU'LL GET THREE CLUES AS TO WHAT THESE OBJECTS ARE.
THEN WHEN YOU PUT ALL THE CLUES TOGETHER, IT'LL MAKE A FOURTH CLUE TELLING YOU WHERE THEY'VE BEEN HIDDEN!
I HAVE TO ADMIT, UP UNTIL THEN, I WAS IMPRESSED!
BUT THERE WAS ONE MORE THING!
AND HERE'S THE BEST PART...

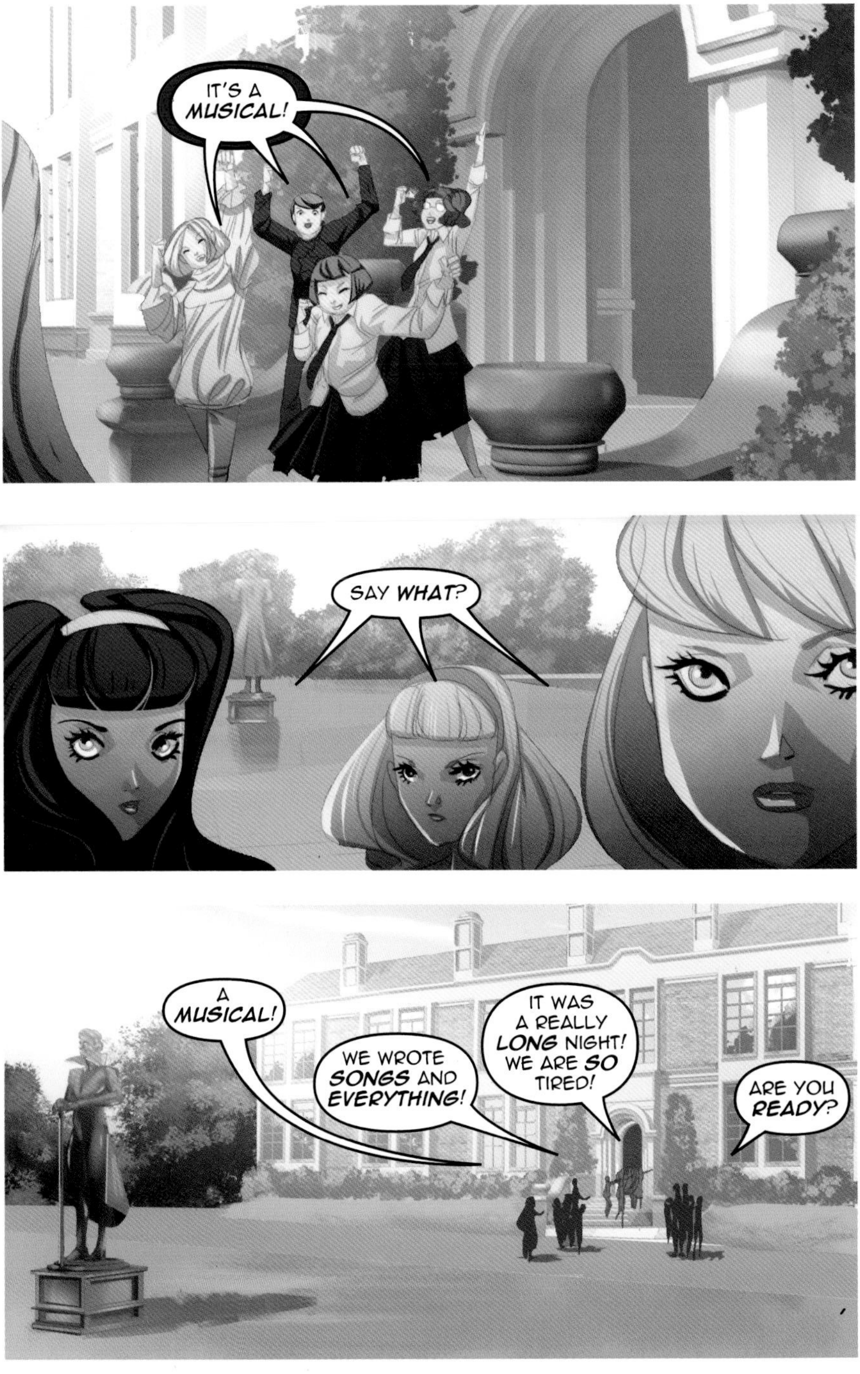
IT'S A MUSICAL!
SAY WHAT?
A MUSICAL!
WE WROTE SONGS AND EVERYTHING!
IT WAS A REALLY LONG NIGHT! WE ARE SO TIRED!
ARE YOU READY?

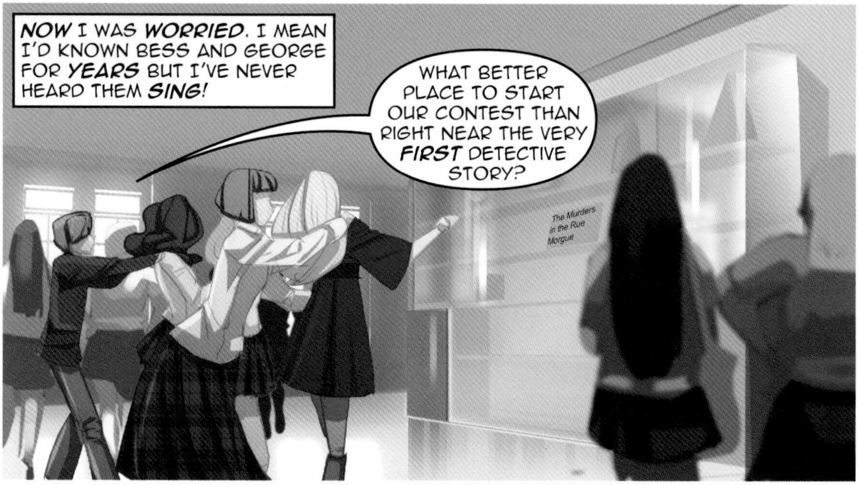
NOW I WAS WORRIED. I MEAN I'D KNOWN BESS AND GEORGE FOR YEARS BUT I'VE NEVER HEARD THEM SING!
WHAT BETTER PLACE TO START OUR CONTEST THAN RIGHT NEAR THE VERY FIRST DETECTIVE STORY?
The Murders in the Rue Morgue

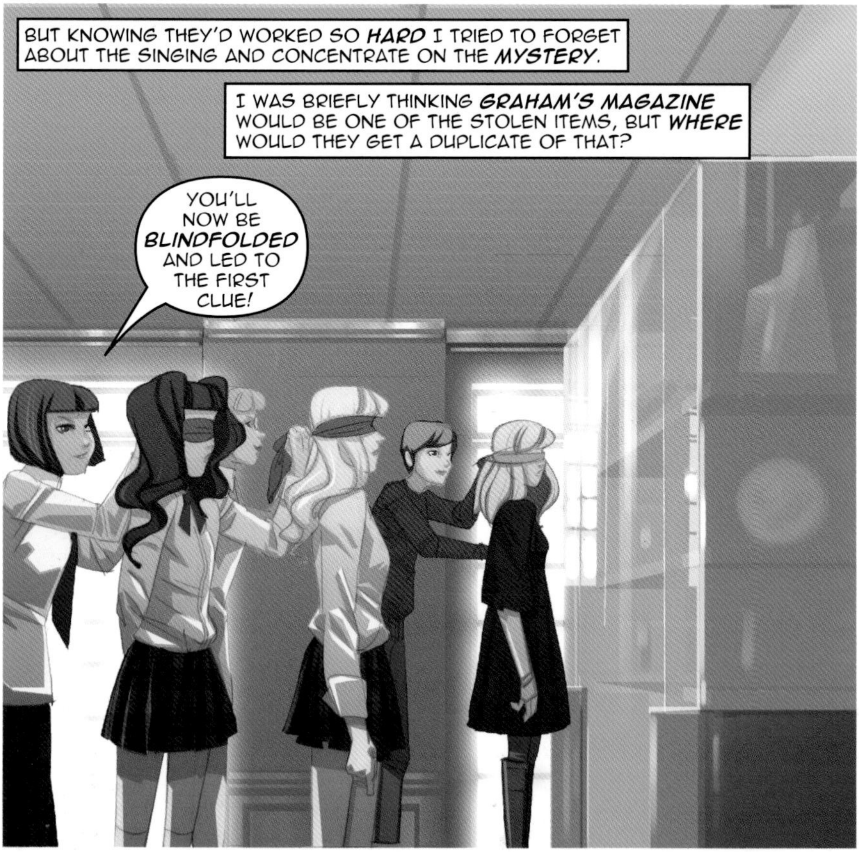
BUT KNOWING THEY'D WORKED SO HARD I TRIED TO FORGET ABOUT THE SINGING AND CONCENTRATE ON THE MYSTERY.
I WAS BRIEFLY THINKING GRAHAM'S MAGAZINE WOULD BE ONE OF THE STOLEN ITEMS, BUT WHERE WOULD THEY GET A DUPLICATE OF THAT?
YOU'LL NOW BE BLINDFOLDED AND LED TO THE FIRST CLUE!

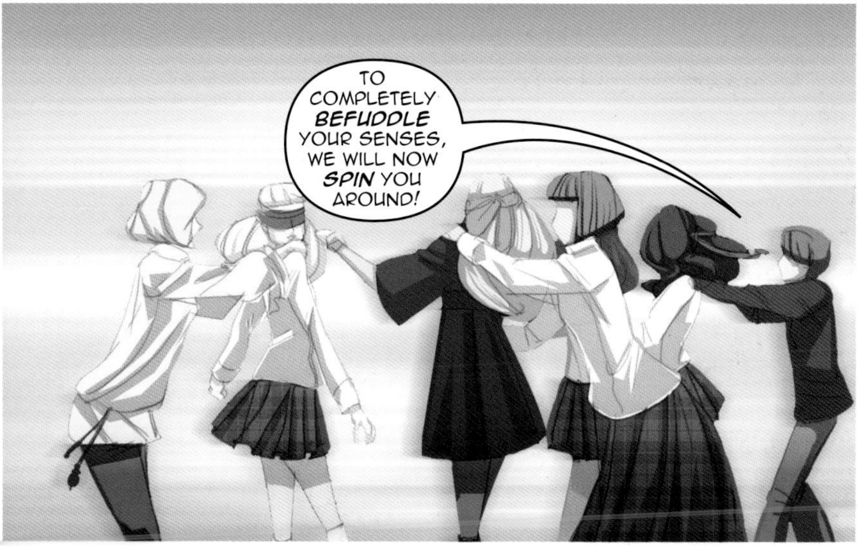
TO COMPLETELY BEFUDDLE YOUR SENSES, WE WILL NOW SPIN YOU AROUND!

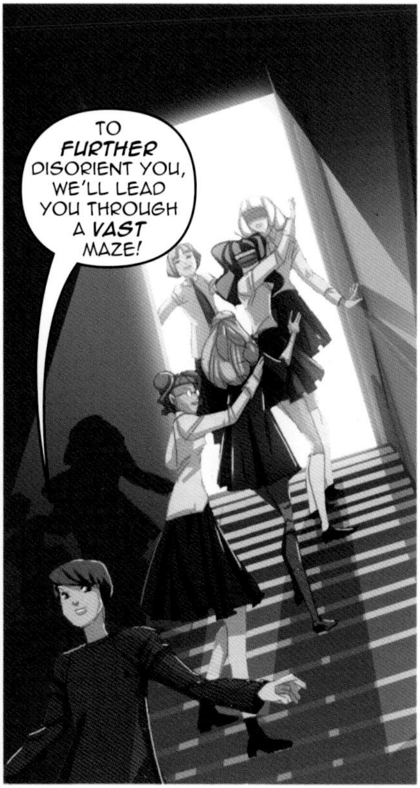
TO FURTHER DISORIENT YOU, WE'LL LEAD YOU THROUGH A VAST MAZE!

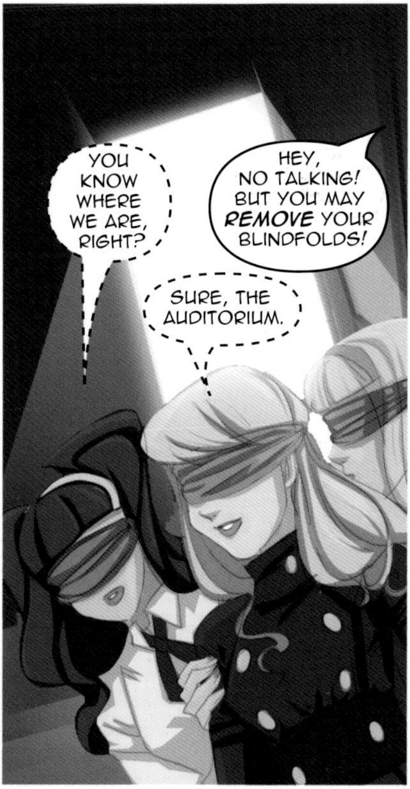
YOU KNOW WHERE WE ARE, RIGHT?
HEY, NO TALKING! BUT YOU MAY REMOVE YOUR BLINDFOLDS!
SURE, THE AUDITORIUM.

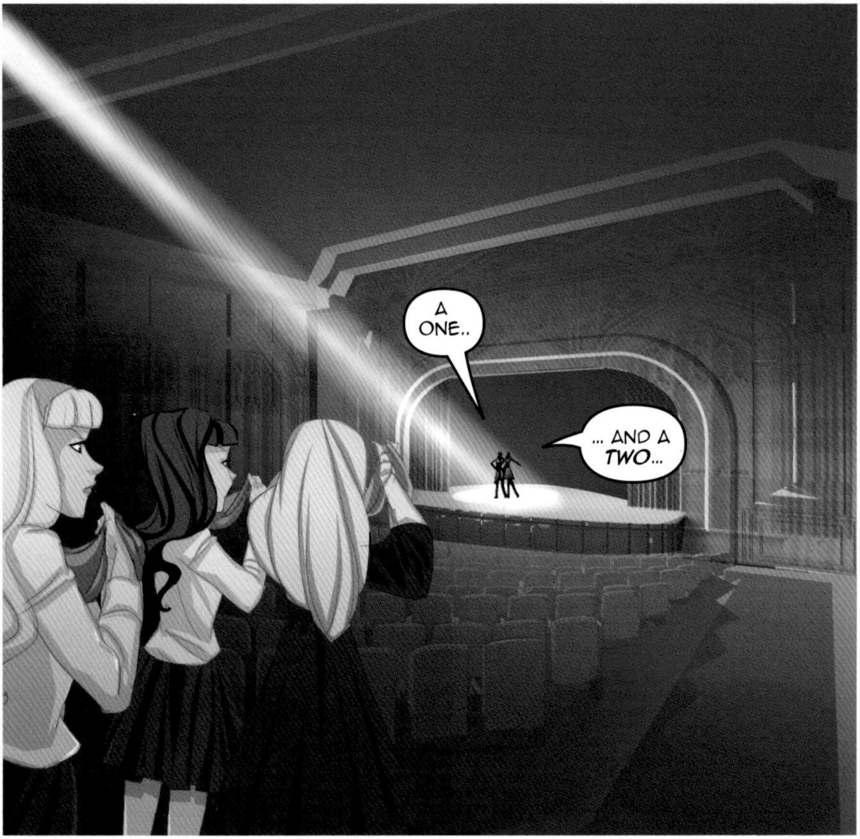
A ONE..
... AND A TWO...

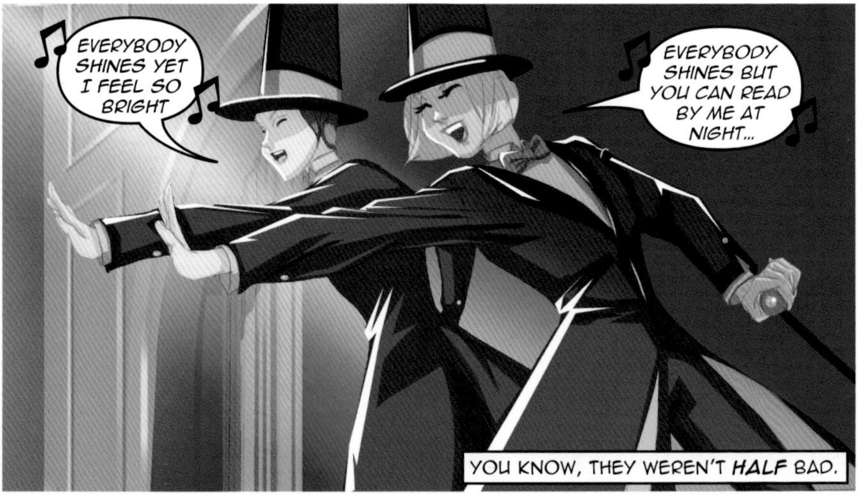
EVERYBODY SHINES YET I FEEL SO BRIGHT
EVERYBODY SHINES BUT YOU CAN READ BY ME AT NIGHT...
YOU KNOW, THEY WEREN'T HALF BAD.

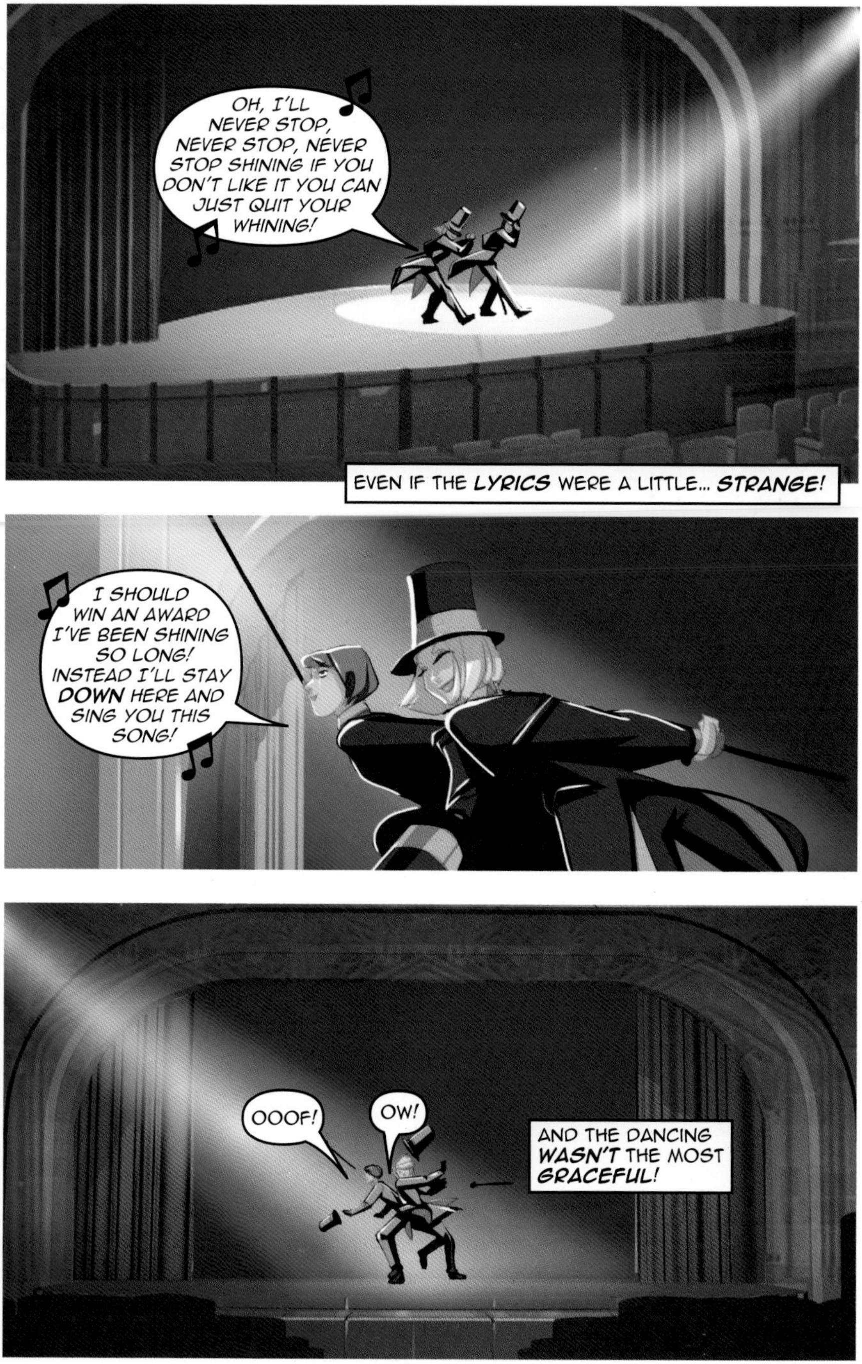
OH, I'LL NEVER STOP, NEVER STOP, NEVER STOP SHINING IF YOU DON'T LIKE IT YOU CAN JUST QUIT YOUR WHINING!
EVEN IF THE LYRICS WERE A LITTLE... STRANGE!
I SHOULD WIN AN AWARD I'VE BEEN SHINING SO LONG! INSTEAD I'LL STAY DOWN HERE AND SING YOU THIS SONG!
OOOF!
OW!
AND THE DANCING WASN'T THE MOST GRACEFUL!

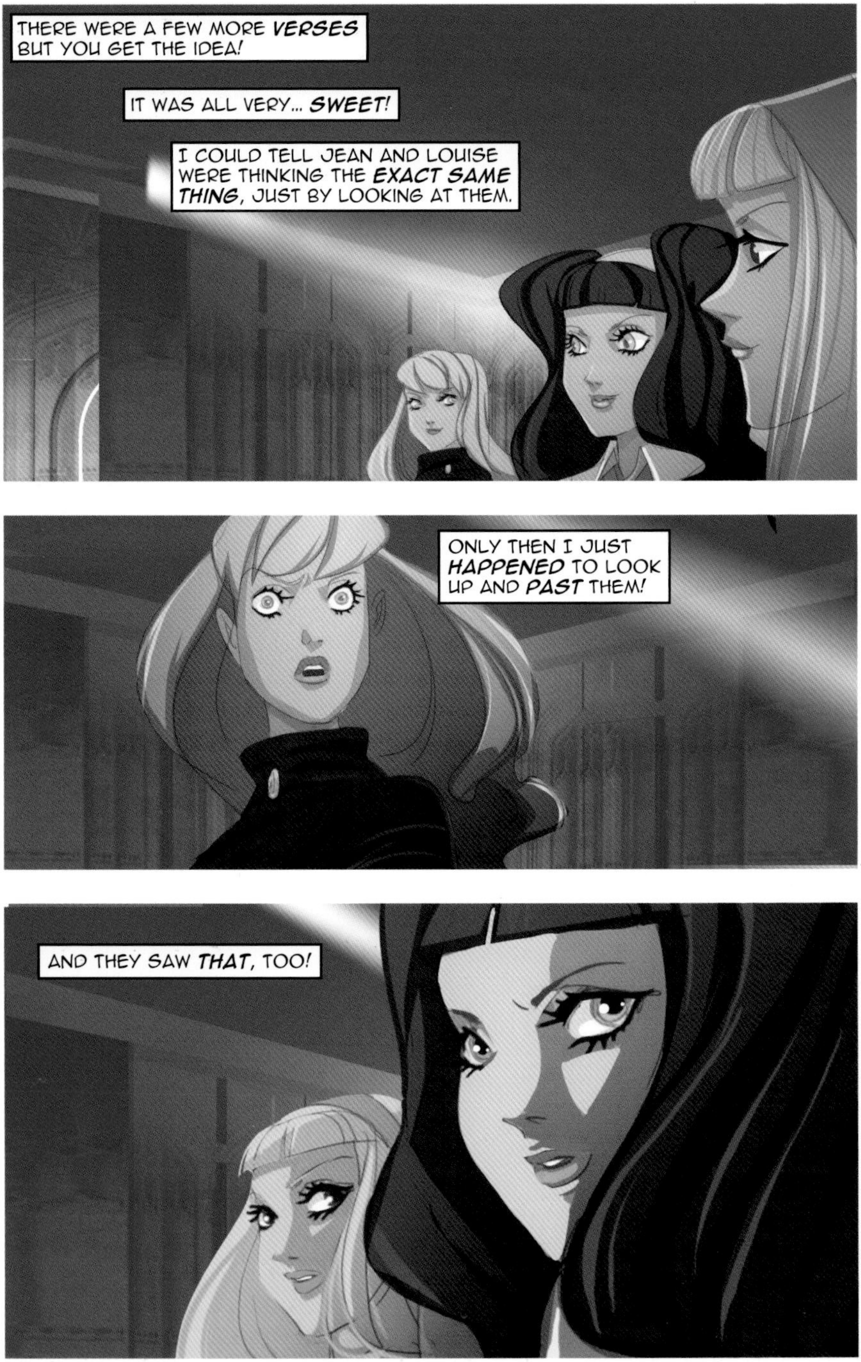
THERE WERE A FEW MORE VERSES BUT YOU GET THE IDEA!
IT WAS ALL VERY... SWEET!
I COULD TELL JEAN AND LOUISE WERE THINKING THE EXACT SAME THING, JUST BY LOOKING AT THEM.
ONLY THEN I JUST HAPPENED TO LOOK UP AND PAST THEM!
AND THEY SAW THAT, TOO!

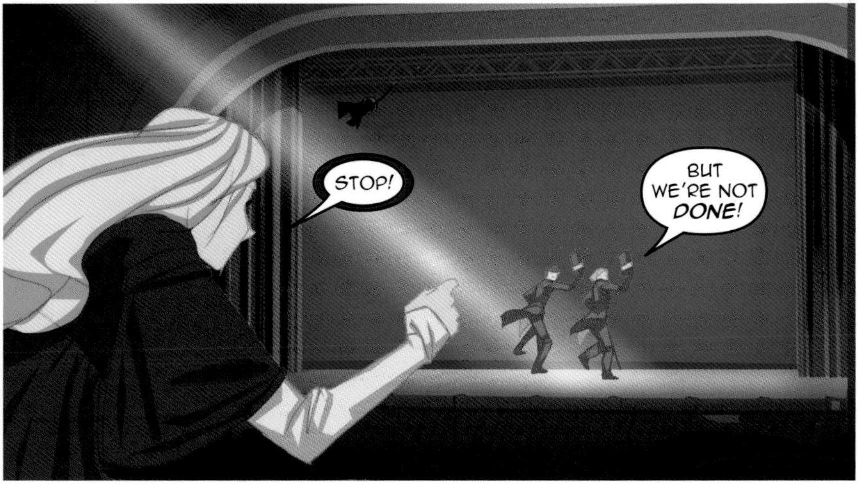
STOP!
BUT WE'RE NOT DONE!

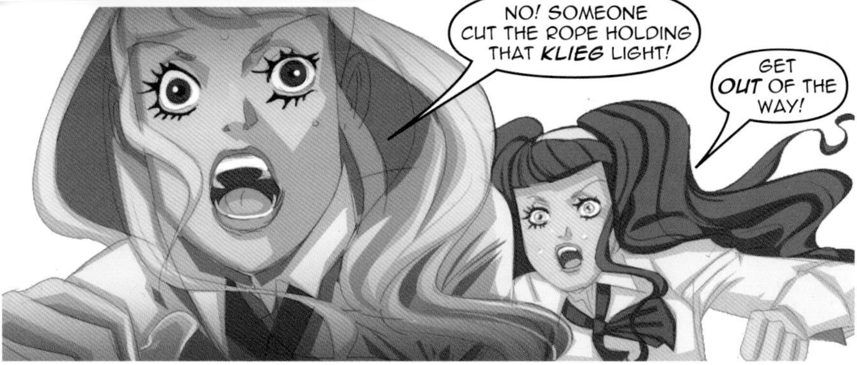
NO! SOMEONE CUT THE ROPE HOLDING THAT KLIEG LIGHT!
GET OUT OF THE WAY!

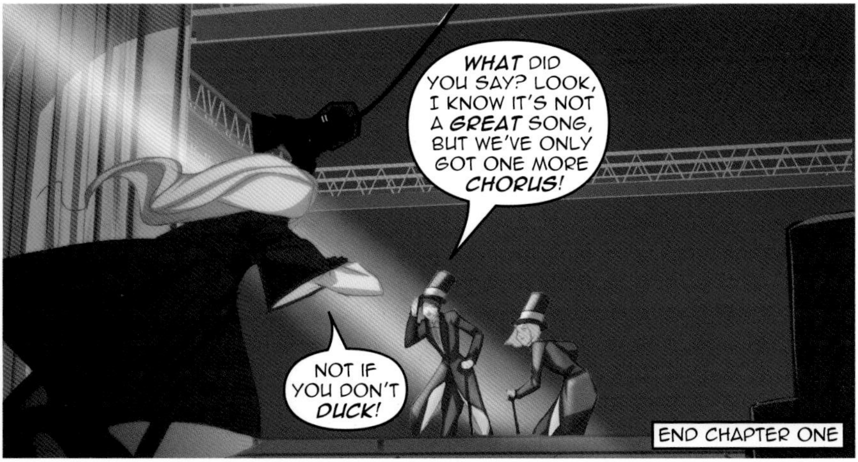
WHAT DID YOU SAY? LOOK, I KNOW IT'S NOT A GREAT SONG, BUT WE'VE ONLY GOT ONE MORE CHORUS!
NOT IF YOU DON'T DUCK!
END CHAPTER ONE

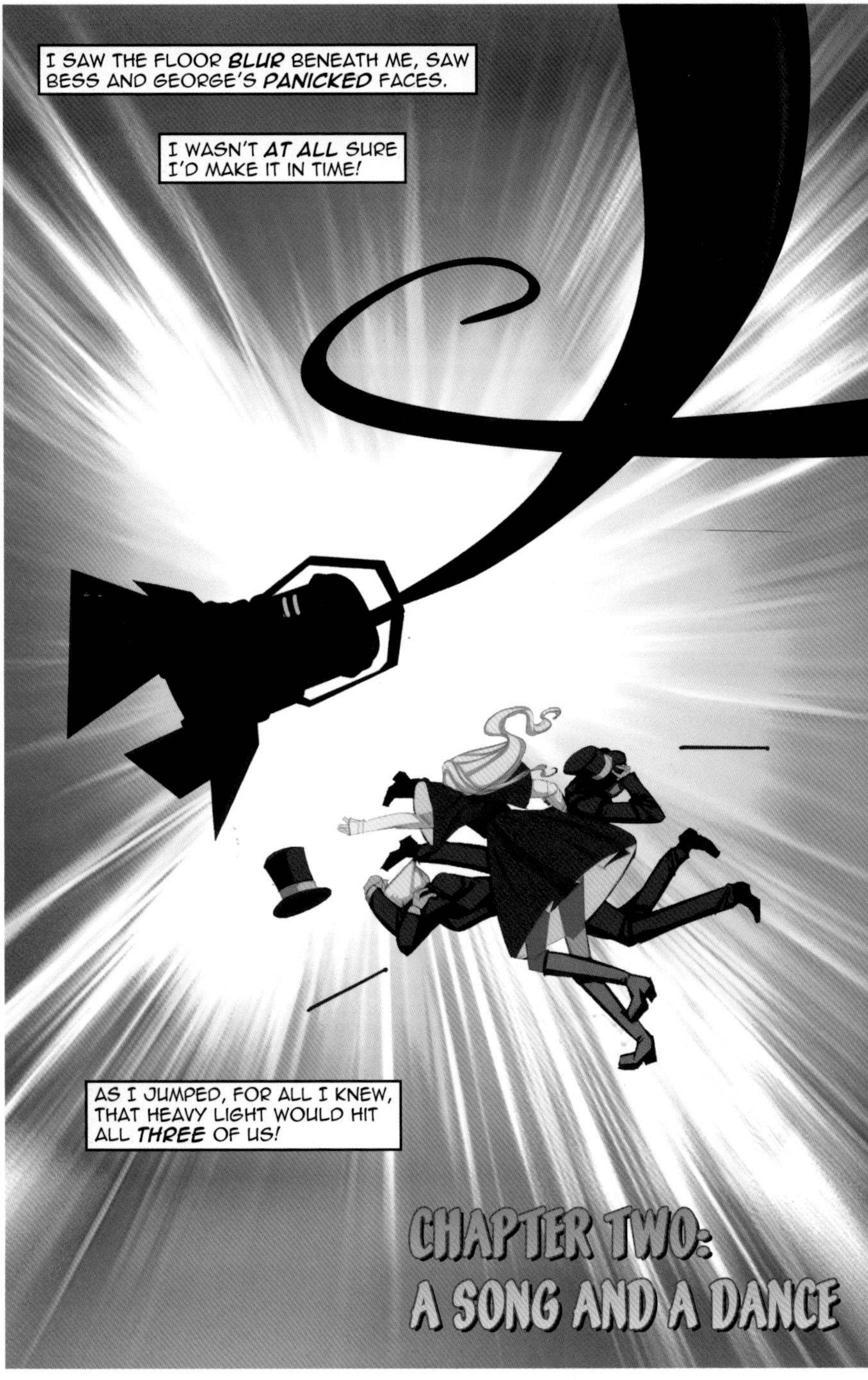
I SAW THE FLOOR BLUR BENEATH ME, SAW BESS AND GEORGE'S PANICKED FACES.
I WASN'T AT ALL SURE I'D MAKE IT IN TIME!
AS I JUMPED, FOR ALL I KNEW, THAT HEAVY LIGHT WOULD HIT ALL THREE OF US!
CHAPTER TWO: A SONG AND A DANCE

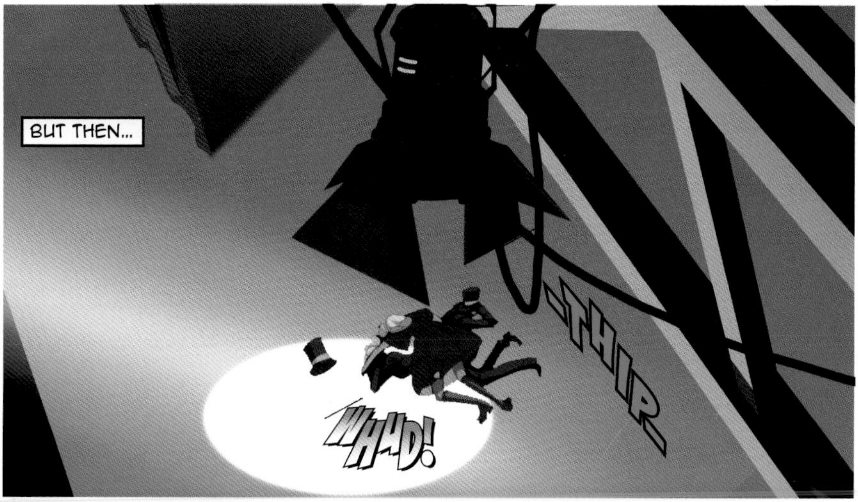
BUT THEN...
-THIP-
WHUD!

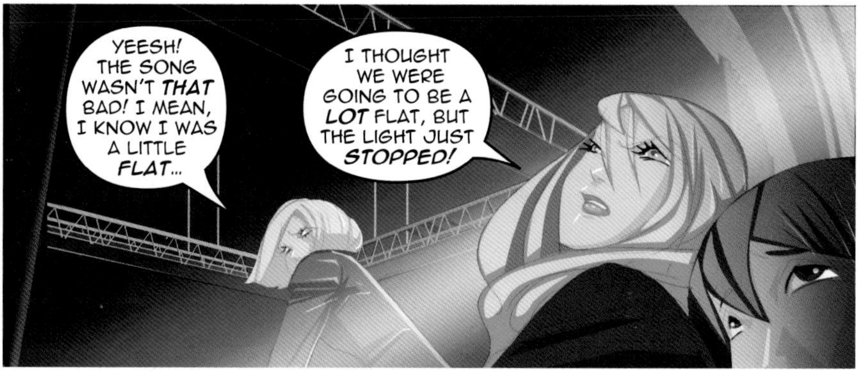
YEESH! THE SONG WASN'T *THAT* BAD! I MEAN, I KNOW I WAS A LITTLE *FLAT*...
I THOUGHT WE WERE GOING TO BE A *LOT* FLAT, BUT THE LIGHT JUST *STOPPED!*

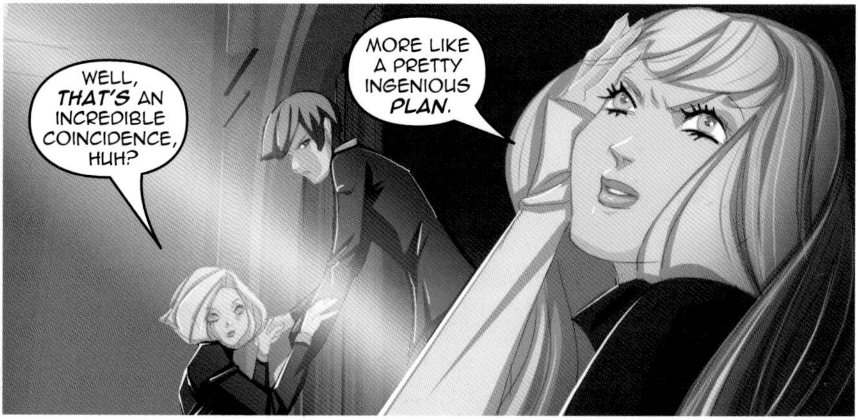
WELL, *THAT'S* AN INCREDIBLE COINCIDENCE, HUH?
MORE LIKE A PRETTY INGENIOUS *PLAN*.

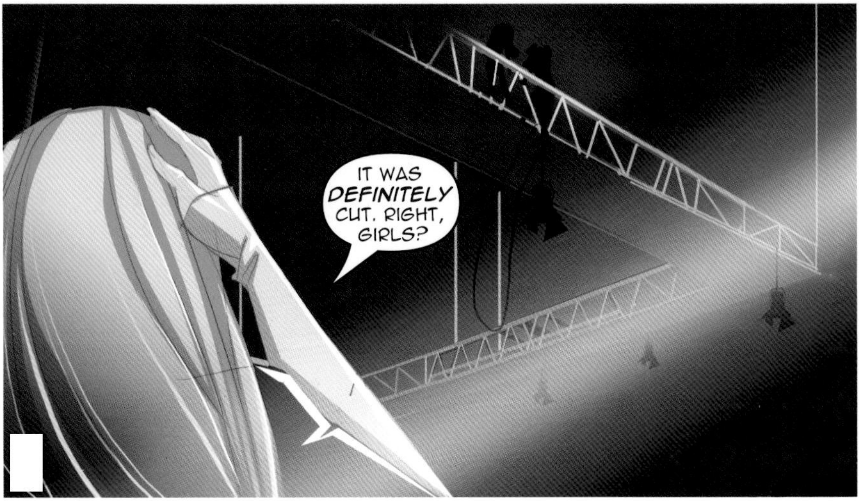
IT WAS DEFINITELY CUT. RIGHT, GIRLS?

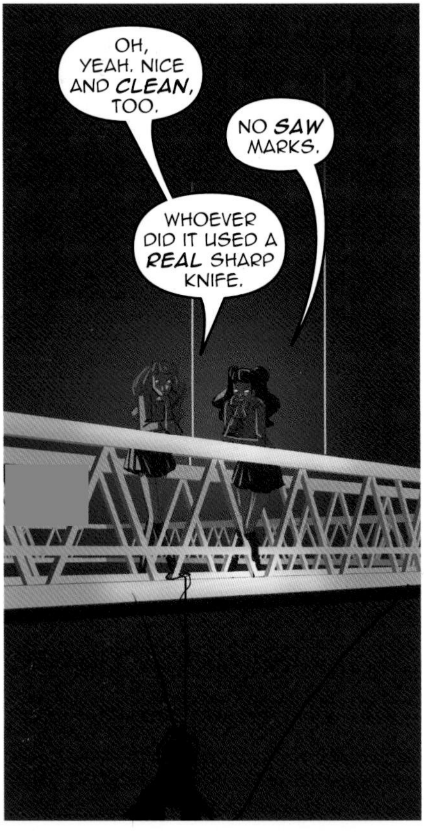
OH, YEAH. NICE AND CLEAN, TOO.
NO SAW MARKS.
WHOEVER DID IT USED A REAL SHARP KNIFE.

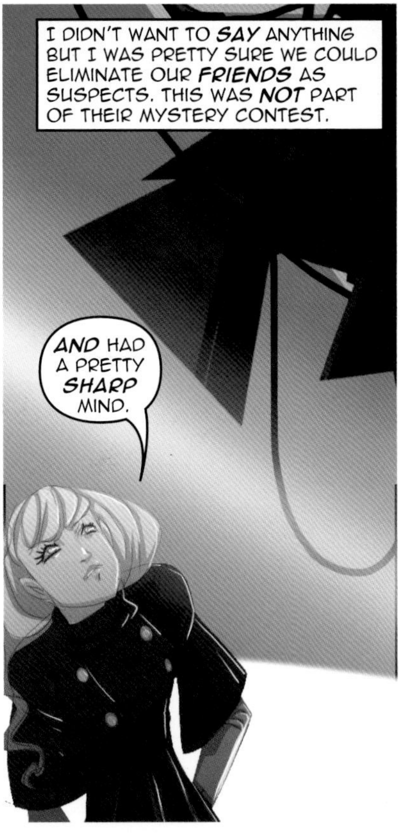
I DIDN'T WANT TO SAY ANYTHING BUT I WAS PRETTY SURE WE COULD ELIMINATE OUR FRIENDS AS SUSPECTS. THIS WAS NOT PART OF THEIR MYSTERY CONTEST.
AND HAD A PRETTY SHARP MIND.

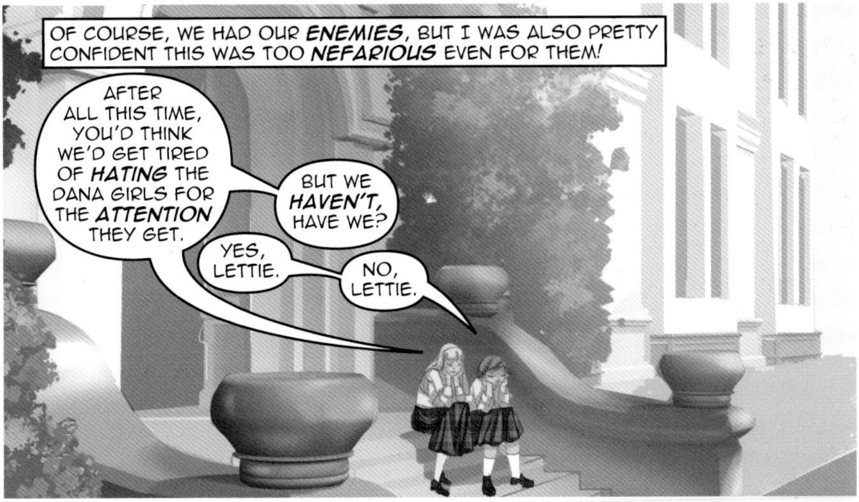
OF COURSE, WE HAD OUR ENEMIES, BUT I WAS ALSO PRETTY CONFIDENT THIS WAS TOO NEFARIOUS EVEN FOR THEM!
AFTER ALL THIS TIME, YOU'D THINK WE'D GET TIRED OF HATING THE DANA GIRLS FOR THE ATTENTION THEY GET.
BUT WE HAVEN'T, HAVE WE?
YES, LETTIE.
NO, LETTIE.
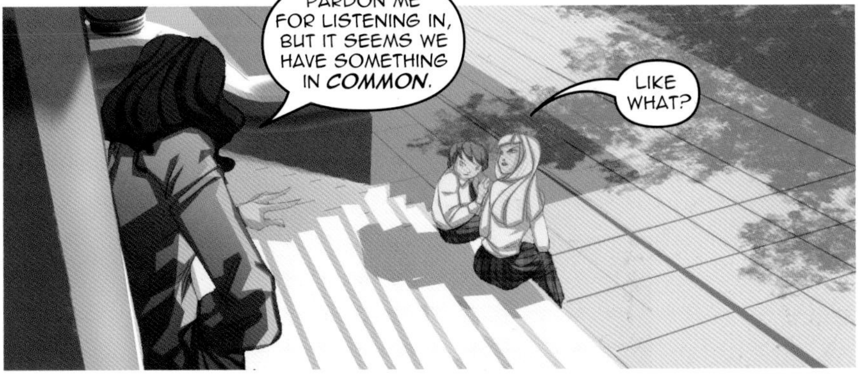
PARDON ME FOR LISTENING IN, BUT IT SEEMS WE HAVE SOMETHING IN COMMON.
LIKE WHAT?
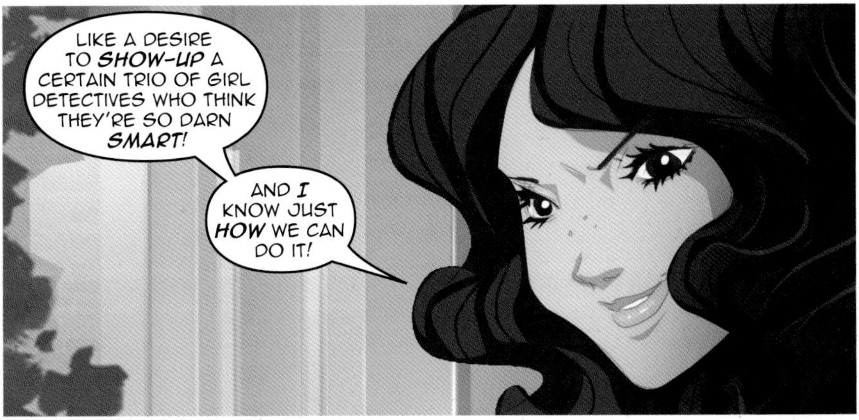
LIKE A DESIRE TO SHOW-UP A CERTAIN TRIO OF GIRL DETECTIVES WHO THINK THEY'RE SO DARN SMART!
AND I KNOW JUST HOW WE CAN DO IT!

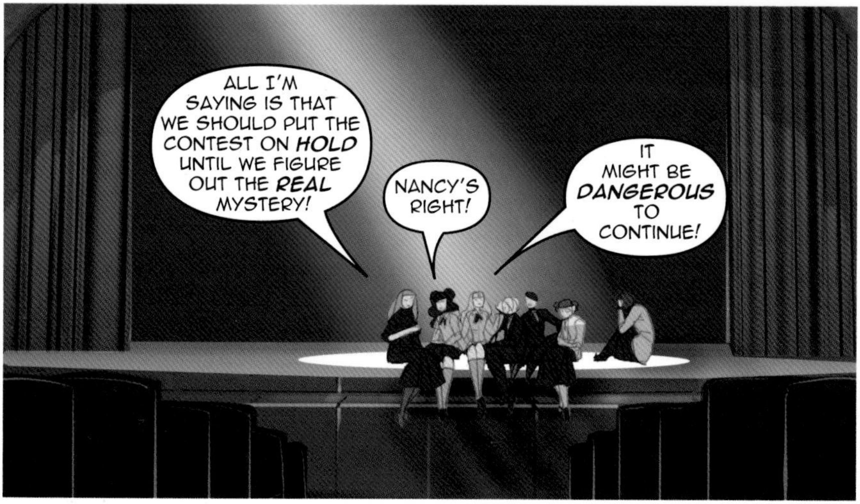
ALL I'M SAYING IS THAT WE SHOULD PUT THE CONTEST ON HOLD UNTIL WE FIGURE OUT THE REAL MYSTERY!
NANCY'S RIGHT!
IT MIGHT BE DANGEROUS TO CONTINUE!

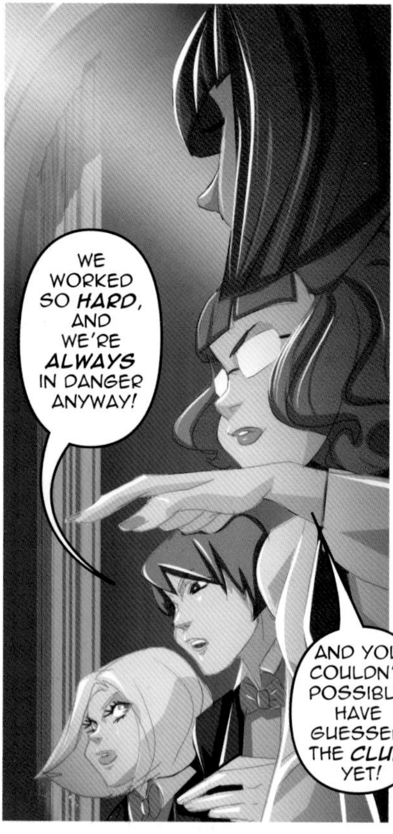
WE WORKED SO HARD, AND WE'RE ALWAYS IN DANGER ANYWAY!
AND YOU COULDN'T POSSIBLY HAVE GUESSED THE CLUE YET!

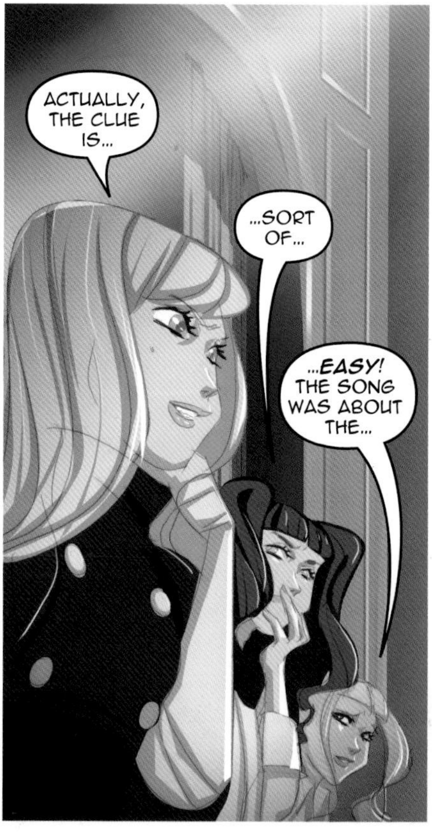
ACTUALLY, THE CLUE IS...
...SORT OF...
...EASY! THE SONG WAS ABOUT THE...

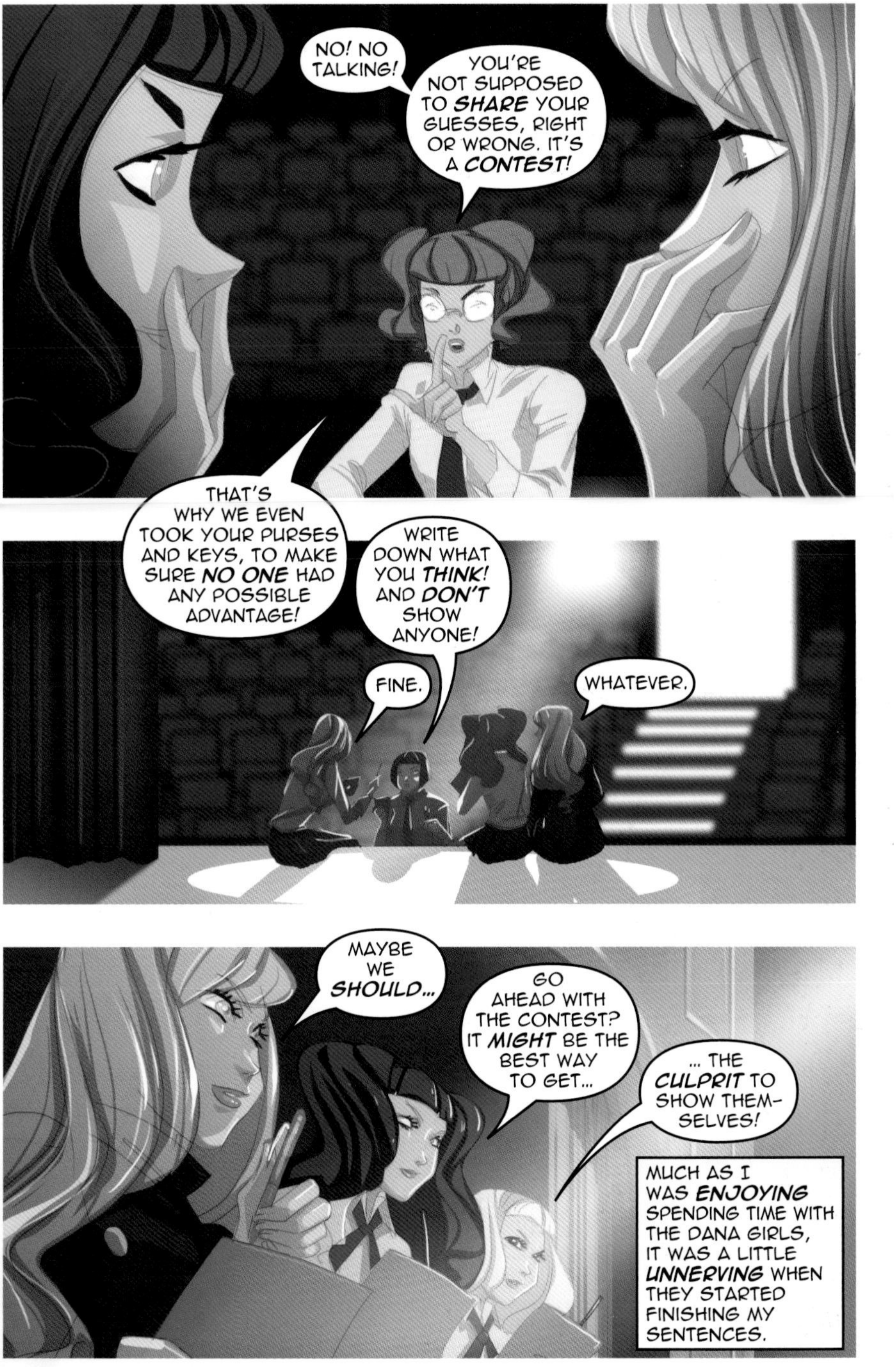
NO! NO TALKING!
YOU'RE NOT SUPPOSED TO SHARE YOUR GUESSES, RIGHT OR WRONG. IT'S A CONTEST!
THAT'S WHY WE EVEN TOOK YOUR PURSES AND KEYS, TO MAKE SURE NO ONE HAD ANY POSSIBLE ADVANTAGE!
WRITE DOWN WHAT YOU THINK! AND DON'T SHOW ANYONE!
FINE.
WHATEVER.
MAYBE WE SHOULD...
GO AHEAD WITH THE CONTEST? IT MIGHT BE THE BEST WAY TO GET...
... THE CULPRIT TO SHOW THEMSELVES!
MUCH AS I WAS ENJOYING SPENDING TIME WITH THE DANA GIRLS, IT WAS A LITTLE UNNERVING WHEN THEY STARTED FINISHING MY SENTENCES.

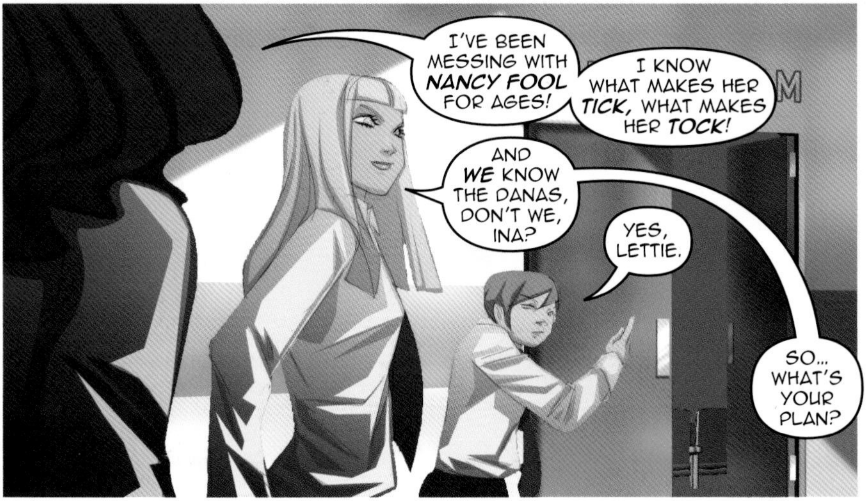
I'VE BEEN MESSING WITH NANCY FOOL FOR AGES!
I KNOW WHAT MAKES HER TICK, WHAT MAKES HER TOCK!
AND WE KNOW THE DANAS, DON'T WE, INA?
YES, LETTIE.
SO... WHAT'S YOUR PLAN?

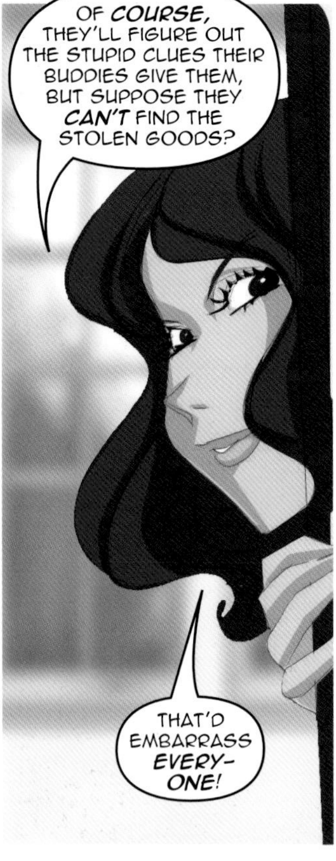
OF COURSE, THEY'LL FIGURE OUT THE STUPID CLUES THEIR BUDDIES GIVE THEM, BUT SUPPOSE THEY CAN'T FIND THE STOLEN GOODS?
THAT'D EMBARRASS EVERY-ONE!

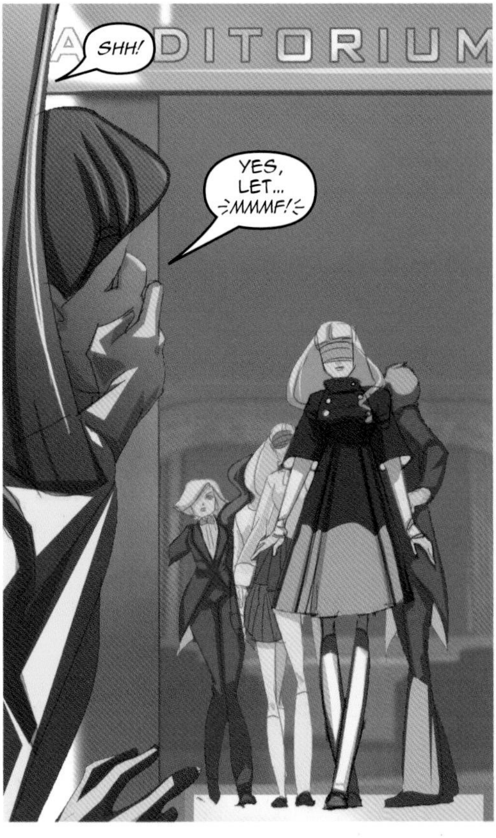
SHH!
ADITORIUM
YES, LET... MMMF!

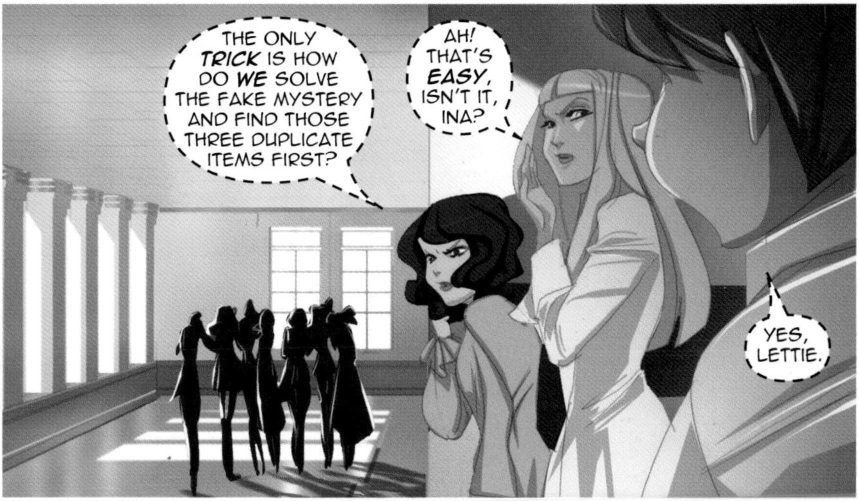
THE ONLY TRICK IS HOW DO WE SOLVE THE FAKE MYSTERY AND FIND THOSE THREE DUPLICATE ITEMS FIRST?
AH! THAT'S EASY, ISN'T IT, INA?
YES, LETTIE.

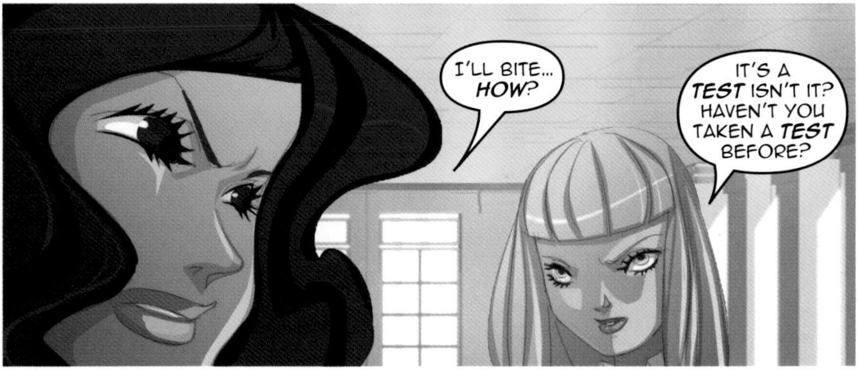
I'LL BITE... HOW?
IT'S A TEST ISN'T IT? HAVEN'T YOU TAKEN A TEST BEFORE?

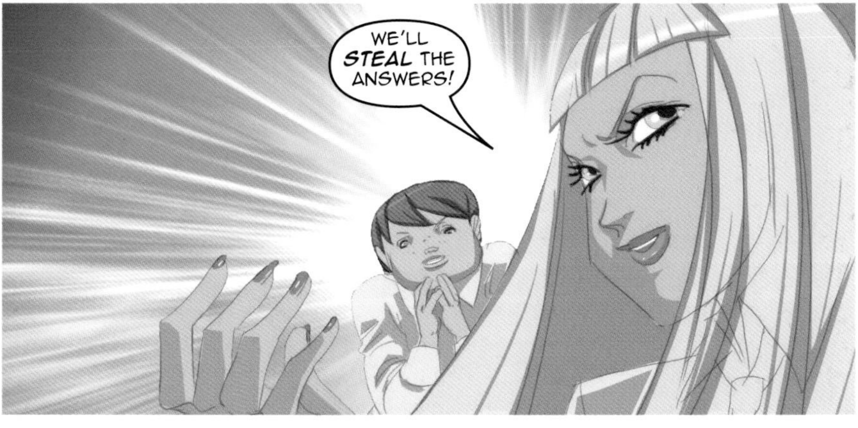
WE'LL STEAL THE ANSWERS!

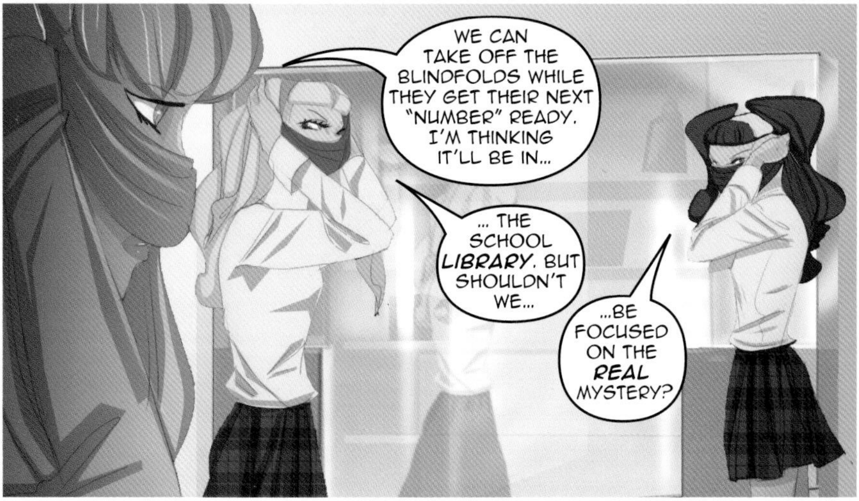
WE CAN TAKE OFF THE BLINDFOLDS WHILE THEY GET THEIR NEXT "NUMBER" READY. I'M THINKING IT'LL BE IN...
... THE SCHOOL LIBRARY. BUT SHOULDN'T WE...
...BE FOCUSED ON THE REAL MYSTERY?

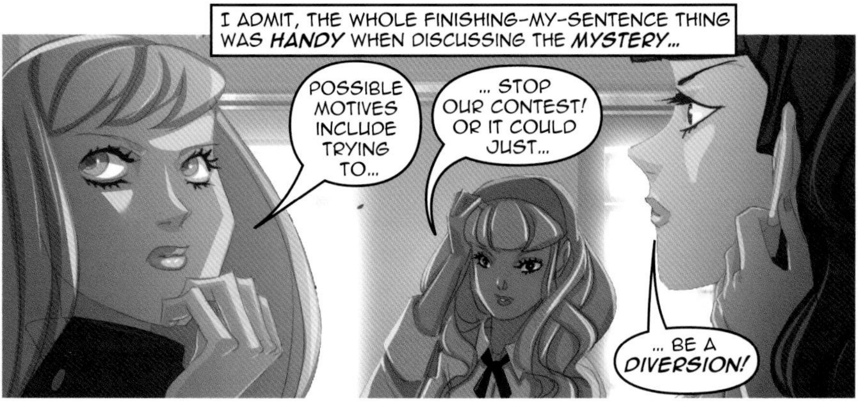
I ADMIT, THE WHOLE FINISHING-MY-SENTENCE THING WAS HANDY WHEN DISCUSSING THE MYSTERY...
POSSIBLE MOTIVES INCLUDE TRYING TO...
... STOP OUR CONTEST! OR IT COULD JUST...
... BE A DIVERSION!

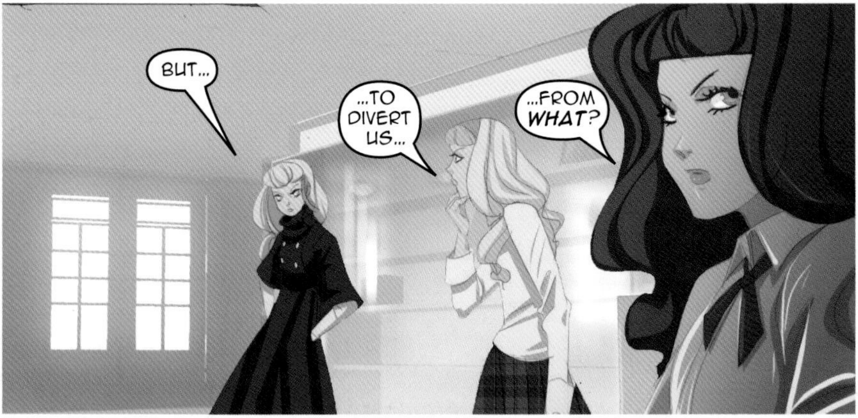
BUT...
...TO DIVERT US...
...FROM WHAT?

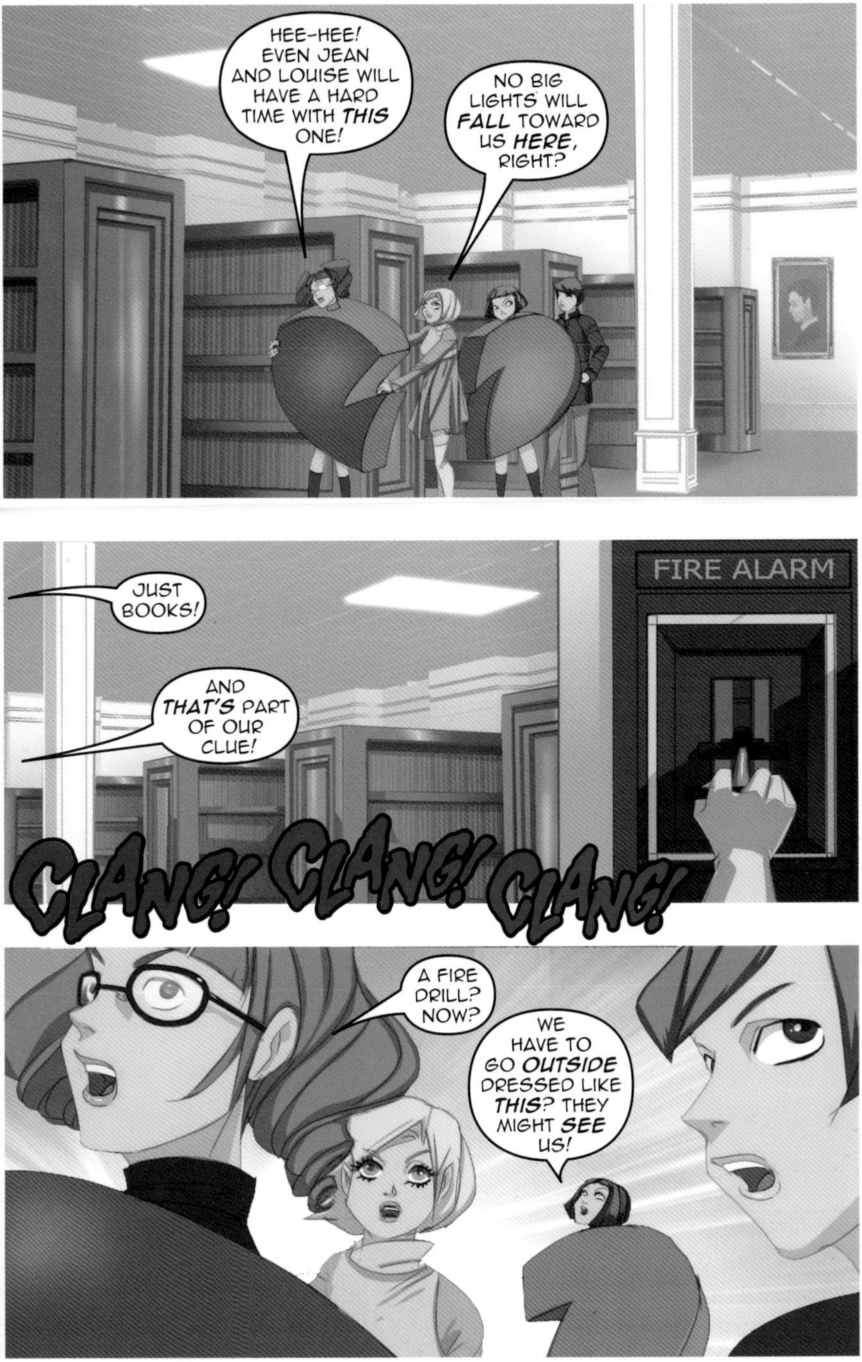
HEE-HEE! EVEN JEAN AND LOUISE WILL HAVE A HARD TIME WITH THIS ONE!
NO BIG LIGHTS WILL FALL TOWARD US HERE, RIGHT?
JUST BOOKS!
AND THAT'S PART OF OUR CLUE!
FIRE ALARM
CLANG! CLANG! CLANG!
A FIRE DRILL? NOW?
WE HAVE TO GO OUTSIDE DRESSED LIKE THIS? THEY MIGHT SEE US!

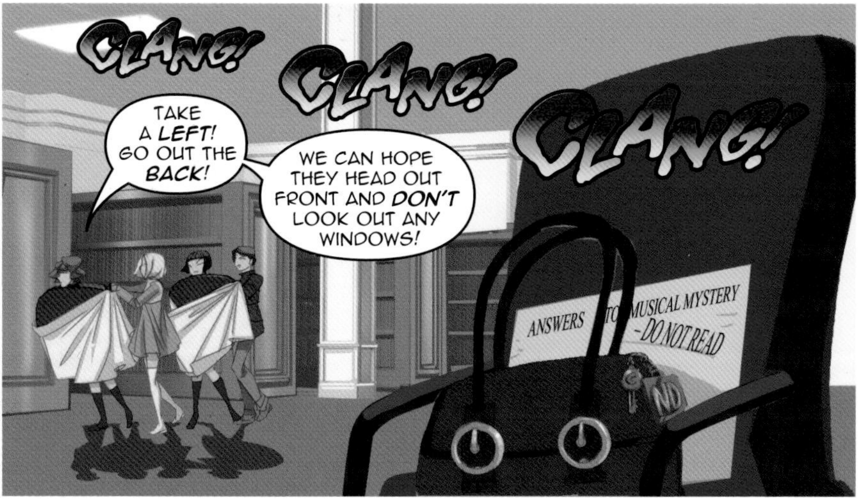
CLANG!
CLANG!
CLANG!
TAKE A LEFT! GO OUT THE BACK!
WE CAN HOPE THEY HEAD OUT FRONT AND DON'T LOOK OUT ANY WINDOWS!
ANSWERS TO MUSICAL MYSTERY -DO NOT READ

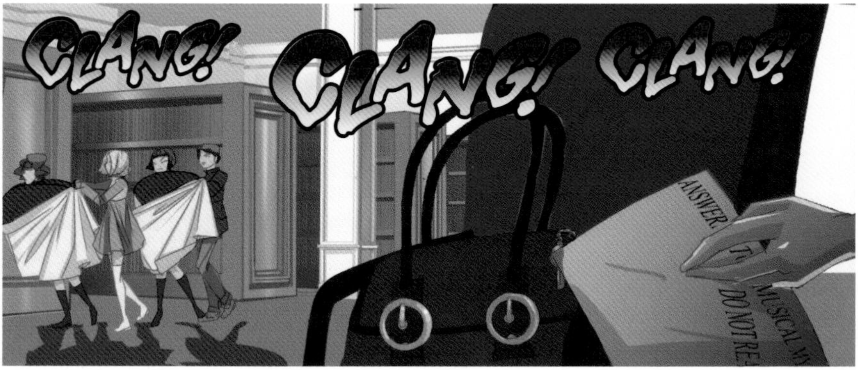
CLANG!
CLANG!
CLANG!

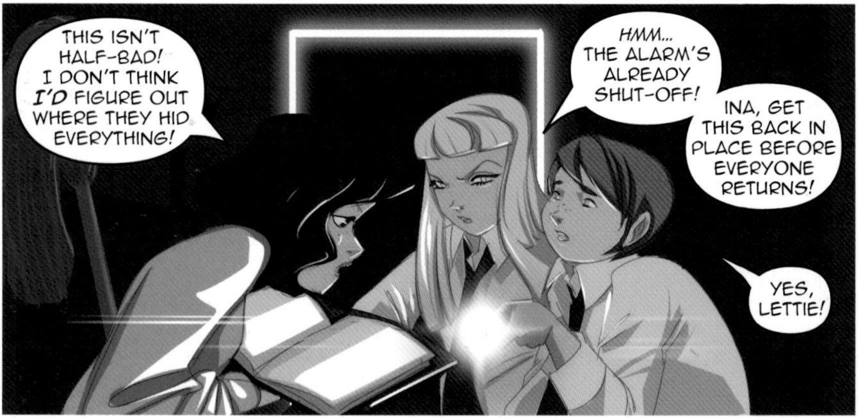
THIS ISN'T HALF-BAD! I DON'T THINK I'D FIGURE OUT WHERE THEY HID EVERYTHING!
HMM... THE ALARM'S ALREADY SHUT-OFF!
INA, GET THIS BACK IN PLACE BEFORE EVERYONE RETURNS!
YES, LETTIE!

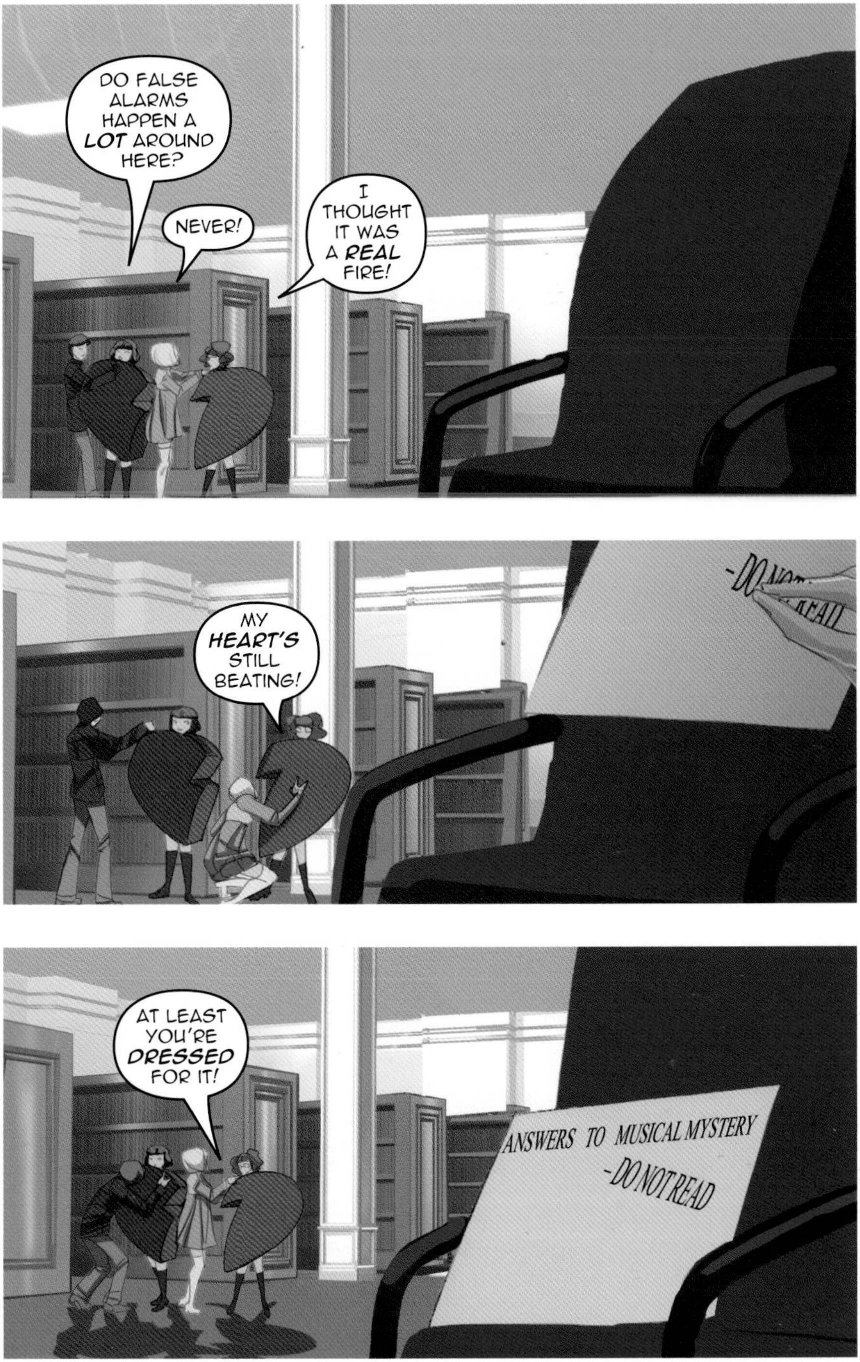
DO FALSE ALARMS HAPPEN A LOT AROUND HERE?
NEVER!
I THOUGHT IT WAS A REAL FIRE!
MY HEART'S STILL BEATING!
AT LEAST YOU'RE DRESSED FOR IT!
ANSWERS TO MUSICAL MYSTERY
-DO NOT READ

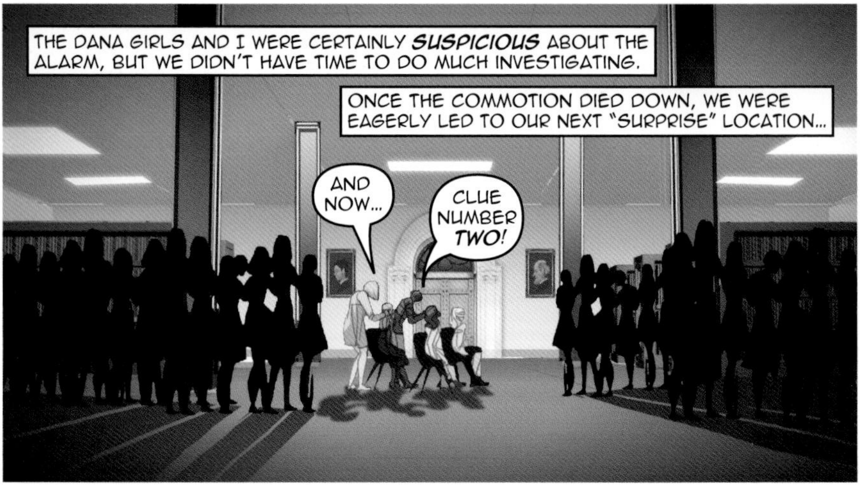
THE DANA GIRLS AND I WERE CERTAINLY SUSPICIOUS ABOUT THE ALARM, BUT WE DIDN'T HAVE TIME TO DO MUCH INVESTIGATING.
ONCE THE COMMOTION DIED DOWN, WE WERE EAGERLY LED TO OUR NEXT "SURPRISE" LOCATION...
AND NOW...
CLUE NUMBER TWO!

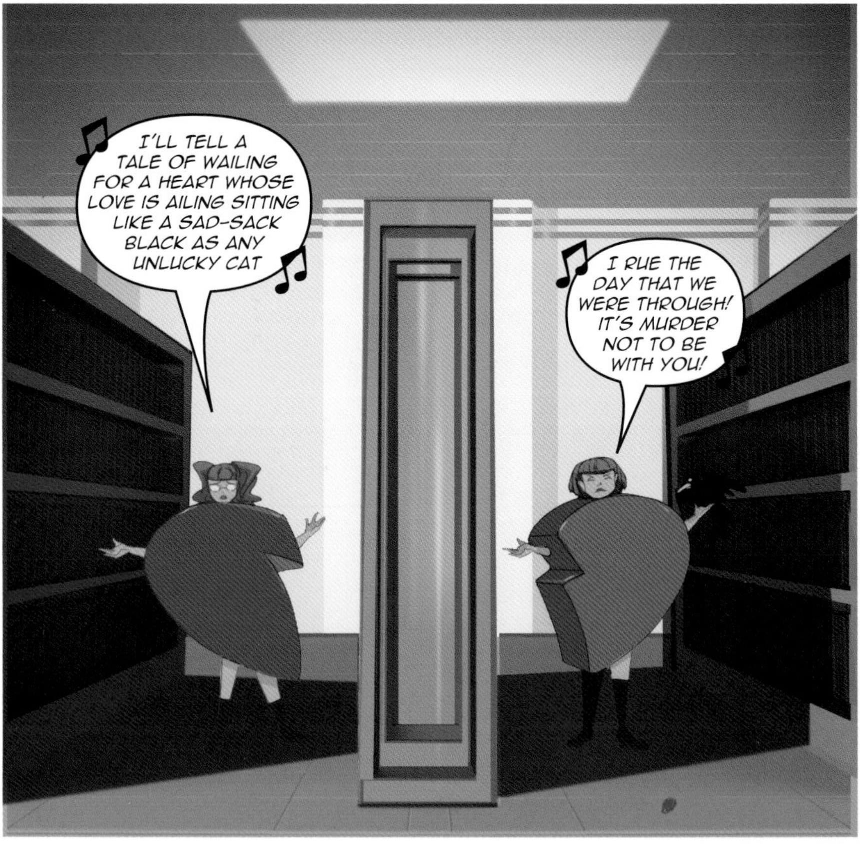
I'LL TELL A TALE OF WAILING FOR A HEART WHOSE LOVE IS AILING SITTING LIKE A SAD-SACK BLACK AS ANY UNLUCKY CAT
I RUE THE DAY THAT WE WERE THROUGH! IT'S MURDER NOT TO BE WITH YOU!

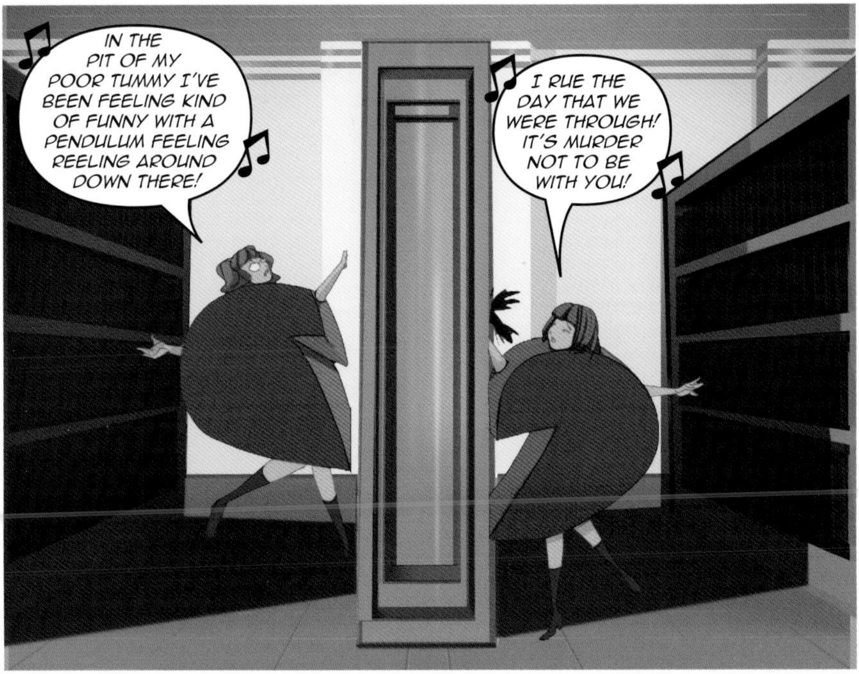
IN THE PIT OF MY POOR TUMMY I'VE BEEN FEELING KIND OF FUNNY WITH A PENDULUM FEELING REELING AROUND DOWN THERE!
I RUE THE DAY THAT WE WERE THROUGH! IT'S MURDER NOT TO BE WITH YOU!

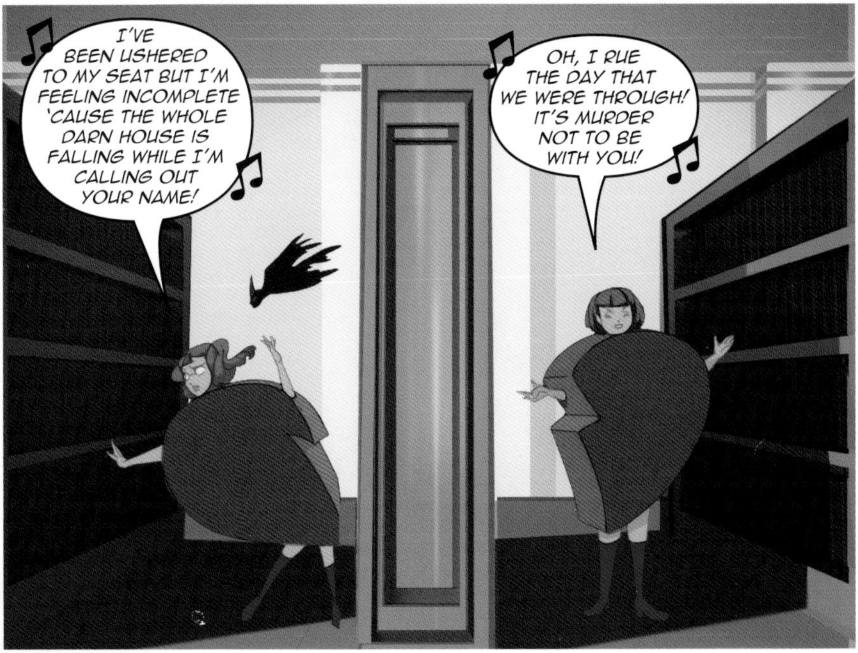
I'VE BEEN USHERED TO MY SEAT BUT I'M FEELING INCOMPLETE 'CAUSE THE WHOLE DARN HOUSE IS FALLING WHILE I'M CALLING OUT YOUR NAME!
OH, I RUE THE DAY THAT WE WERE THROUGH! IT'S MURDER NOT TO BE WITH YOU!

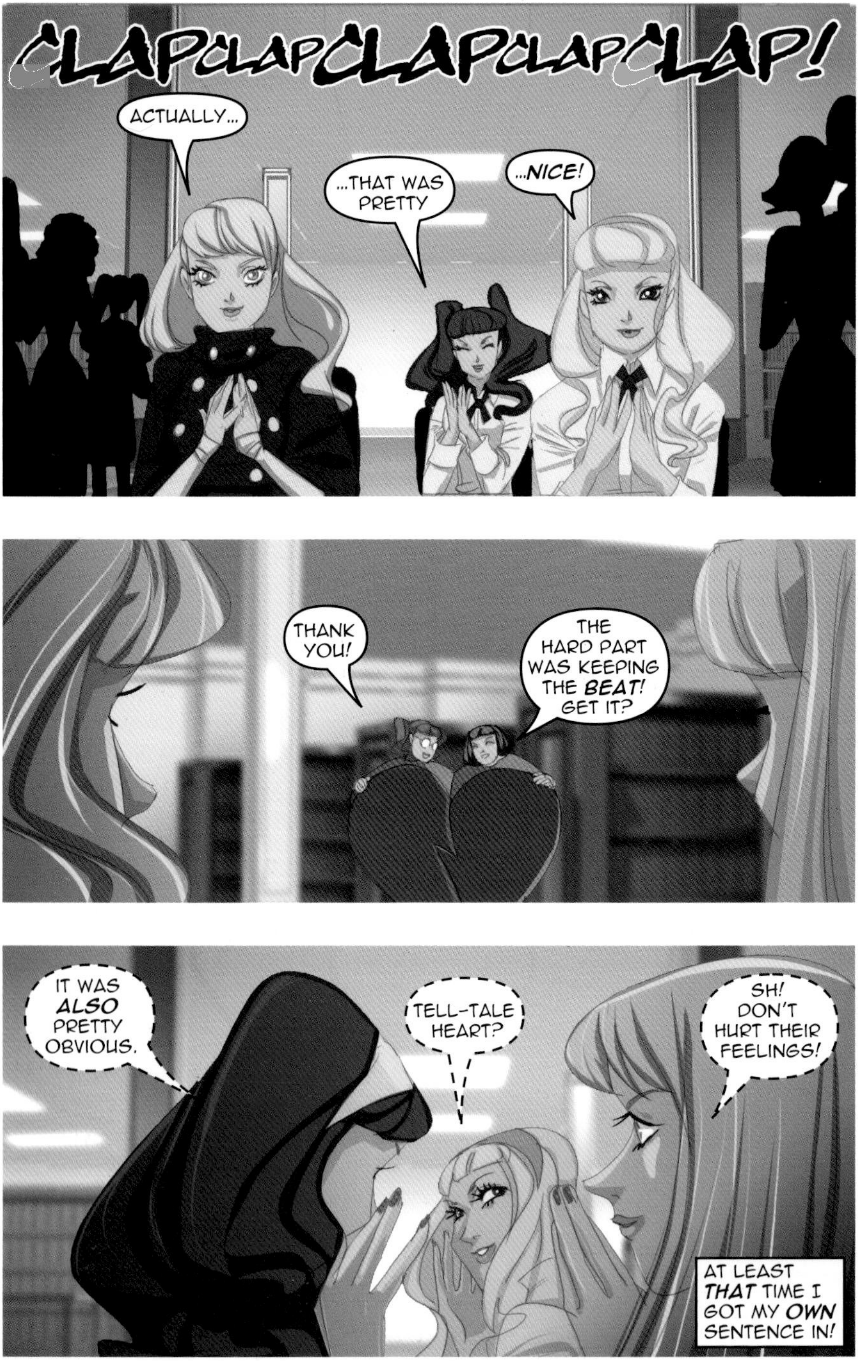
CLAPCLAPCLAPCLAPCLAP!
ACTUALLY...
...THAT WAS PRETTY
...NICE!
THANK YOU!
THE HARD PART WAS KEEPING THE BEAT! GET IT?
IT WAS ALSO PRETTY OBVIOUS.
TELL-TALE HEART?
SH! DON'T HURT THEIR FEELINGS!
AT LEAST THAT TIME I GOT MY OWN SENTENCE IN!

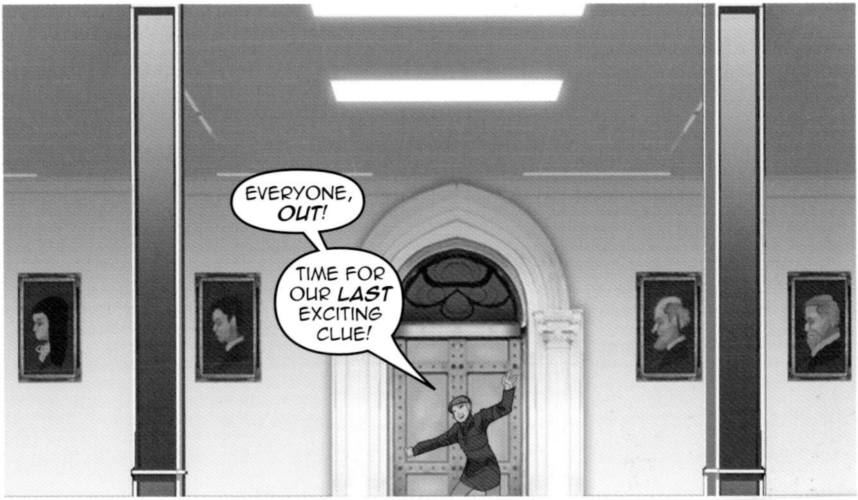
EVERYONE, *OUT*!
TIME FOR OUR *LAST* EXCITING CLUE!

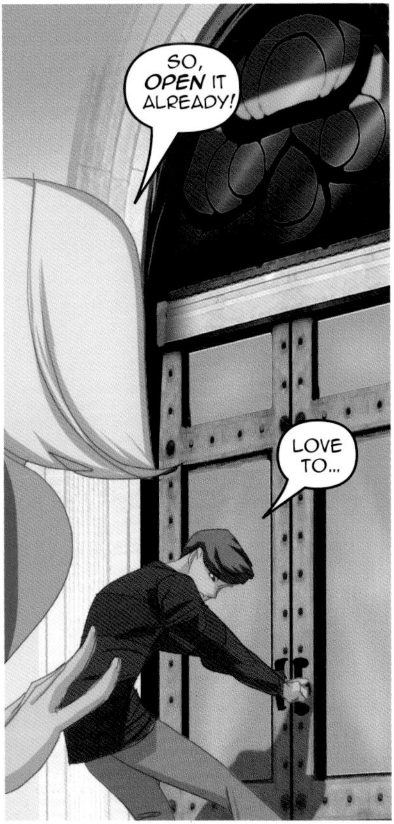
SO, *OPEN* IT ALREADY!
LOVE TO...

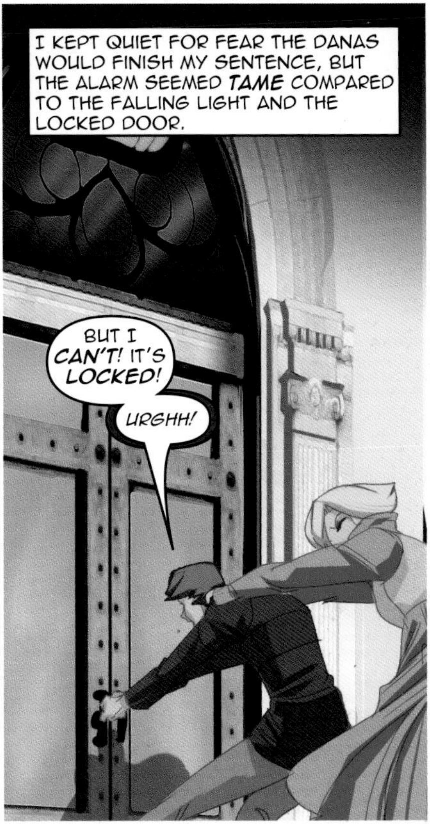
I KEPT QUIET FOR FEAR THE DANAS WOULD FINISH MY SENTENCE, BUT THE ALARM SEEMED *TAME* COMPARED TO THE FALLING LIGHT AND THE LOCKED DOOR.
BUT I *CAN'T*! IT'S *LOCKED*!
URGHH!

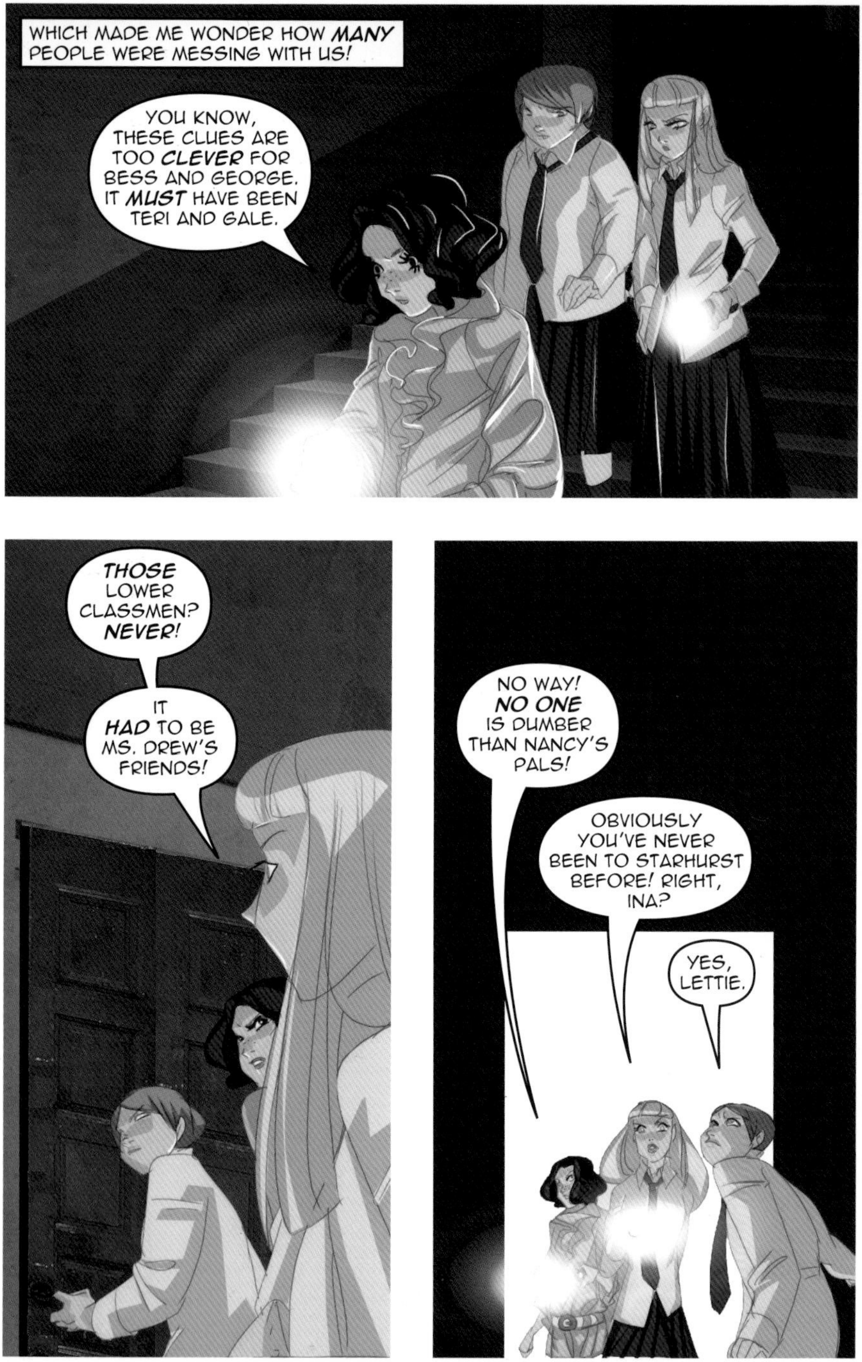
WHICH MADE ME WONDER HOW *MANY* PEOPLE WERE MESSING WITH US!
YOU KNOW, THESE CLUES ARE TOO *CLEVER* FOR BESS AND GEORGE. IT *MUST* HAVE BEEN TERI AND GALE.
THOSE LOWER CLASSMEN? *NEVER!*
IT *HAD* TO BE MS. DREW'S FRIENDS!
NO WAY! *NO ONE* IS DUMBER THAN NANCY'S PALS!
OBVIOUSLY YOU'VE NEVER BEEN TO STARHURST BEFORE! RIGHT, INA?
YES, LETTIE.

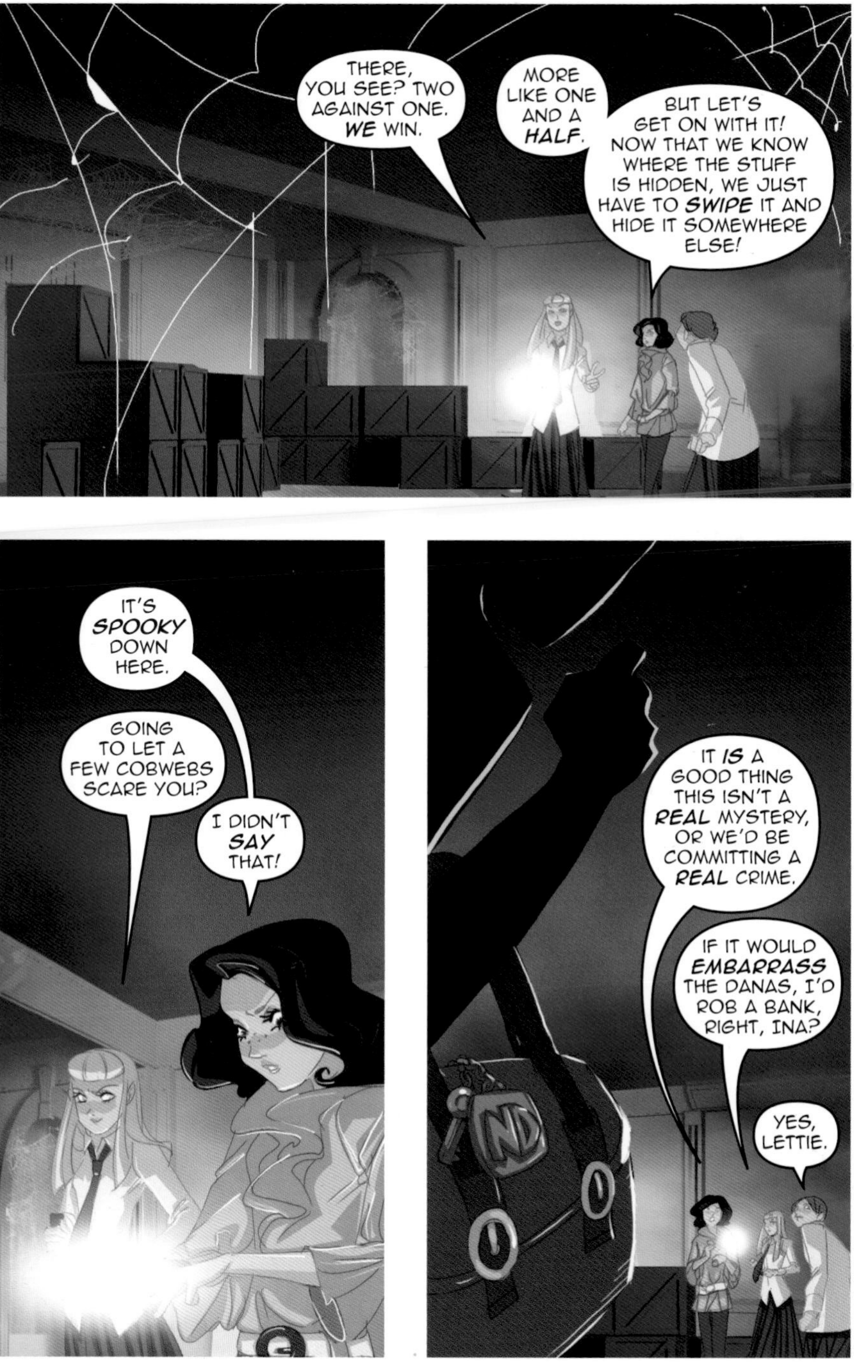
THERE, YOU SEE? TWO AGAINST ONE. WE WIN.
MORE LIKE ONE AND A HALF.
BUT LET'S GET ON WITH IT! NOW THAT WE KNOW WHERE THE STUFF IS HIDDEN, WE JUST HAVE TO SWIPE IT AND HIDE IT SOMEWHERE ELSE!
IT'S SPOOKY DOWN HERE.
GOING TO LET A FEW COBWEBS SCARE YOU?
I DIDN'T SAY THAT!
IT IS A GOOD THING THIS ISN'T A REAL MYSTERY, OR WE'D BE COMMITTING A REAL CRIME.
IF IT WOULD EMBARRASS THE DANAS, I'D ROB A BANK, RIGHT, INA?
YES, LETTIE.
ND

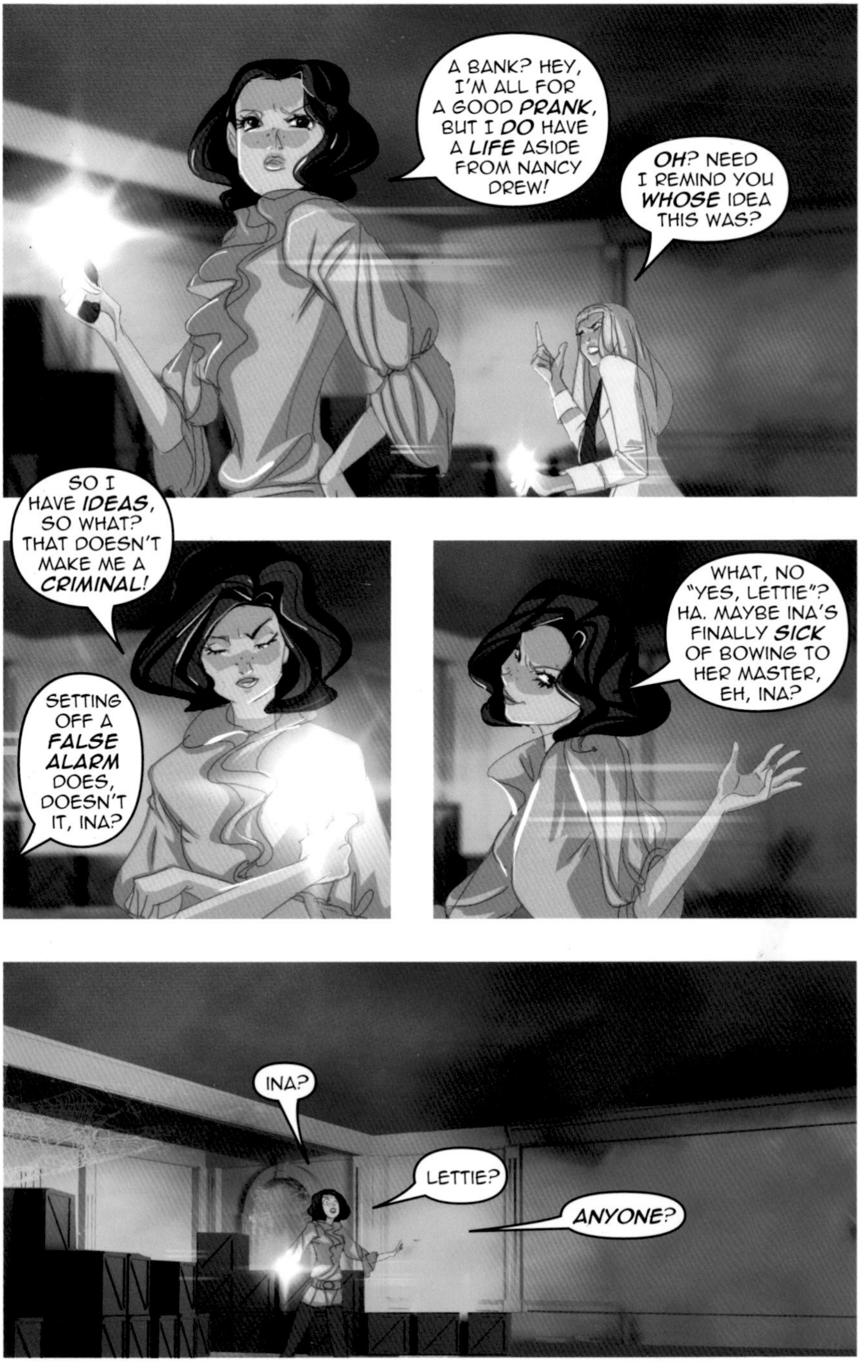
A BANK? HEY, I'M ALL FOR A GOOD PRANK, BUT I DO HAVE A LIFE ASIDE FROM NANCY DREW!
OH? NEED I REMIND YOU WHOSE IDEA THIS WAS?
SO I HAVE IDEAS, SO WHAT? THAT DOESN'T MAKE ME A CRIMINAL!
SETTING OFF A FALSE ALARM DOES, DOESN'T IT, INA?
WHAT, NO "YES, LETTIE"? HA. MAYBE INA'S FINALLY SICK OF BOWING TO HER MASTER, EH, INA?
INA?
LETTIE?
ANYONE?

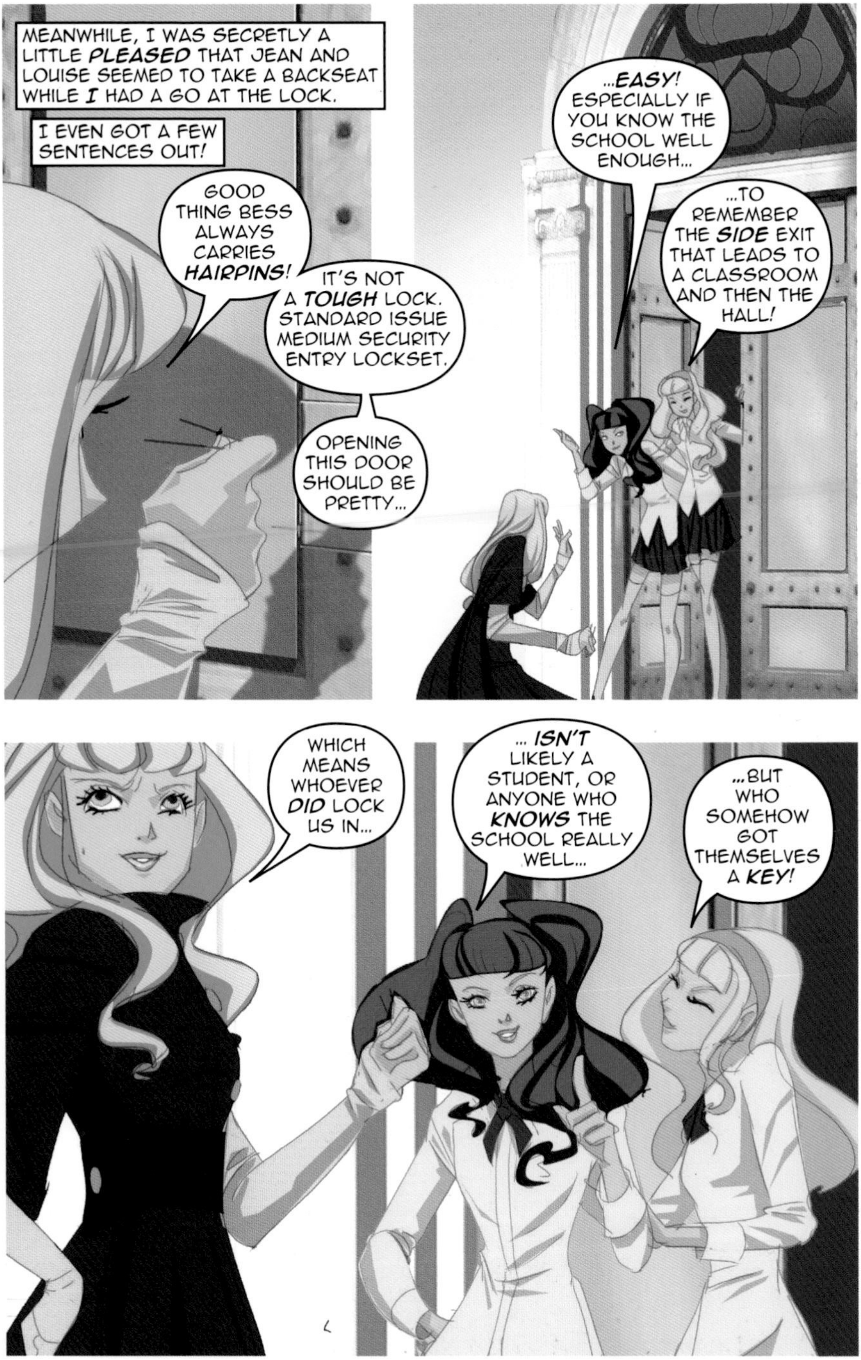
MEANWHILE, I WAS SECRETLY A LITTLE PLEASED THAT JEAN AND LOUISE SEEMED TO TAKE A BACKSEAT WHILE I HAD A GO AT THE LOCK.
I EVEN GOT A FEW SENTENCES OUT!
GOOD THING BESS ALWAYS CARRIES HAIRPINS!
IT'S NOT A TOUGH LOCK. STANDARD ISSUE MEDIUM SECURITY ENTRY LOCKSET.
OPENING THIS DOOR SHOULD BE PRETTY...
...EASY! ESPECIALLY IF YOU KNOW THE SCHOOL WELL ENOUGH...
...TO REMEMBER THE SIDE EXIT THAT LEADS TO A CLASSROOM AND THEN THE HALL!
WHICH MEANS WHOEVER DID LOCK US IN...
... ISN'T LIKELY A STUDENT, OR ANYONE WHO KNOWS THE SCHOOL REALLY WELL...
...BUT WHO SOMEHOW GOT THEMSELVES A KEY!

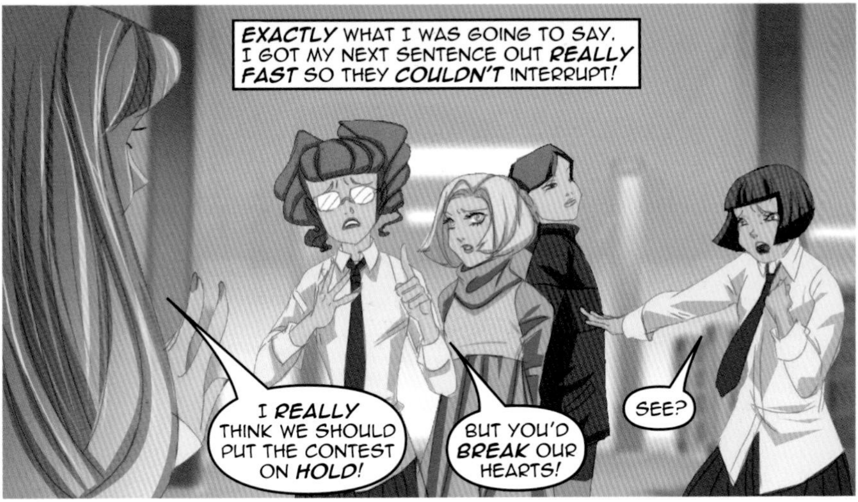
EXACTLY WHAT I WAS GOING TO SAY. I GOT MY NEXT SENTENCE OUT REALLY FAST SO THEY COULDN'T INTERRUPT!
I REALLY THINK WE SHOULD PUT THE CONTEST ON HOLD!
BUT YOU'D BREAK OUR HEARTS!
SEE?

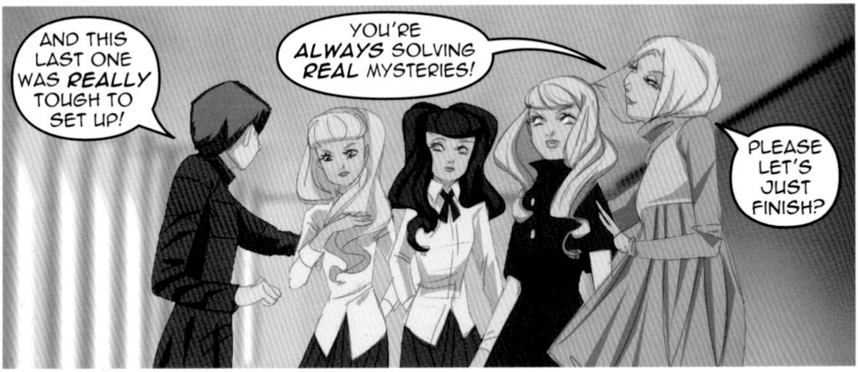
AND THIS LAST ONE WAS REALLY TOUGH TO SET UP!
YOU'RE ALWAYS SOLVING REAL MYSTERIES!
PLEASE LET'S JUST FINISH?

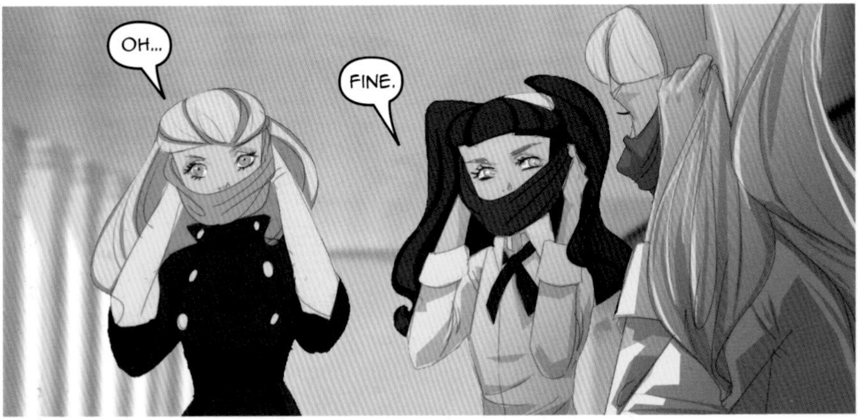
OH...
FINE.

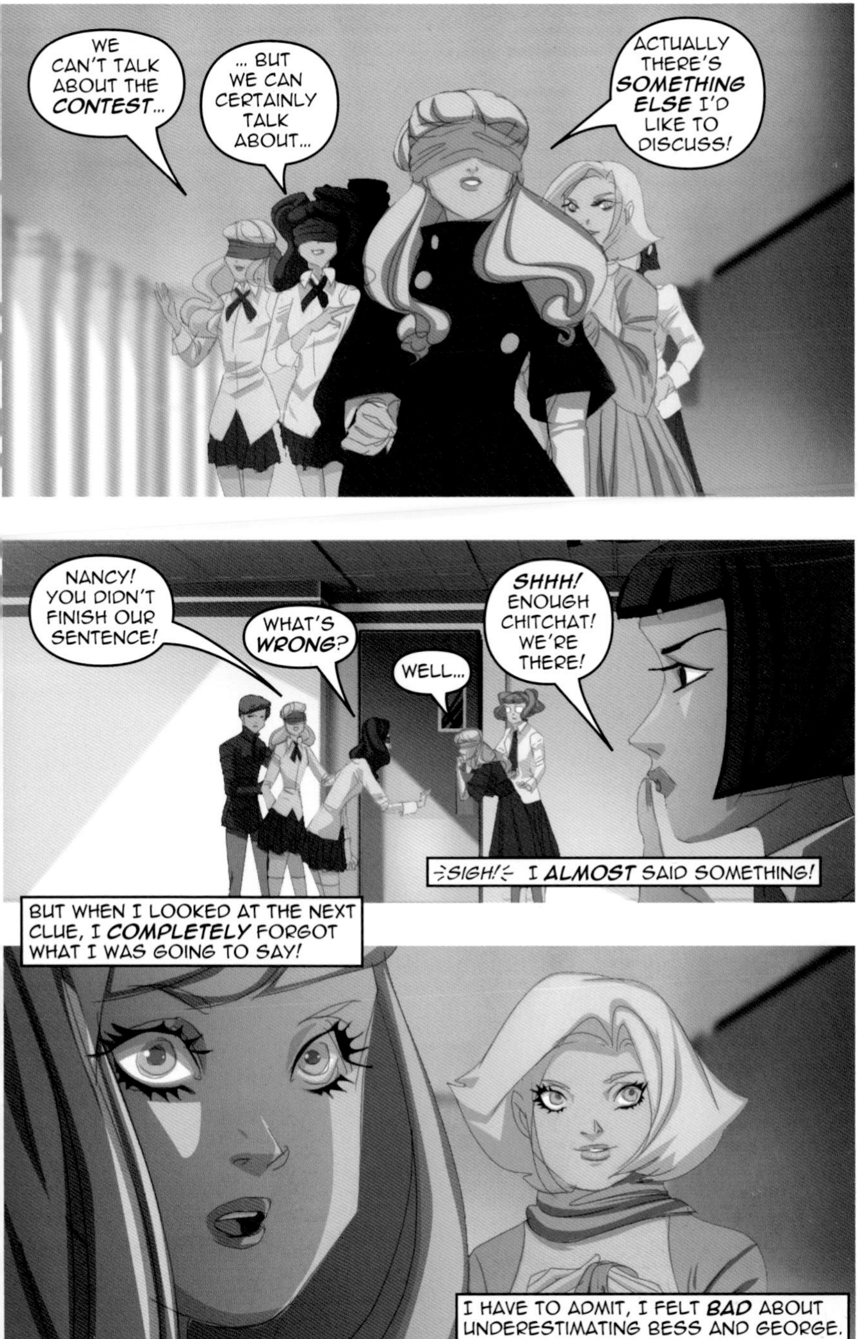

WE CAN'T TALK ABOUT THE CONTEST...
... BUT WE CAN CERTAINLY TALK ABOUT...
ACTUALLY THERE'S SOMETHING ELSE I'D LIKE TO DISCUSS!
NANCY! YOU DIDN'T FINISH OUR SENTENCE!
WHAT'S WRONG?
WELL...
SHHH! ENOUGH CHITCHAT! WE'RE THERE!
SIGH! I ALMOST SAID SOMETHING!
BUT WHEN I LOOKED AT THE NEXT CLUE, I COMPLETELY FORGOT WHAT I WAS GOING TO SAY!
I HAVE TO ADMIT, I FELT BAD ABOUT UNDERESTIMATING BESS AND GEORGE.

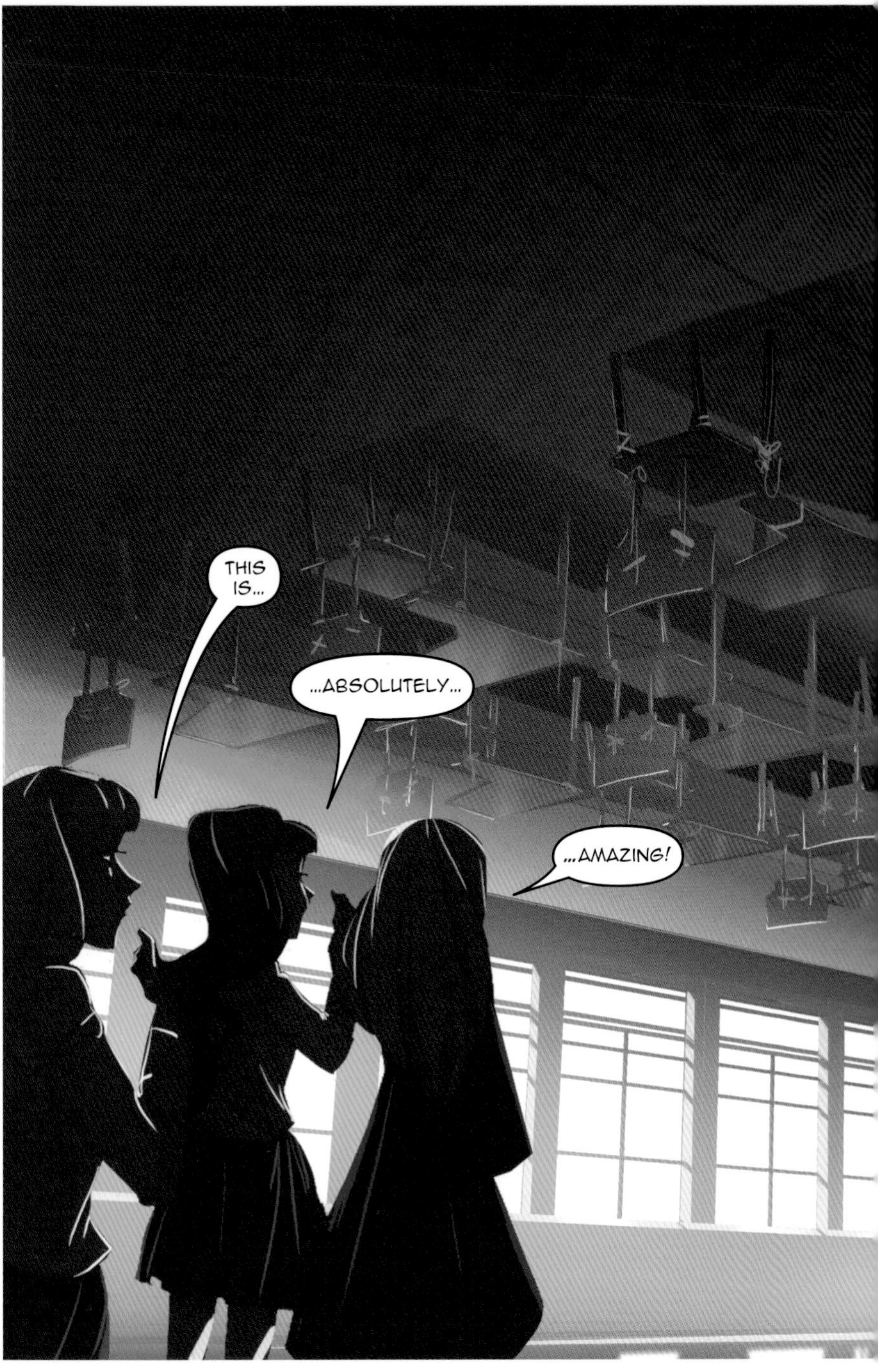
THIS IS...
...ABSOLUTELY...
...AMAZING!

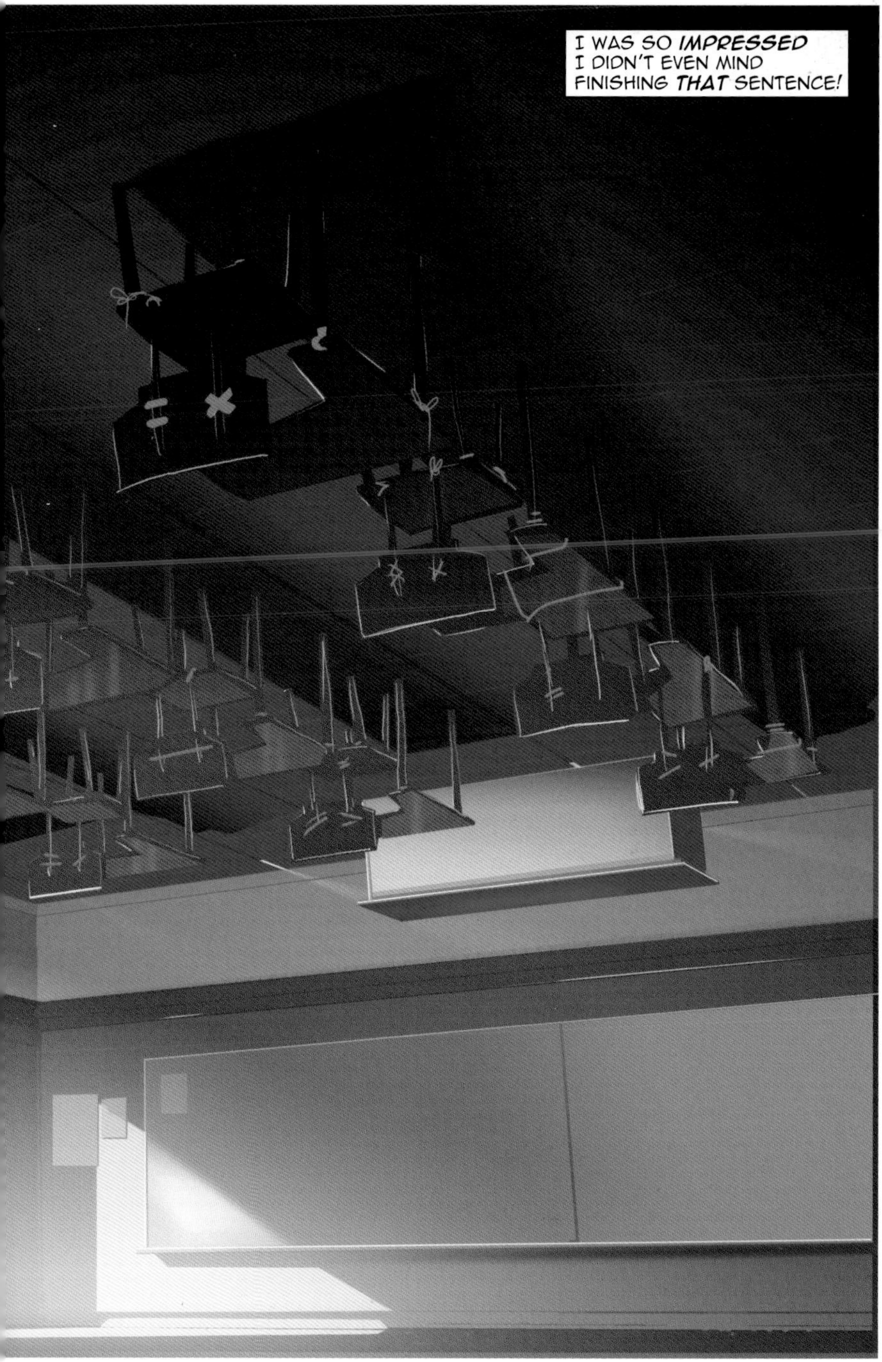
I WAS SO IMPRESSED I DIDN'T EVEN MIND FINISHING THAT SENTENCE!

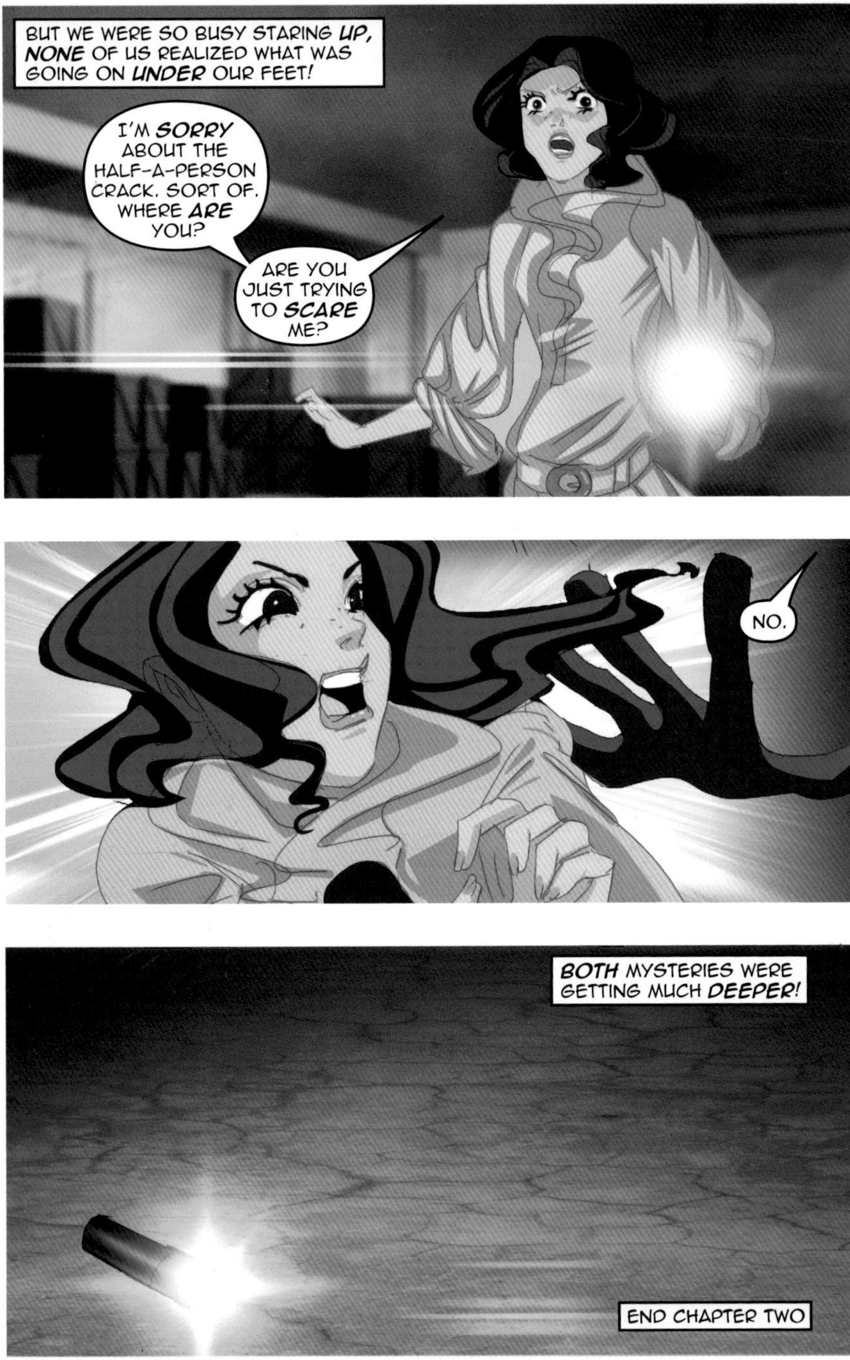
BUT WE WERE SO BUSY STARING *UP*, *NONE* OF US REALIZED WHAT WAS GOING ON *UNDER* OUR FEET!
I'M *SORRY* ABOUT THE HALF-A-PERSON CRACK. SORT OF. WHERE *ARE* YOU?
ARE YOU JUST TRYING TO *SCARE* ME?
NO.
BOTH MYSTERIES WERE GETTING MUCH *DEEPER*!
END CHAPTER TWO

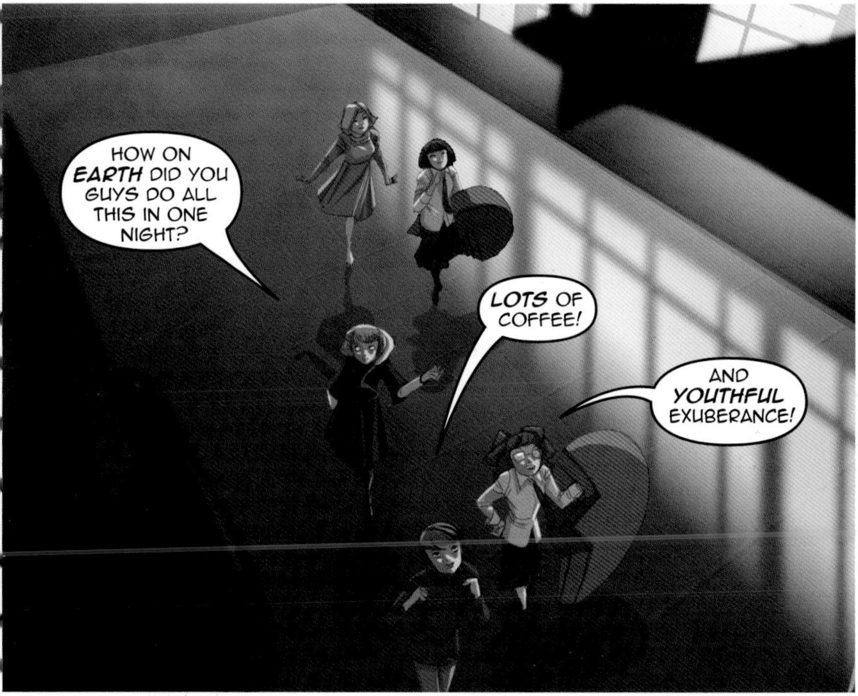
HOW ON EARTH DID YOU GUYS DO ALL THIS IN ONE NIGHT?
LOTS OF COFFEE!
AND YOUTHFUL EXUBERANCE!

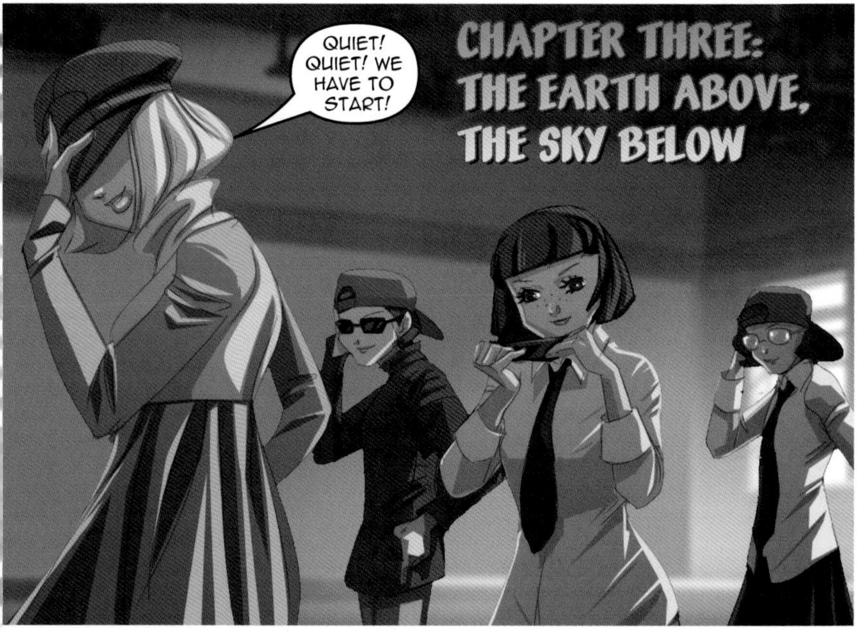
QUIET! QUIET! WE HAVE TO START!
CHAPTER THREE: THE EARTH ABOVE, THE SKY BELOW

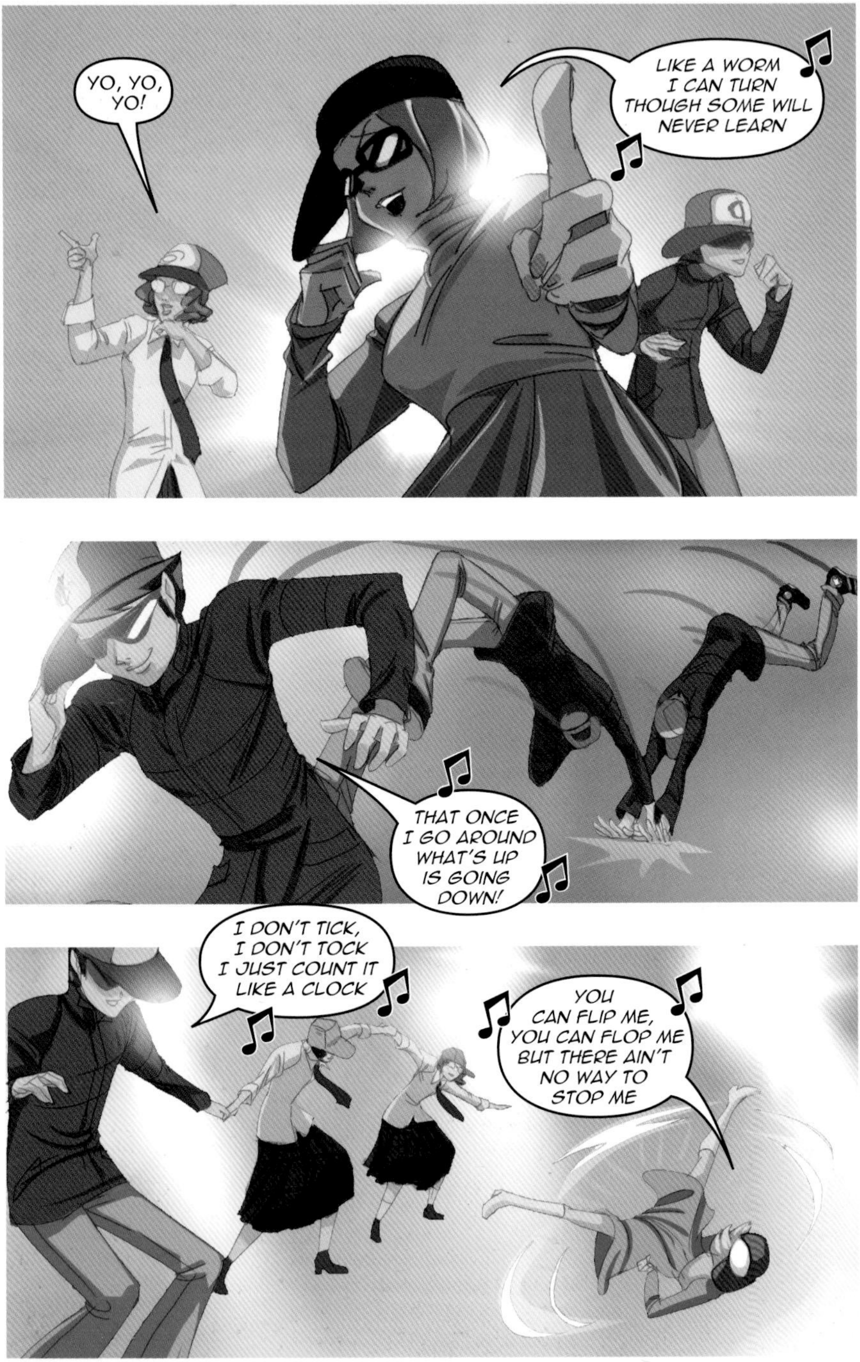
YO, YO, YO!
LIKE A WORM I CAN TURN THOUGH SOME WILL NEVER LEARN
THAT ONCE I GO AROUND WHAT'S UP IS GOING DOWN!
I DON'T TICK, I DON'T TOCK I JUST COUNT IT LIKE A CLOCK
YOU CAN FLIP ME, YOU CAN FLOP ME BUT THERE AIN'T NO WAY TO STOP ME

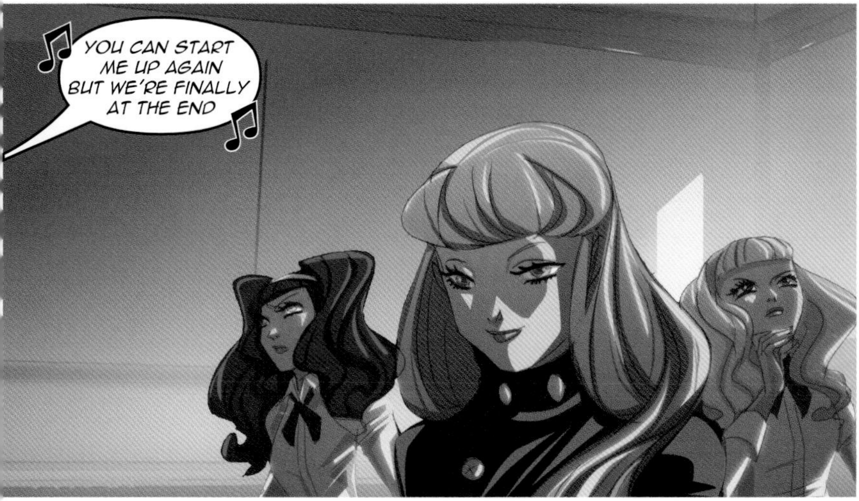
YOU CAN START ME UP AGAIN BUT WE'RE FINALLY AT THE END

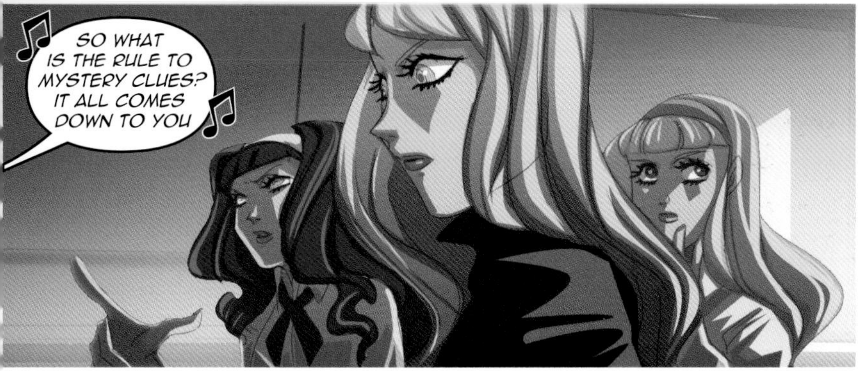
SO WHAT IS THE RULE TO MYSTERY CLUES? IT ALL COMES DOWN TO YOU

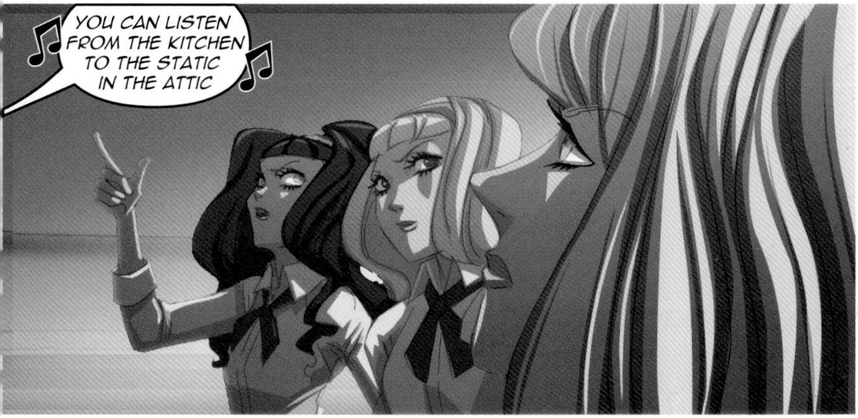
YOU CAN LISTEN FROM THE KITCHEN TO THE STATIC IN THE ATTIC

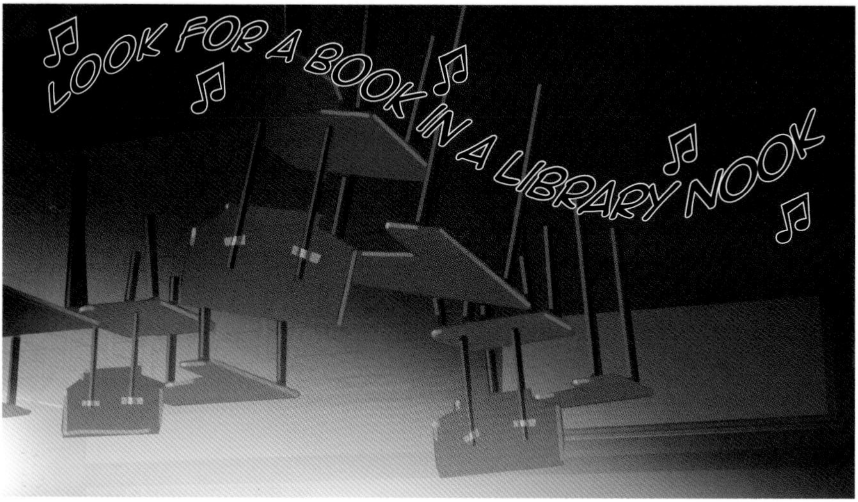
LOOK FOR A BOOK IN A LIBRARY NOOK

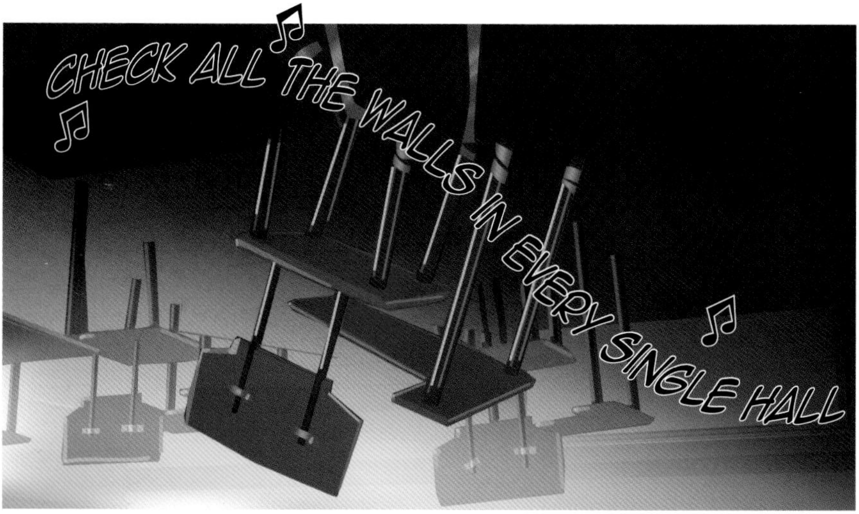
CHECK ALL THE WALLS IN EVERY SINGLE HALL

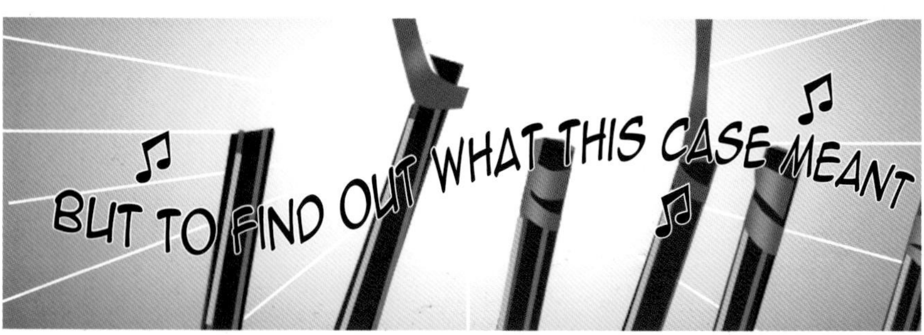
BUT TO FIND OUT WHAT THIS CASE MEANT

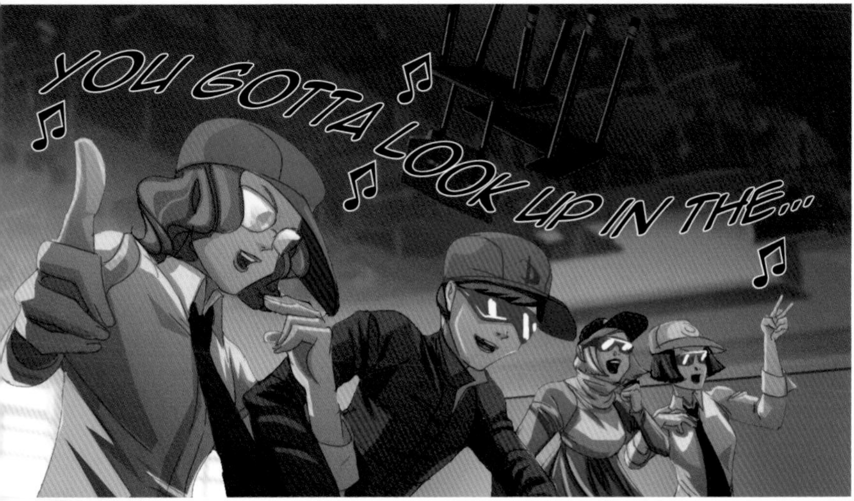

YOU GOTTA LOOK UP IN THE...

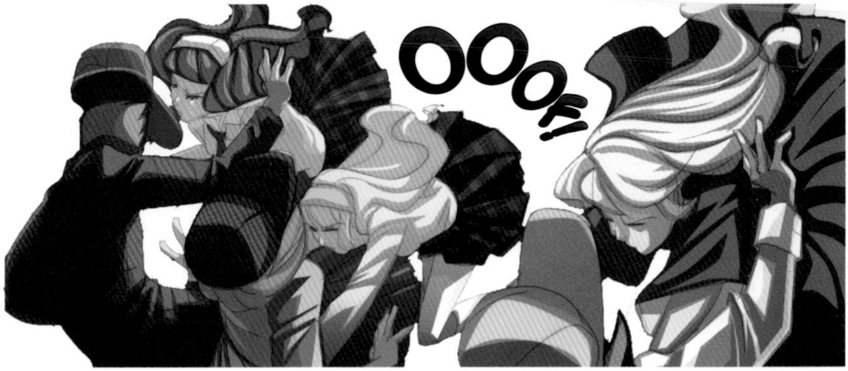

OOOF!

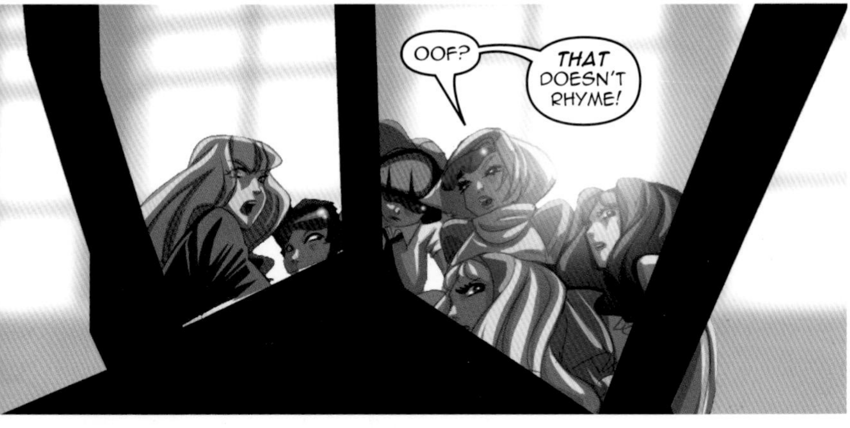

OOF?
THAT DOESN'T RHYME!

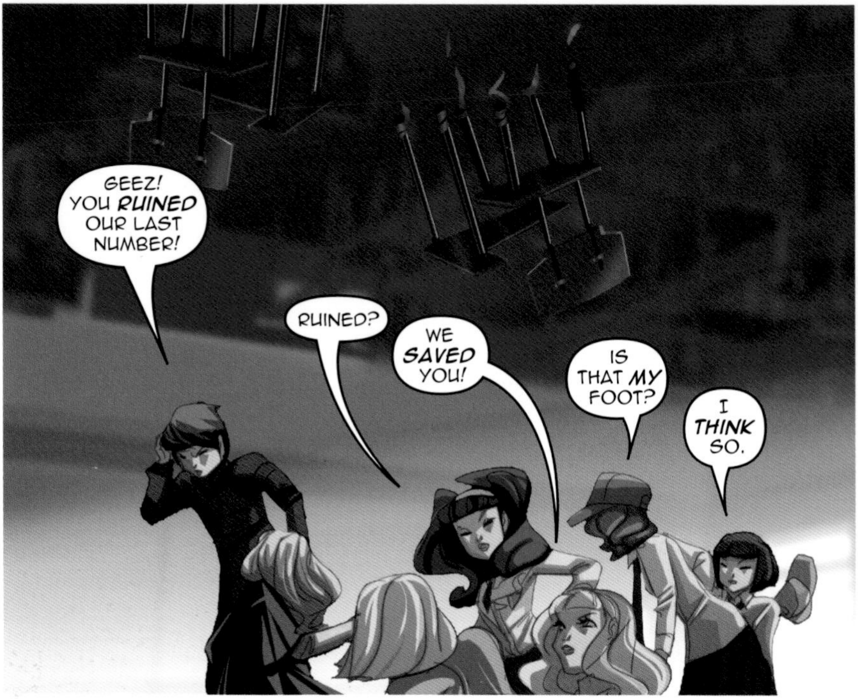
GEEZ! YOU RUINED OUR LAST NUMBER!
RUINED?
WE SAVED YOU!
IS THAT MY FOOT?
I THINK SO.

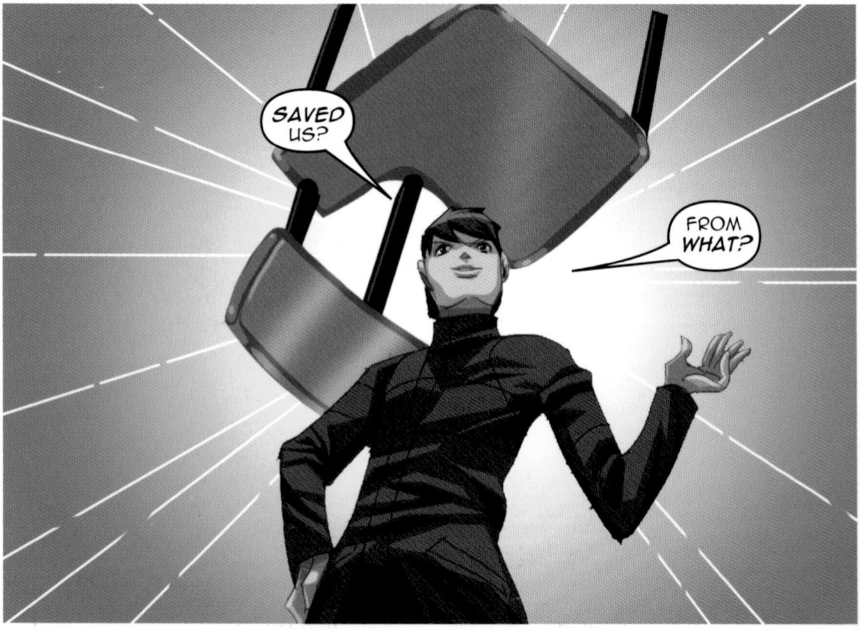
SAVED US?
FROM WHAT?

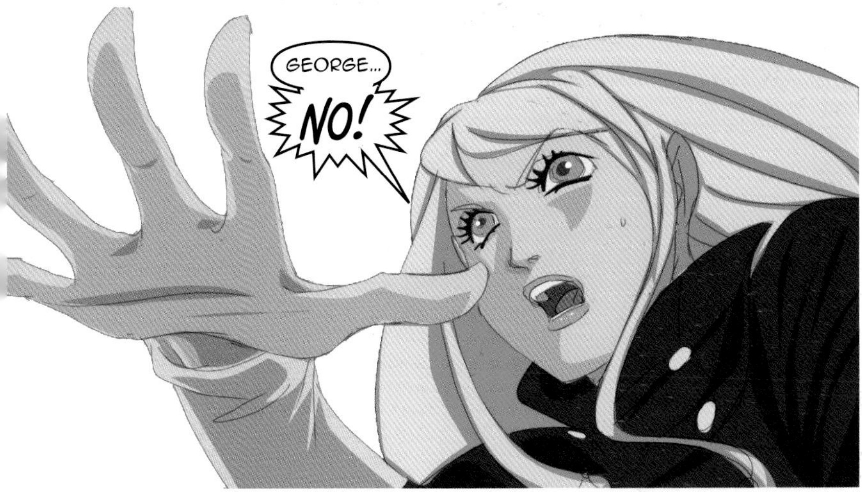
GEORGE...
NO!

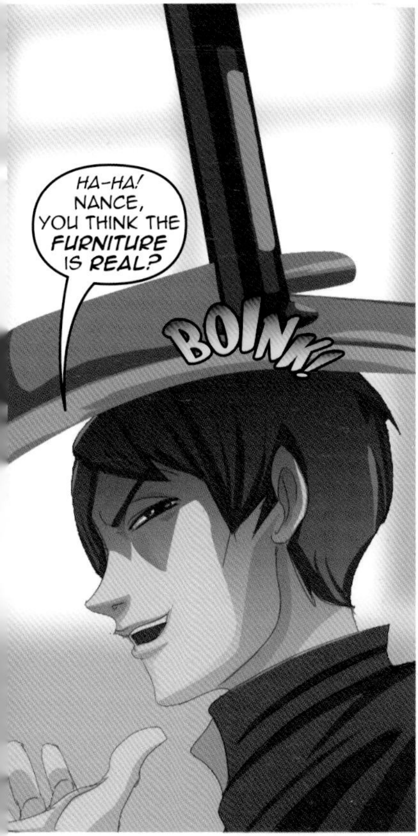
HA-HA! NANCE, YOU THINK THE FURNITURE IS REAL?
BOINK!

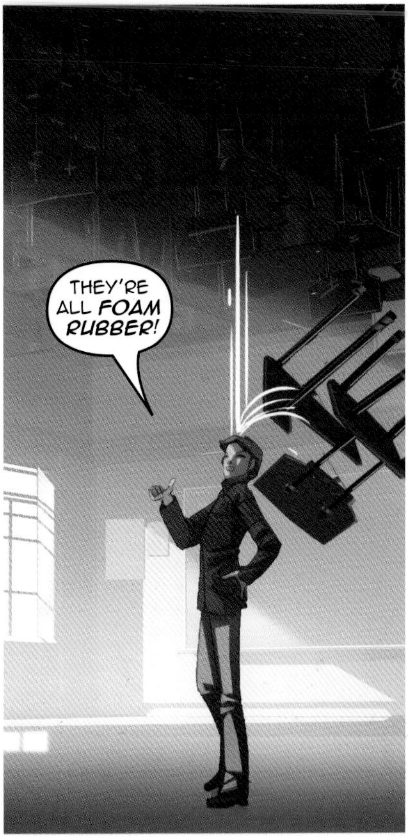
THEY'RE ALL FOAM RUBBER!

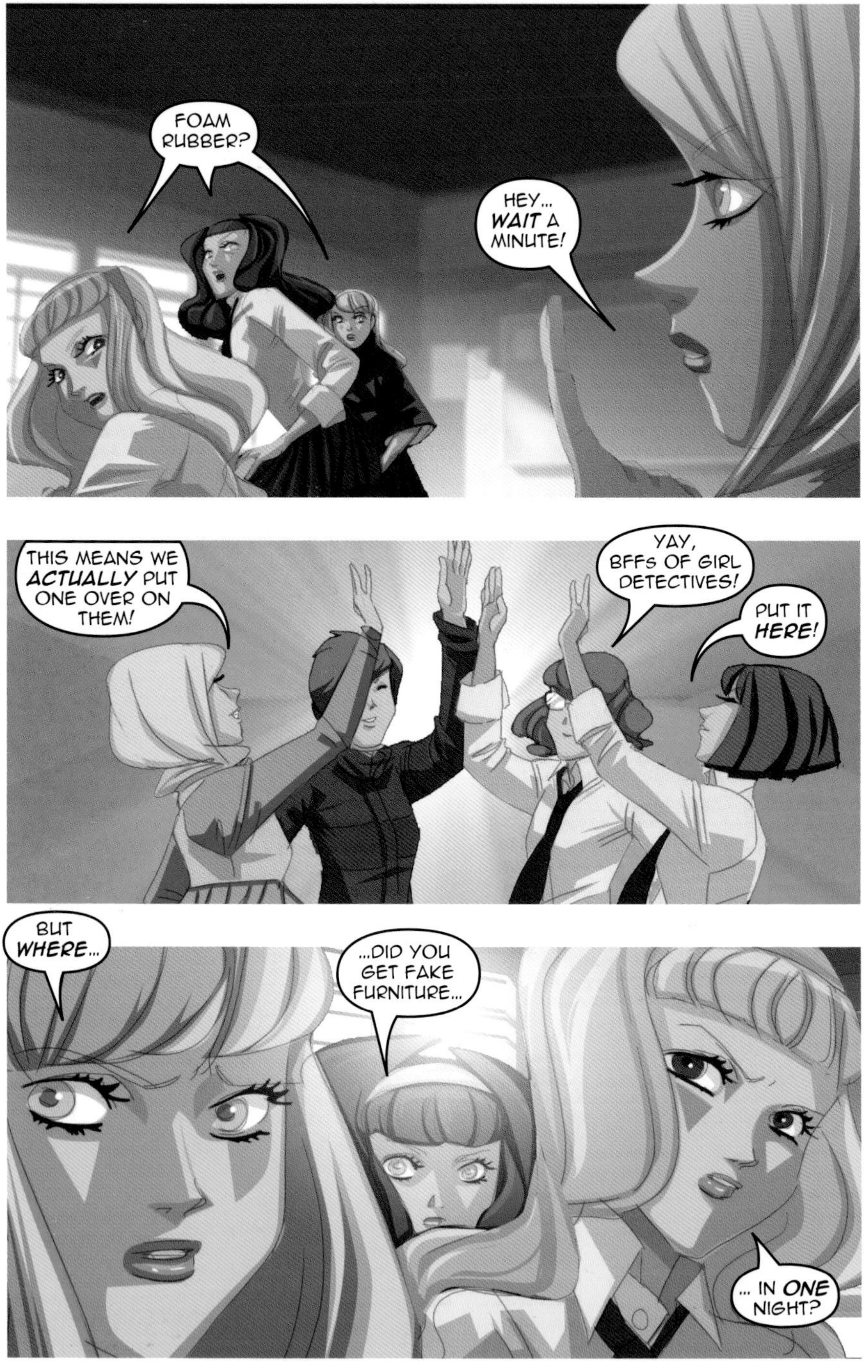
FOAM RUBBER?
HEY... WAIT A MINUTE!
THIS MEANS WE ACTUALLY PUT ONE OVER ON THEM!
YAY, BFFs OF GIRL DETECTIVES!
PUT IT HERE!
BUT WHERE...
...DID YOU GET FAKE FURNITURE...
... IN ONE NIGHT?

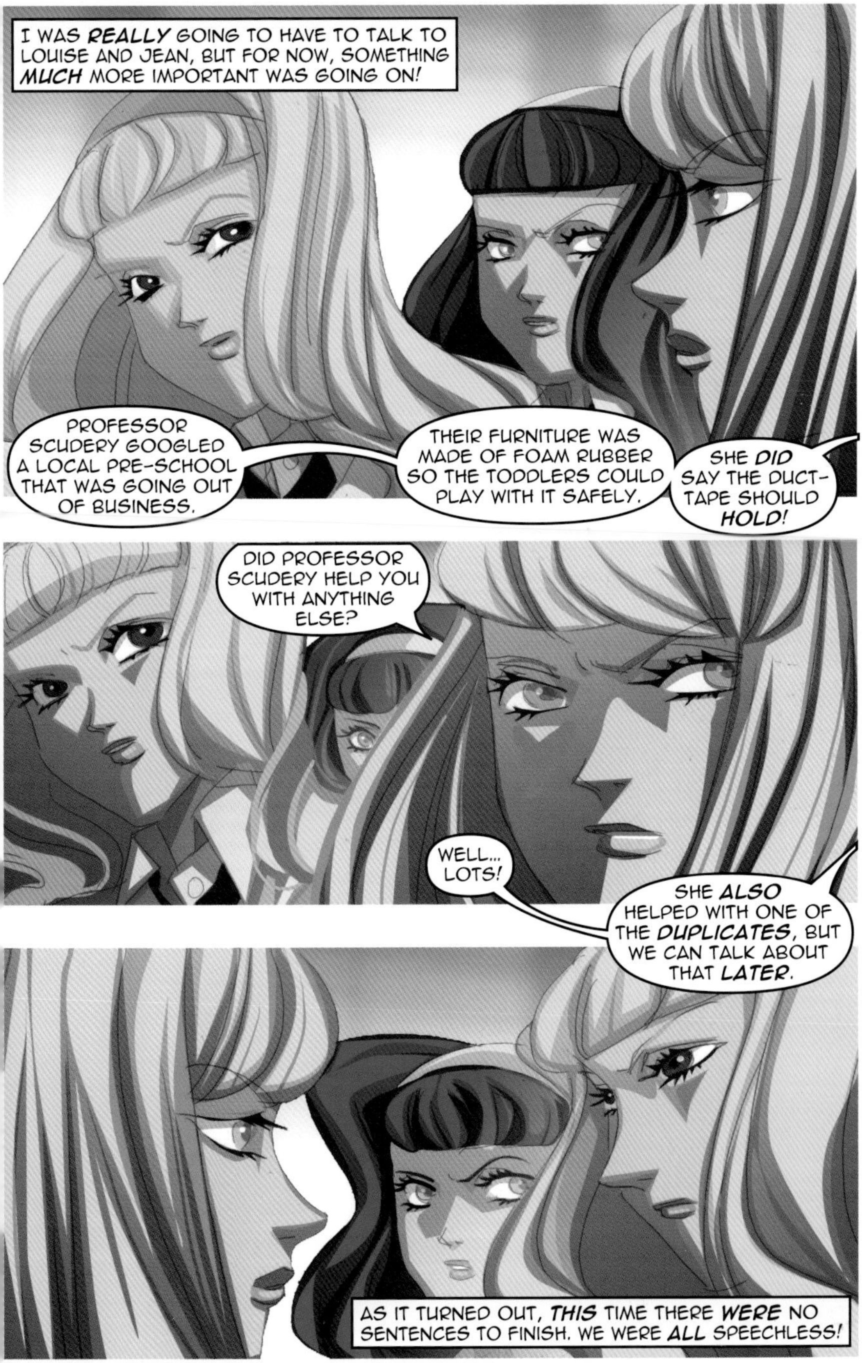
I WAS REALLY GOING TO HAVE TO TALK TO LOUISE AND JEAN, BUT FOR NOW, SOMETHING MUCH MORE IMPORTANT WAS GOING ON!
PROFESSOR SCUDERY GOOGLED A LOCAL PRE-SCHOOL THAT WAS GOING OUT OF BUSINESS.
THEIR FURNITURE WAS MADE OF FOAM RUBBER SO THE TODDLERS COULD PLAY WITH IT SAFELY.
SHE DID SAY THE DUCT-TAPE SHOULD HOLD!
DID PROFESSOR SCUDERY HELP YOU WITH ANYTHING ELSE?
WELL... LOTS!
SHE ALSO HELPED WITH ONE OF THE DUPLICATES, BUT WE CAN TALK ABOUT THAT LATER.
AS IT TURNED OUT, THIS TIME THERE WERE NO SENTENCES TO FINISH. WE WERE ALL SPEECHLESS!

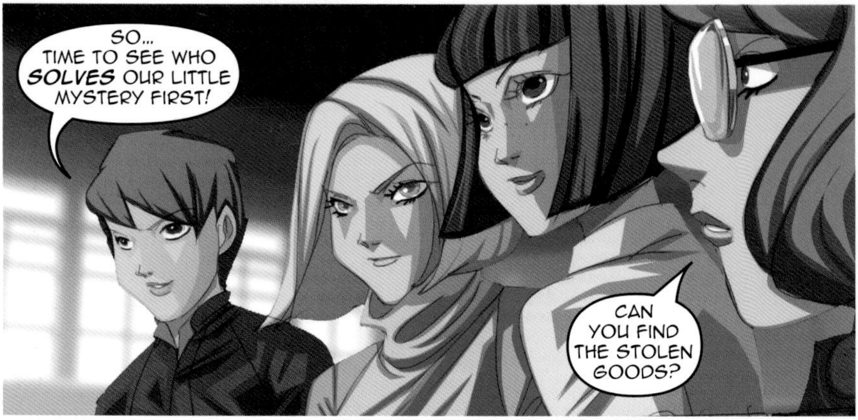
SO... TIME TO SEE WHO SOLVES OUR LITTLE MYSTERY FIRST!
CAN YOU FIND THE STOLEN GOODS?

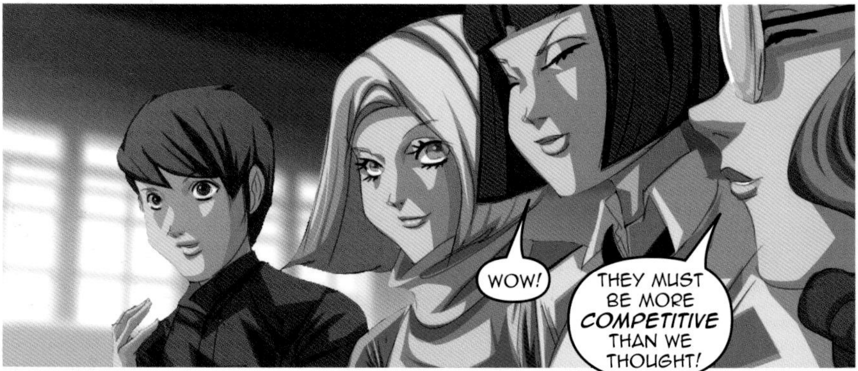
WOW!
THEY MUST BE MORE COMPETITIVE THAN WE THOUGHT!

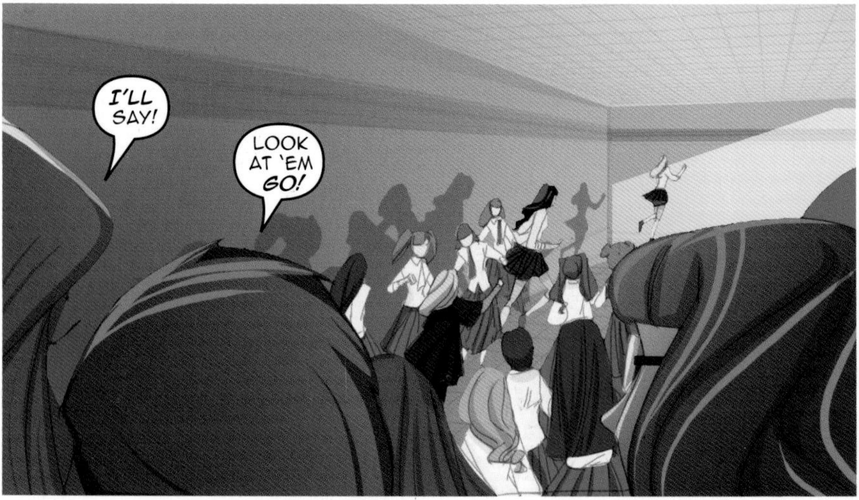
I'LL SAY!
LOOK AT 'EM GO!

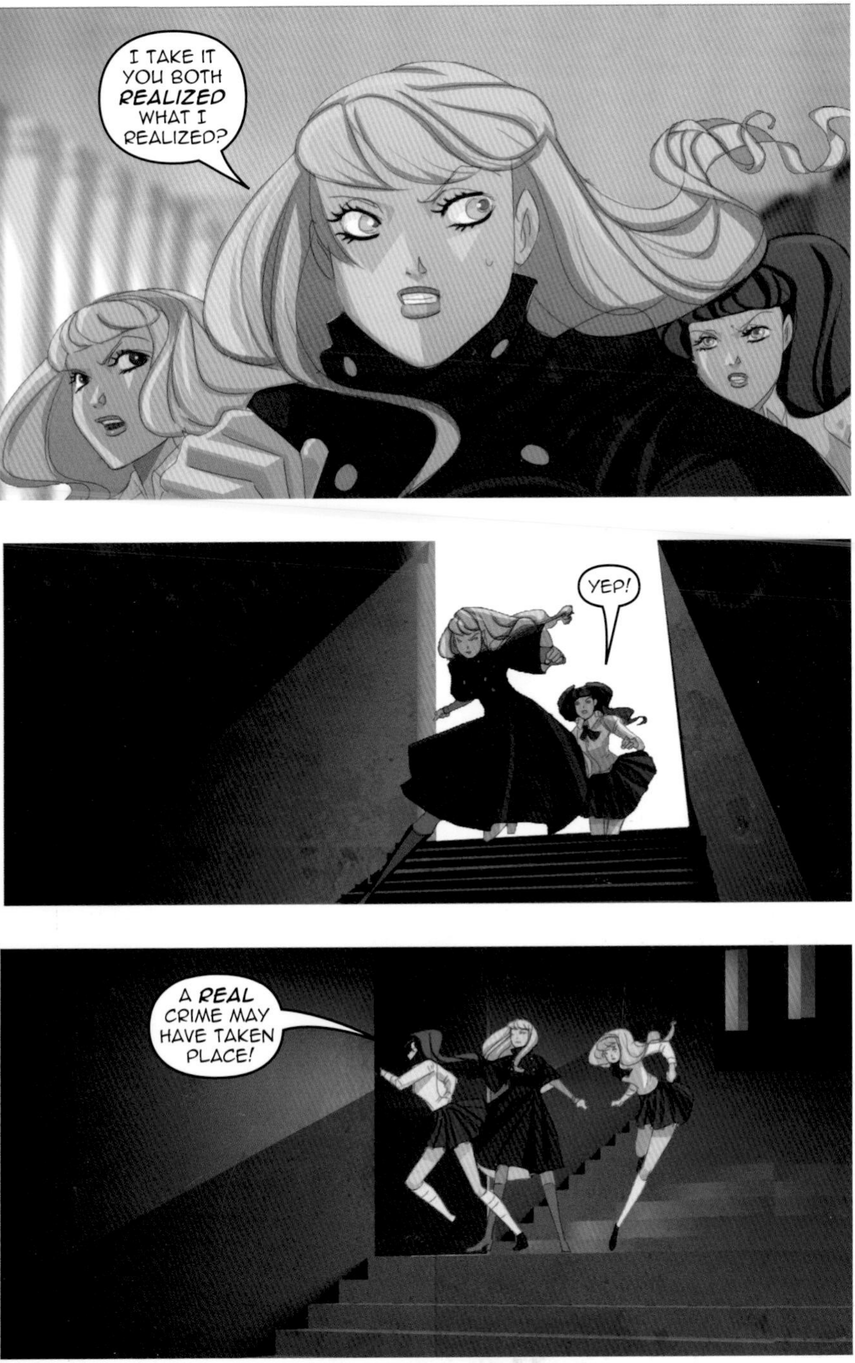
I TAKE IT YOU BOTH REALIZED WHAT I REALIZED?
YEP!
A REAL CRIME MAY HAVE TAKEN PLACE!

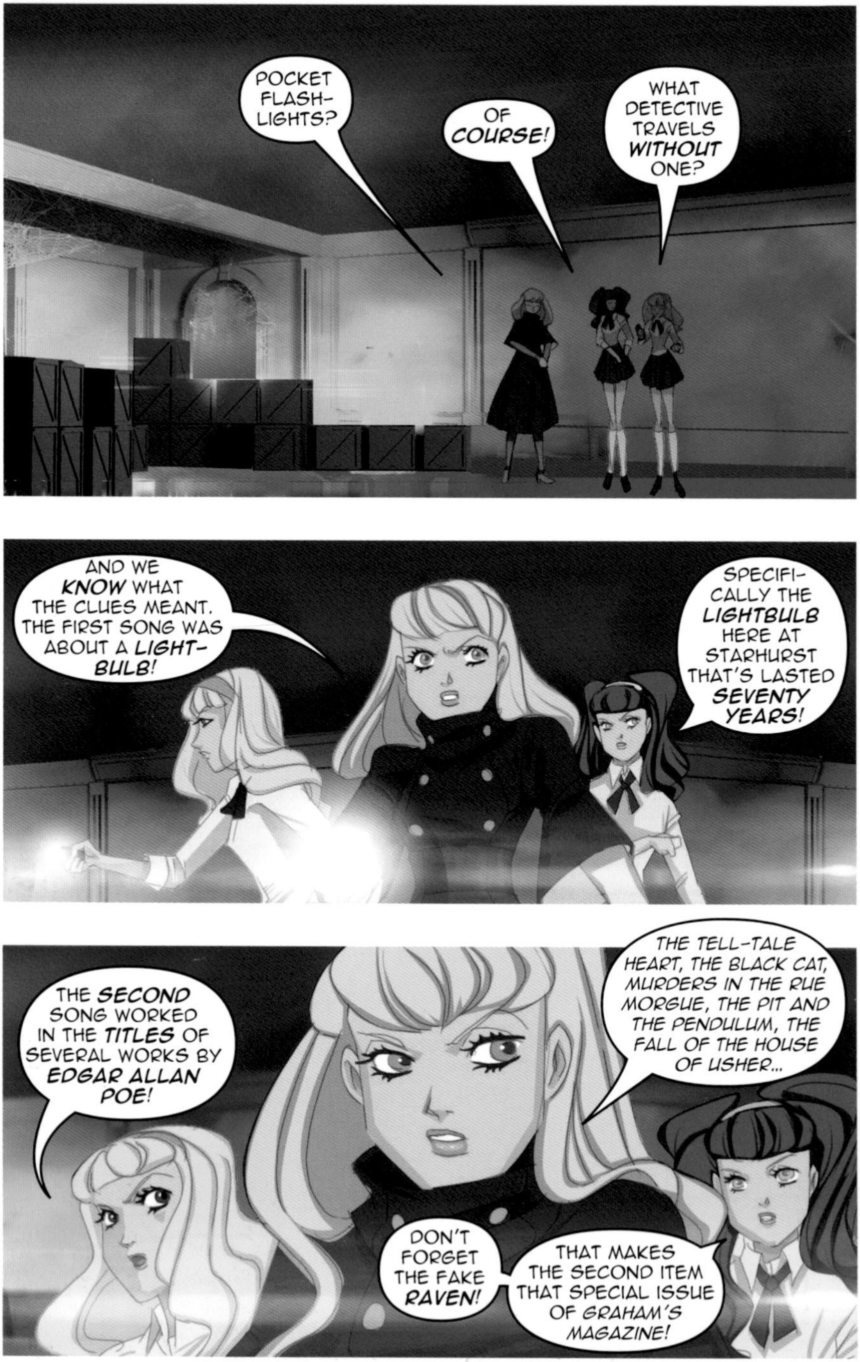
POCKET FLASH-LIGHTS?
OF COURSE!
WHAT DETECTIVE TRAVELS WITHOUT ONE?
AND WE KNOW WHAT THE CLUES MEANT. THE FIRST SONG WAS ABOUT A LIGHT-BULB!
SPECIFI-CALLY THE LIGHTBULB HERE AT STARHURST THAT'S LASTED SEVENTY YEARS!
THE SECOND SONG WORKED IN THE TITLES OF SEVERAL WORKS BY EDGAR ALLAN POE!
THE TELL-TALE HEART, THE BLACK CAT, MURDERS IN THE RUE MORGUE, THE PIT AND THE PENDULUM, THE FALL OF THE HOUSE OF USHER...
DON'T FORGET THE FAKE RAVEN!
THAT MAKES THE SECOND ITEM THAT SPECIAL ISSUE OF GRAHAM'S MAGAZINE!

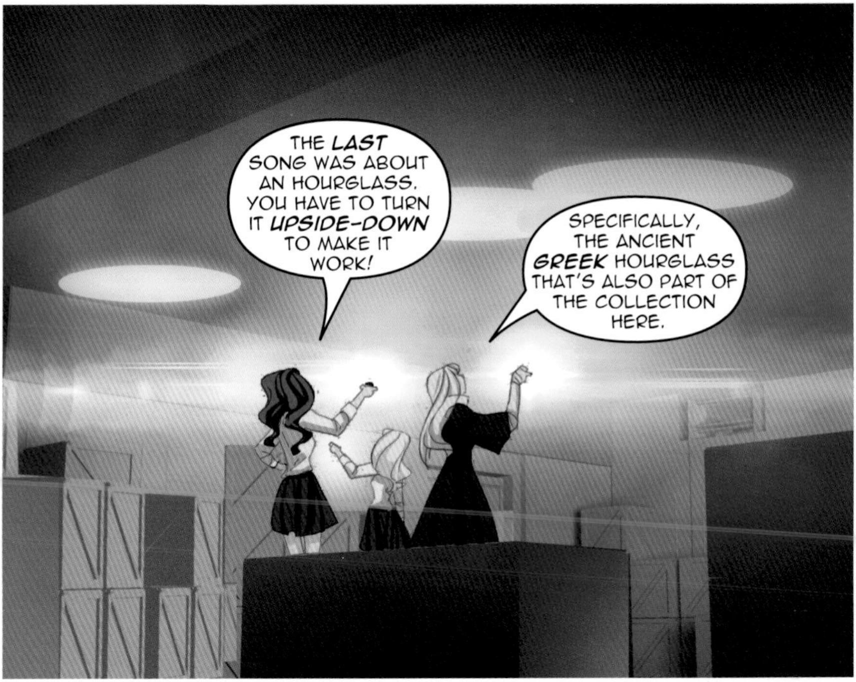
THE LAST SONG WAS ABOUT AN HOURGLASS. YOU HAVE TO TURN IT UPSIDE-DOWN TO MAKE IT WORK!
SPECIFICALLY, THE ANCIENT GREEK HOURGLASS THAT'S ALSO PART OF THE COLLECTION HERE.

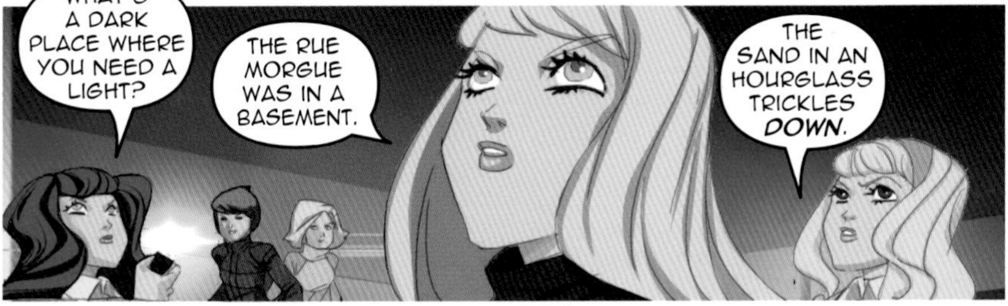
WHAT'S A DARK PLACE WHERE YOU NEED A LIGHT?
THE RUE MORGUE WAS IN A BASEMENT.
THE SAND IN AN HOURGLASS TRICKLES DOWN.

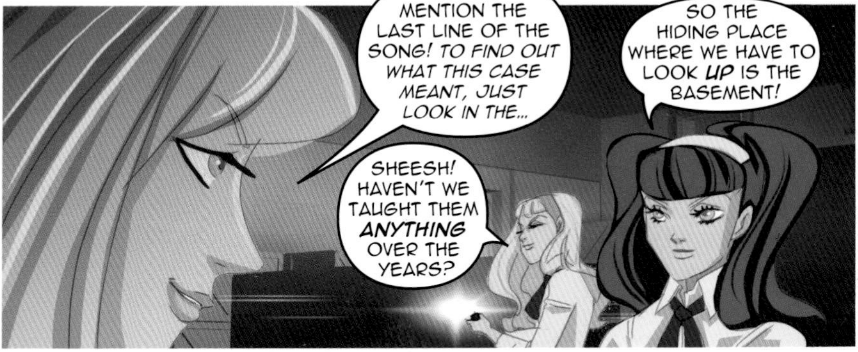
NOT TO MENTION THE LAST LINE OF THE SONG! TO FIND OUT WHAT THIS CASE MEANT, JUST LOOK IN THE...
SO THE HIDING PLACE WHERE WE HAVE TO LOOK UP IS THE BASEMENT!
SHEESH! HAVEN'T WE TAUGHT THEM ANYTHING OVER THE YEARS?

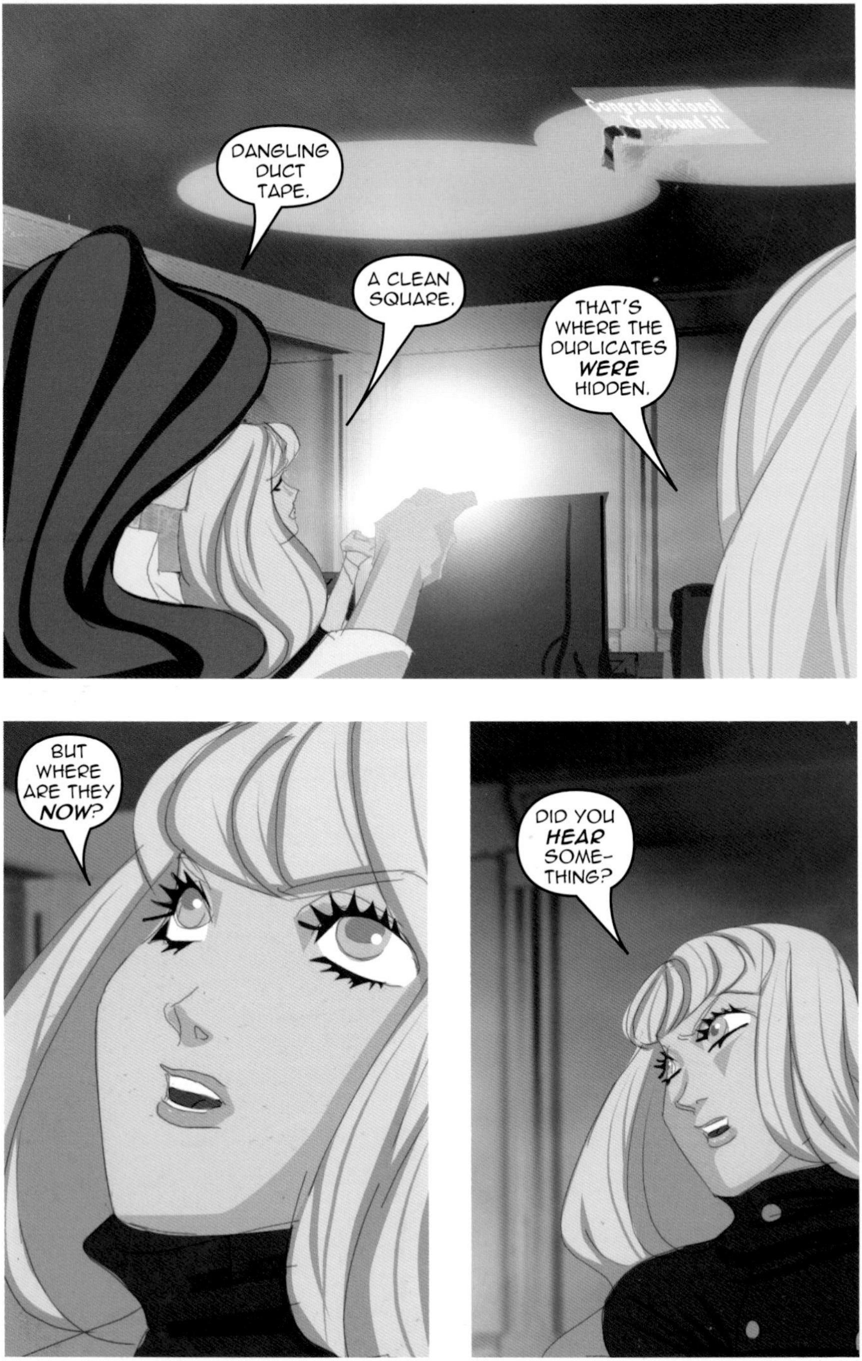
Congratulations! You found it!
DANGLING DUCT TAPE.
A CLEAN SQUARE.
THAT'S WHERE THE DUPLICATES *WERE* HIDDEN.
BUT WHERE ARE THEY *NOW*?
DID YOU *HEAR* SOMETHING?

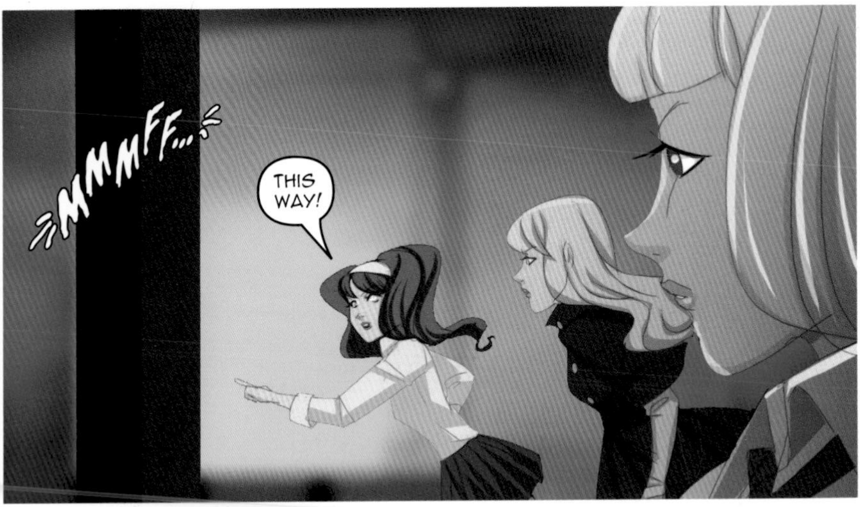
MMMFF...
THIS WAY!

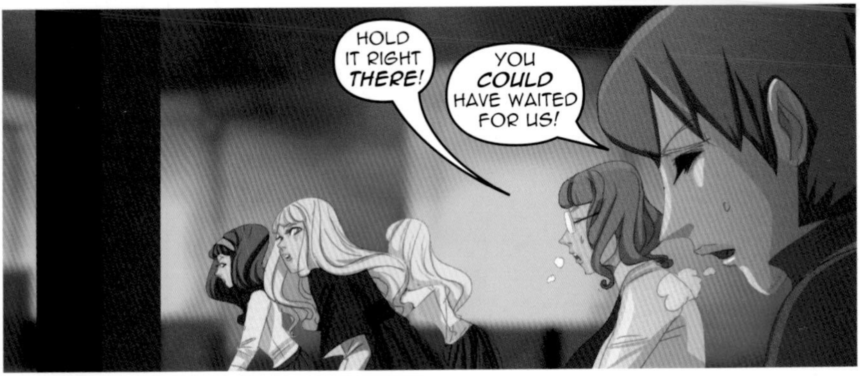
HOLD IT RIGHT THERE!
YOU COULD HAVE WAITED FOR US!

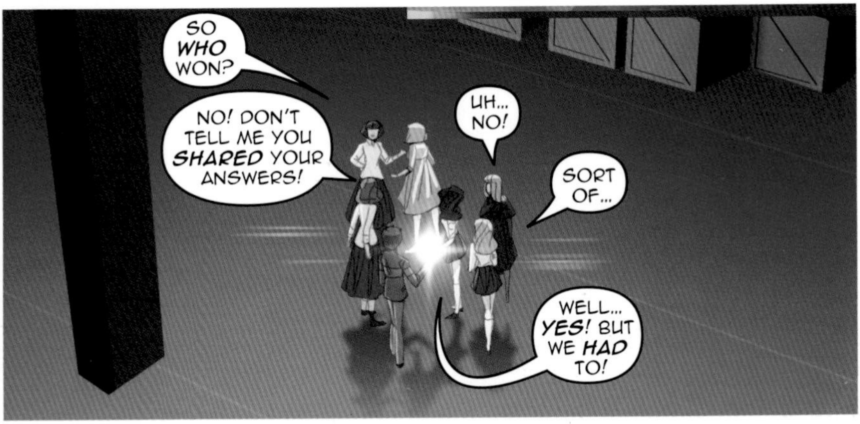
SO WHO WON?
NO! DON'T TELL ME YOU SHARED YOUR ANSWERS!
UH... NO!
SORT OF...
WELL... YES! BUT WE HAD TO!

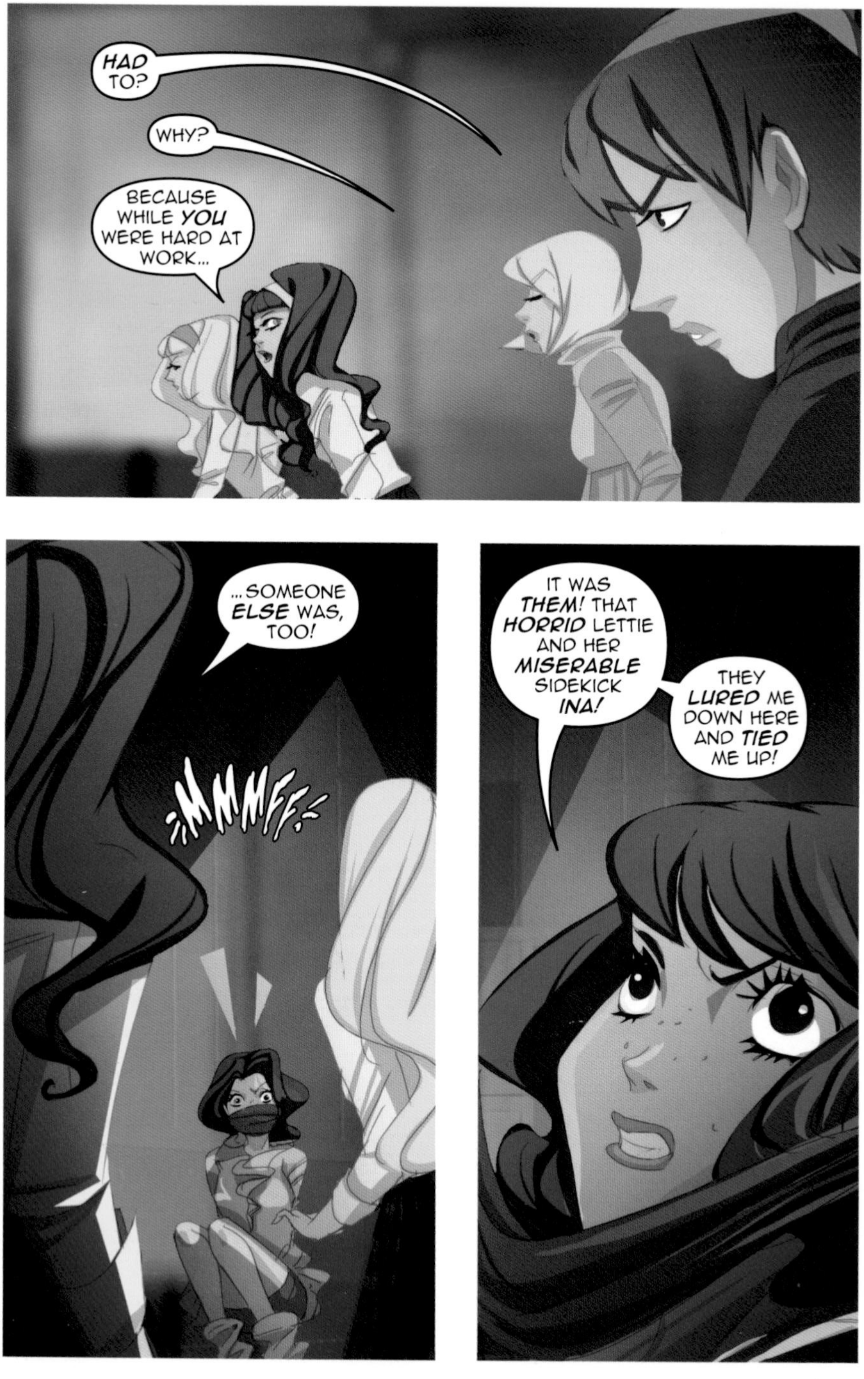
HAD TO?
WHY?
BECAUSE WHILE YOU WERE HARD AT WORK...
...SOMEONE ELSE WAS, TOO!
MMMFF
IT WAS THEM! THAT HORRID LETTIE AND HER MISERABLE SIDEKICK INA!
THEY LURED ME DOWN HERE AND TIED ME UP!

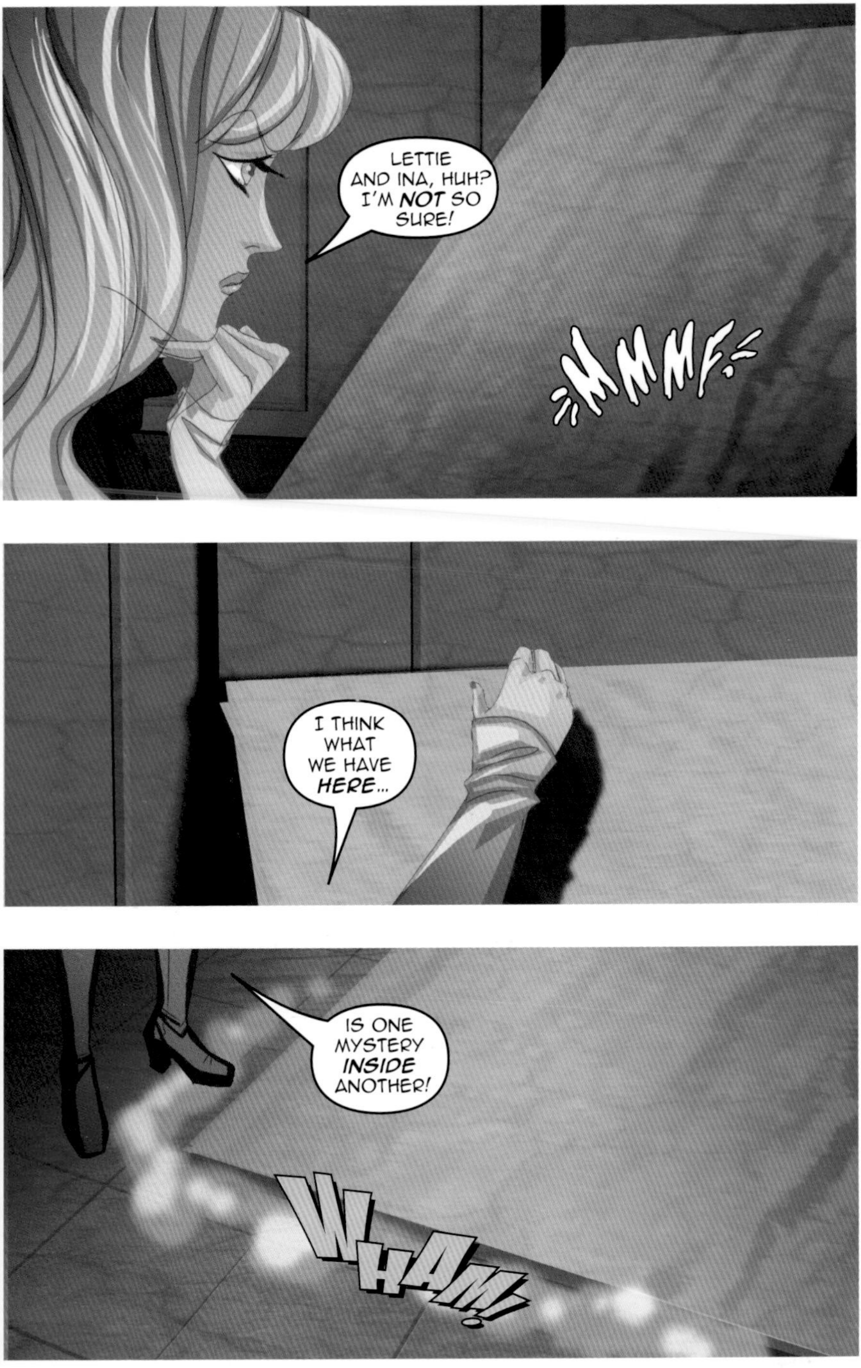
LETTIE AND INA, HUH? I'M NOT SO SURE!
MMMF
I THINK WHAT WE HAVE HERE...
IS ONE MYSTERY INSIDE ANOTHER!
WHAM!

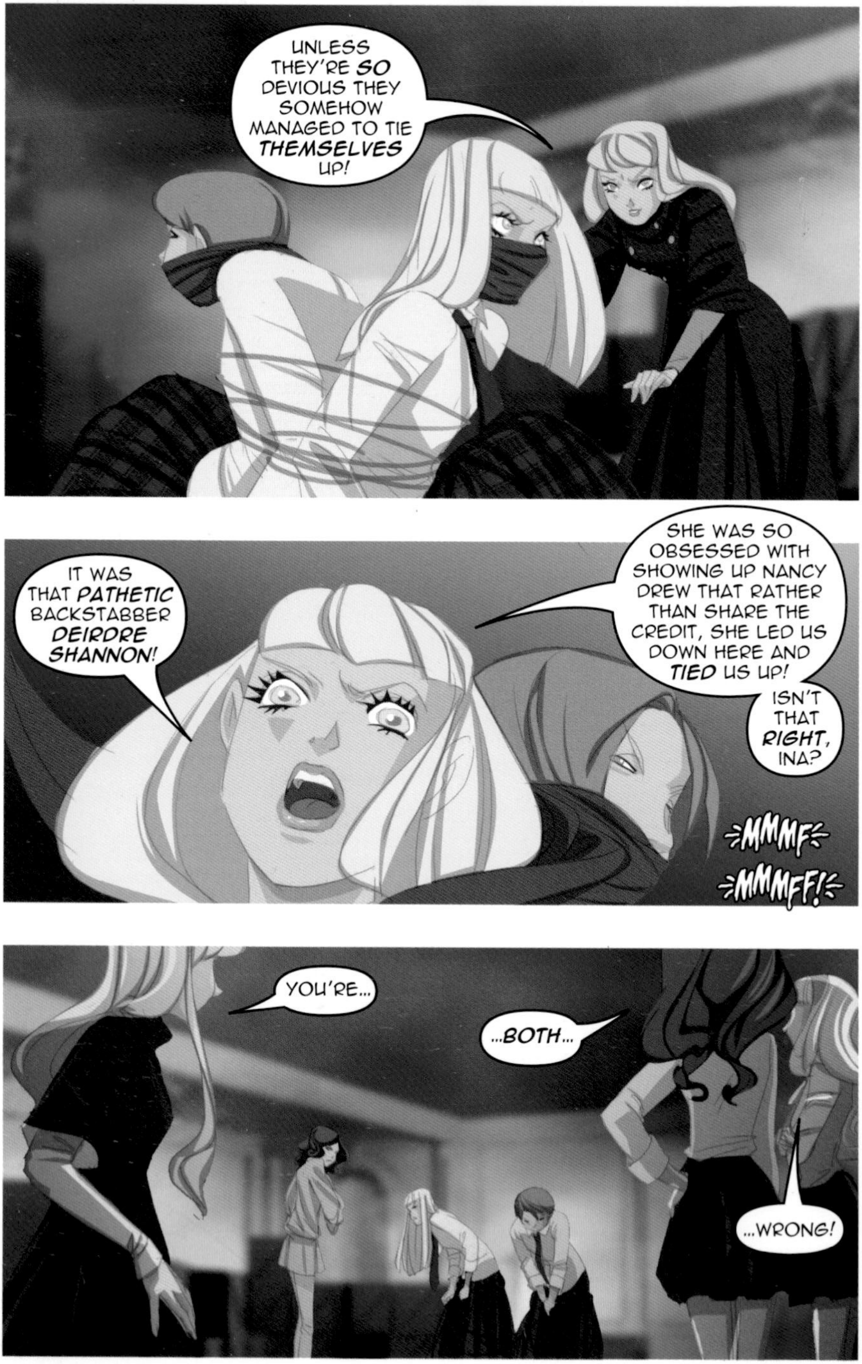
UNLESS THEY'RE SO DEVIOUS THEY SOMEHOW MANAGED TO TIE THEMSELVES UP!
IT WAS THAT PATHETIC BACKSTABBER DEIRDRE SHANNON!
SHE WAS SO OBSESSED WITH SHOWING UP NANCY DREW THAT RATHER THAN SHARE THE CREDIT, SHE LED US DOWN HERE AND TIED US UP!
ISN'T THAT RIGHT, INA?
MMMF
MMMFF!
YOU'RE...
...BOTH...
...WRONG!

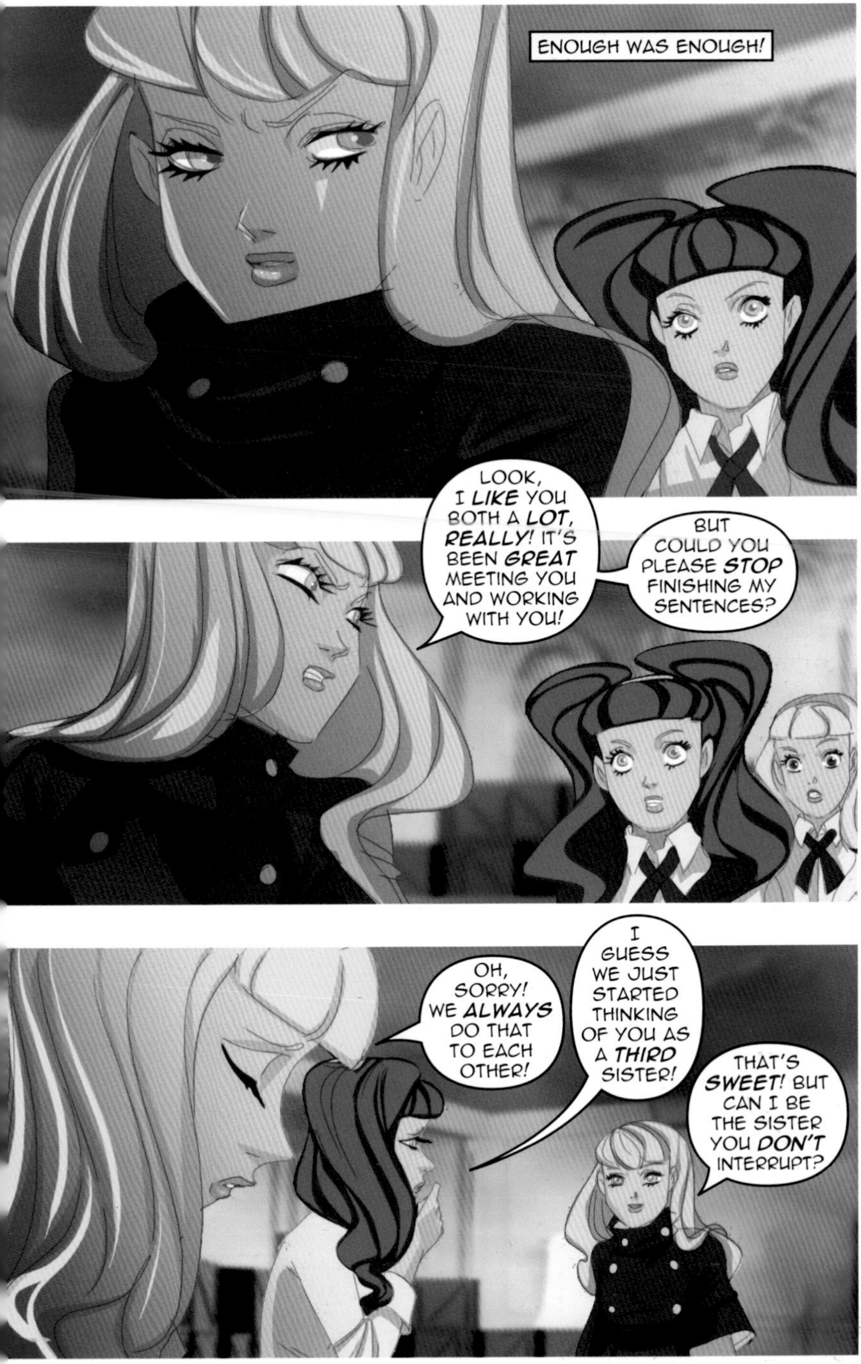
ENOUGH WAS ENOUGH!
LOOK, I LIKE YOU BOTH A LOT, REALLY! IT'S BEEN GREAT MEETING YOU AND WORKING WITH YOU!
BUT COULD YOU PLEASE STOP FINISHING MY SENTENCES?
OH, SORRY! WE ALWAYS DO THAT TO EACH OTHER!
I GUESS WE JUST STARTED THINKING OF YOU AS A THIRD SISTER!
THAT'S SWEET! BUT CAN I BE THE SISTER YOU DON'T INTERRUPT?

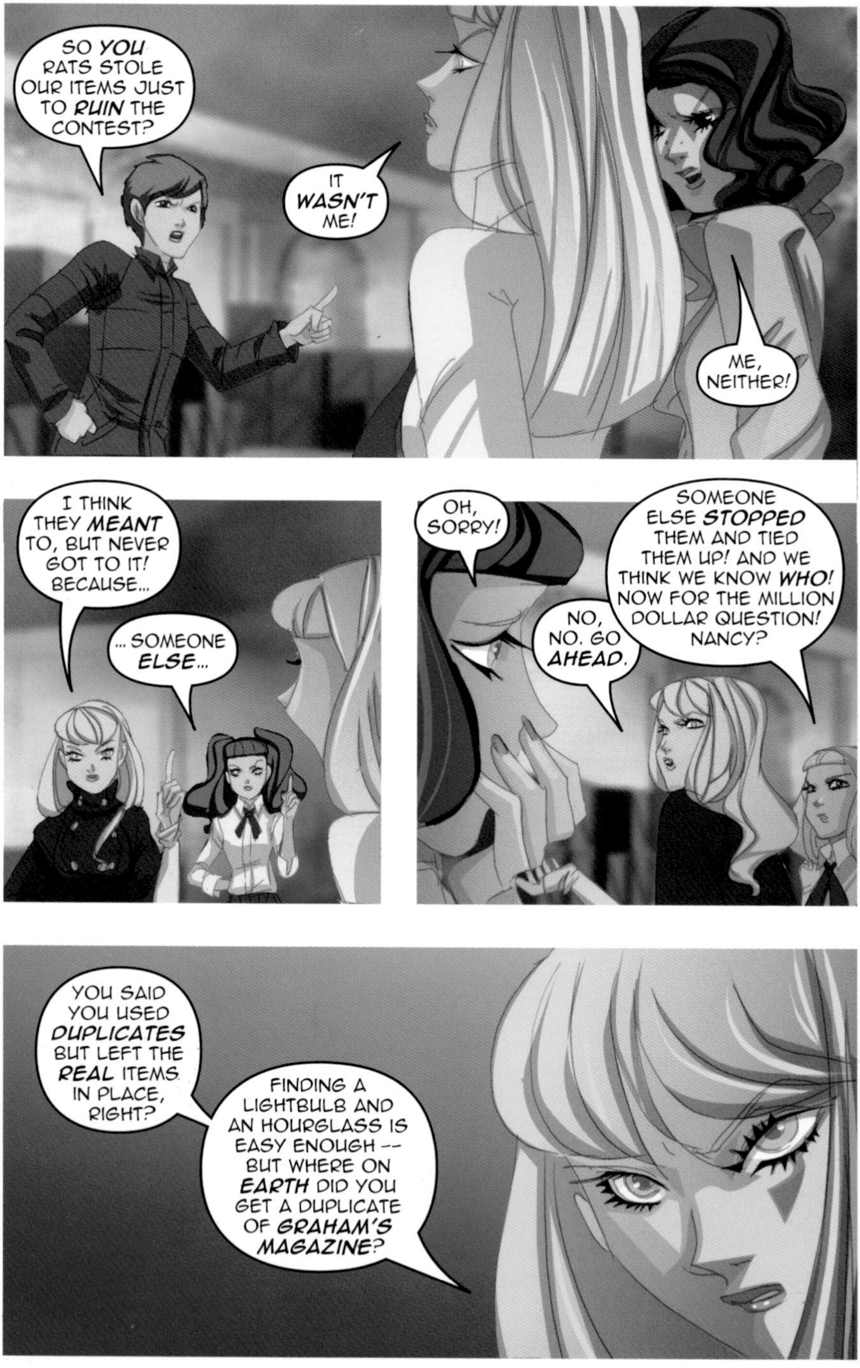
SO YOU RATS STOLE OUR ITEMS JUST TO RUIN THE CONTEST?
IT WASN'T ME!
ME, NEITHER!
I THINK THEY MEANT TO, BUT NEVER GOT TO IT! BECAUSE...
... SOMEONE ELSE...
OH, SORRY!
SOMEONE ELSE STOPPED THEM AND TIED THEM UP! AND WE THINK WE KNOW WHO! NOW FOR THE MILLION DOLLAR QUESTION! NANCY?
NO, NO. GO AHEAD.
YOU SAID YOU USED DUPLICATES BUT LEFT THE REAL ITEMS IN PLACE, RIGHT?
FINDING A LIGHTBULB AND AN HOURGLASS IS EASY ENOUGH -- BUT WHERE ON EARTH DID YOU GET A DUPLICATE OF GRAHAM'S MAGAZINE?

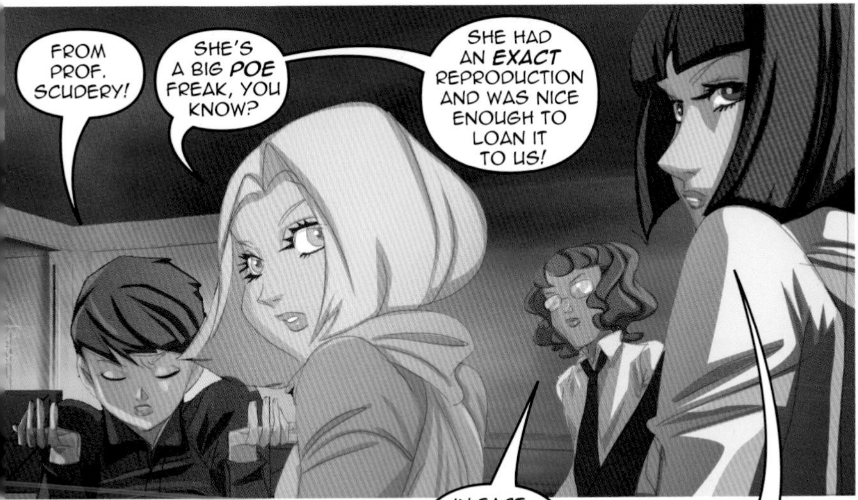
FROM PROF. SCUDERY!
SHE'S A BIG **POE** FREAK, YOU KNOW?
SHE HAD AN **EXACT** REPRODUCTION AND WAS NICE ENOUGH TO LOAN IT TO US!

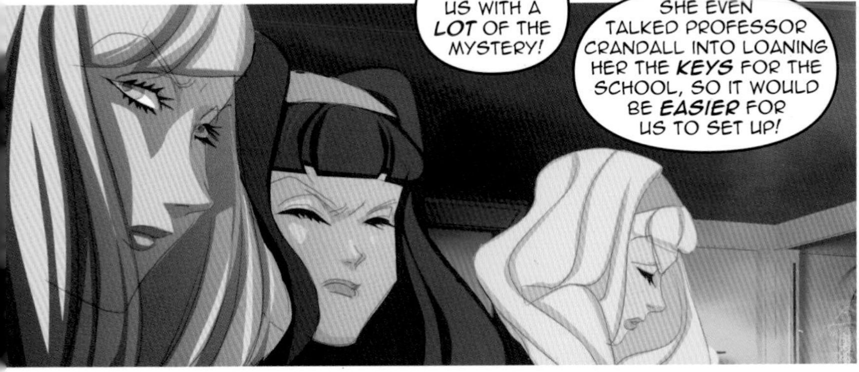
IN FACT, SHE HELPED US WITH A **LOT** OF THE MYSTERY!
SHE EVEN TALKED PROFESSOR CRANDALL INTO LOANING HER THE **KEYS** FOR THE SCHOOL, SO IT WOULD BE **EASIER** FOR US TO SET UP!

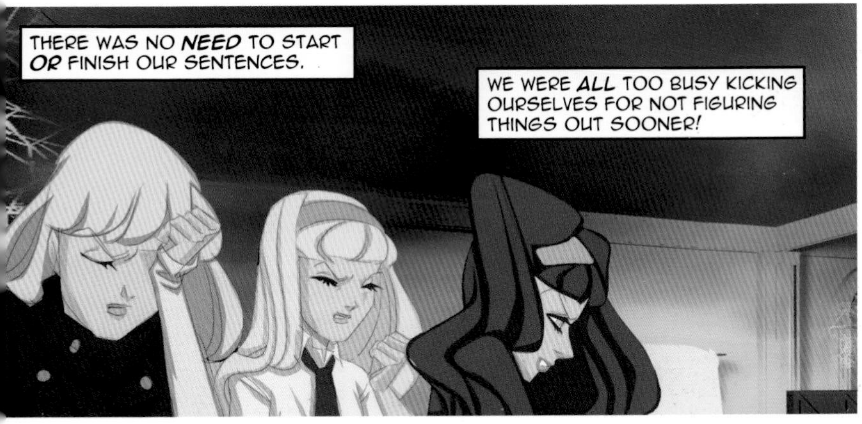
THERE WAS NO **NEED** TO START **OR** FINISH OUR SENTENCES.
WE WERE **ALL** TOO BUSY KICKING OURSELVES FOR NOT FIGURING THINGS OUT SOONER!

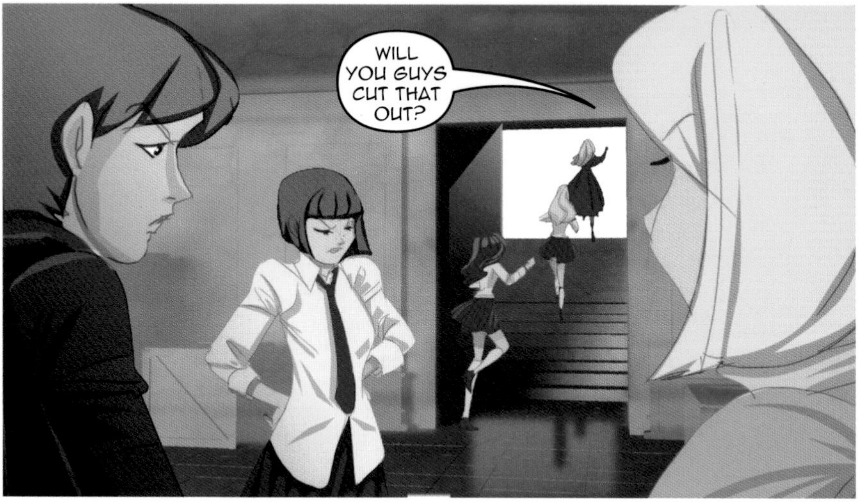
WILL YOU GUYS CUT THAT OUT?

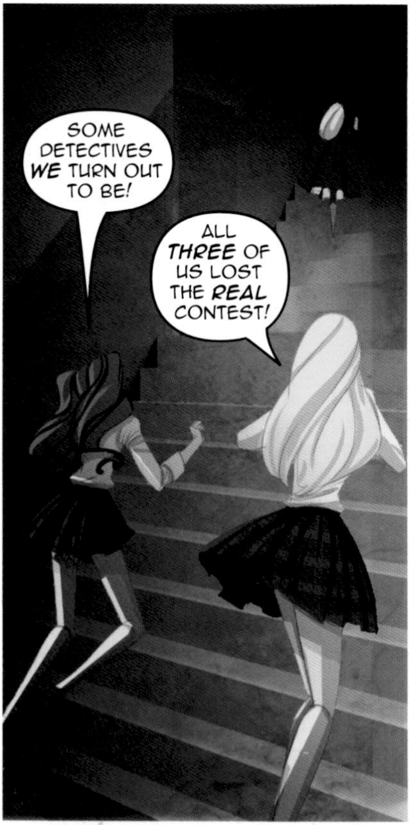
SOME DETECTIVES *WE* TURN OUT TO BE!
ALL *THREE* OF US LOST THE *REAL* CONTEST!

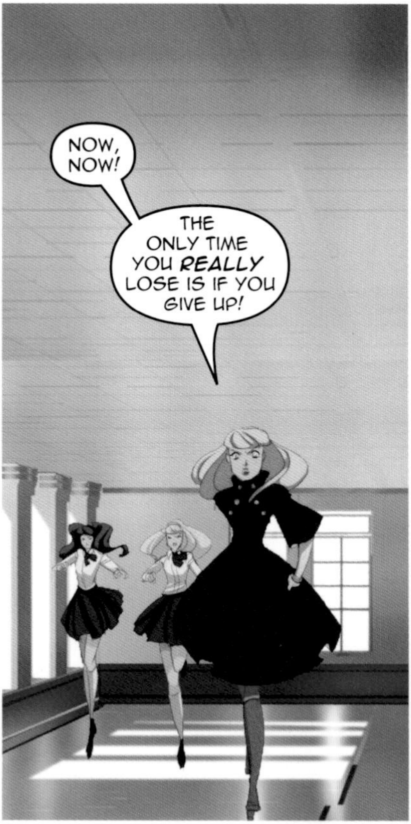
NOW, NOW!
THE ONLY TIME YOU *REALLY* LOSE IS IF YOU GIVE UP!

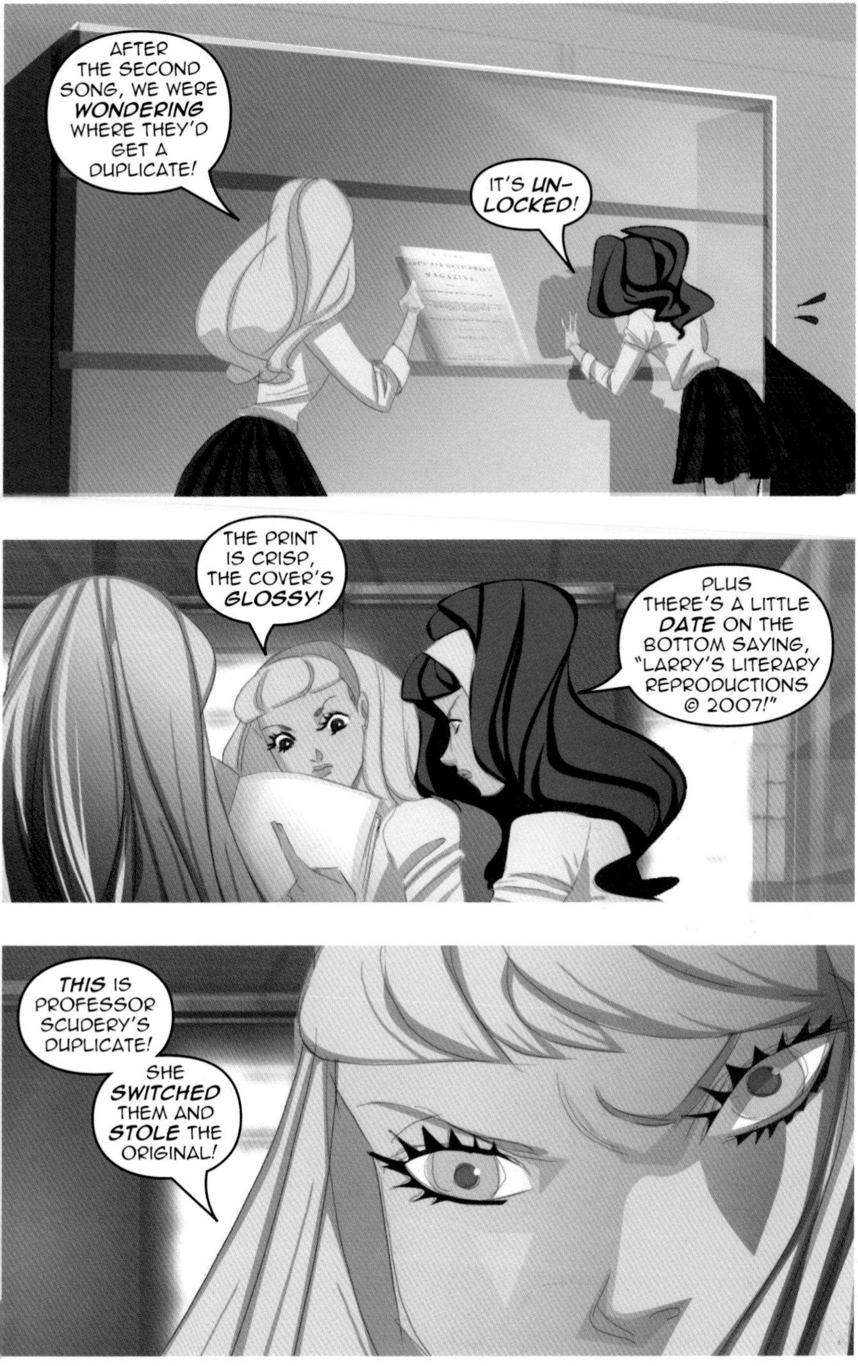
AFTER THE SECOND SONG, WE WERE *WONDERING* WHERE THEY'D GET A DUPLICATE!
IT'S *UN-LOCKED!*
THE PRINT IS CRISP, THE COVER'S *GLOSSY!*
PLUS THERE'S A LITTLE *DATE* ON THE BOTTOM SAYING, "LARRY'S LITERARY REPRODUCTIONS © 2007!"
THIS IS PROFESSOR SCUDERY'S DUPLICATE!
SHE *SWITCHED* THEM AND *STOLE* THE ORIGINAL!

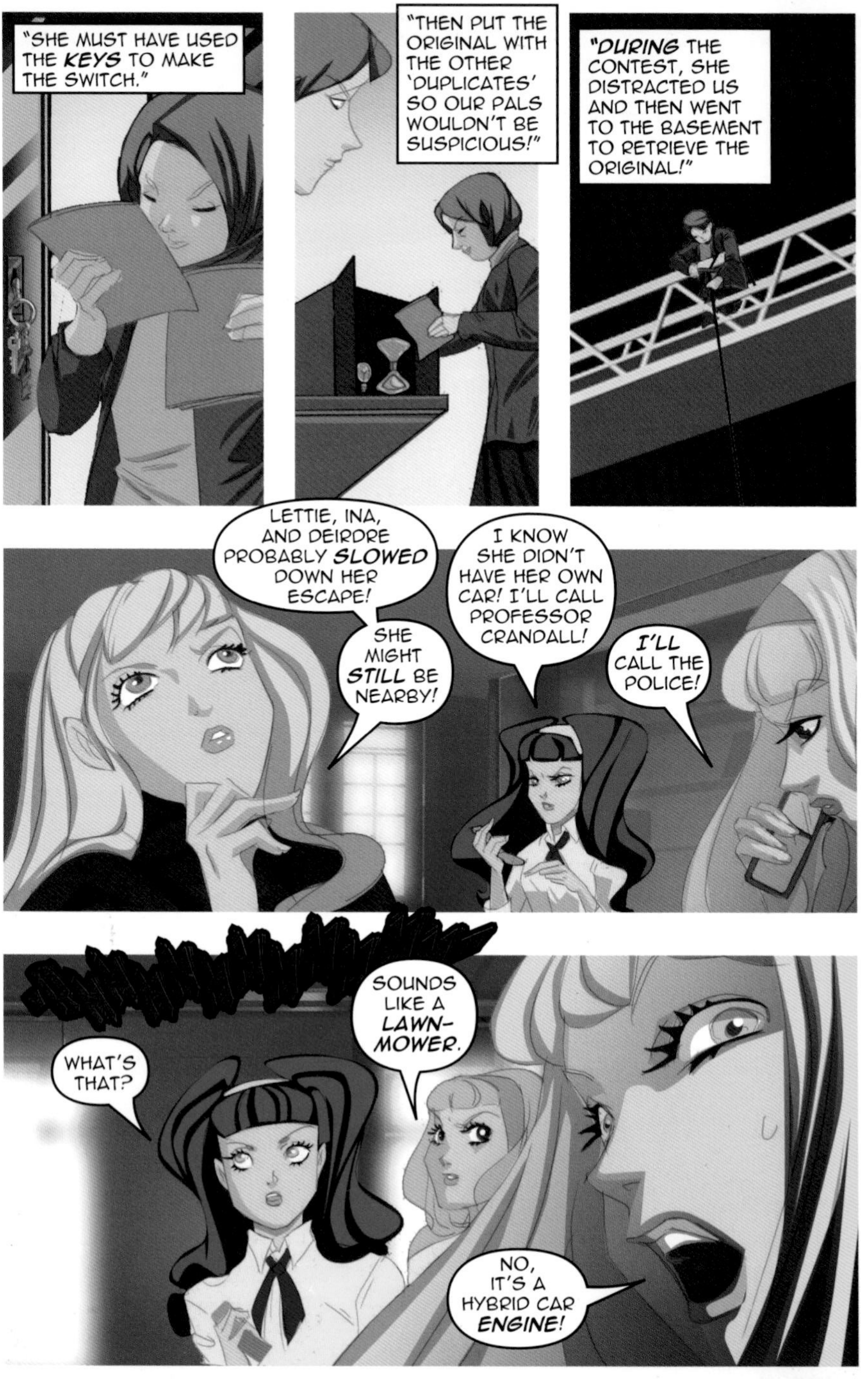
"SHE MUST HAVE USED THE KEYS TO MAKE THE SWITCH."
"THEN PUT THE ORIGINAL WITH THE OTHER 'DUPLICATES' SO OUR PALS WOULDN'T BE SUSPICIOUS!"
"DURING THE CONTEST, SHE DISTRACTED US AND THEN WENT TO THE BASEMENT TO RETRIEVE THE ORIGINAL!"
LETTIE, INA, AND DEIRDRE PROBABLY SLOWED DOWN HER ESCAPE!
SHE MIGHT STILL BE NEARBY!
I KNOW SHE DIDN'T HAVE HER OWN CAR! I'LL CALL PROFESSOR CRANDALL!
I'LL CALL THE POLICE!
WHAT'S THAT?
SOUNDS LIKE A LAWN-MOWER.
NO, IT'S A HYBRID CAR ENGINE!

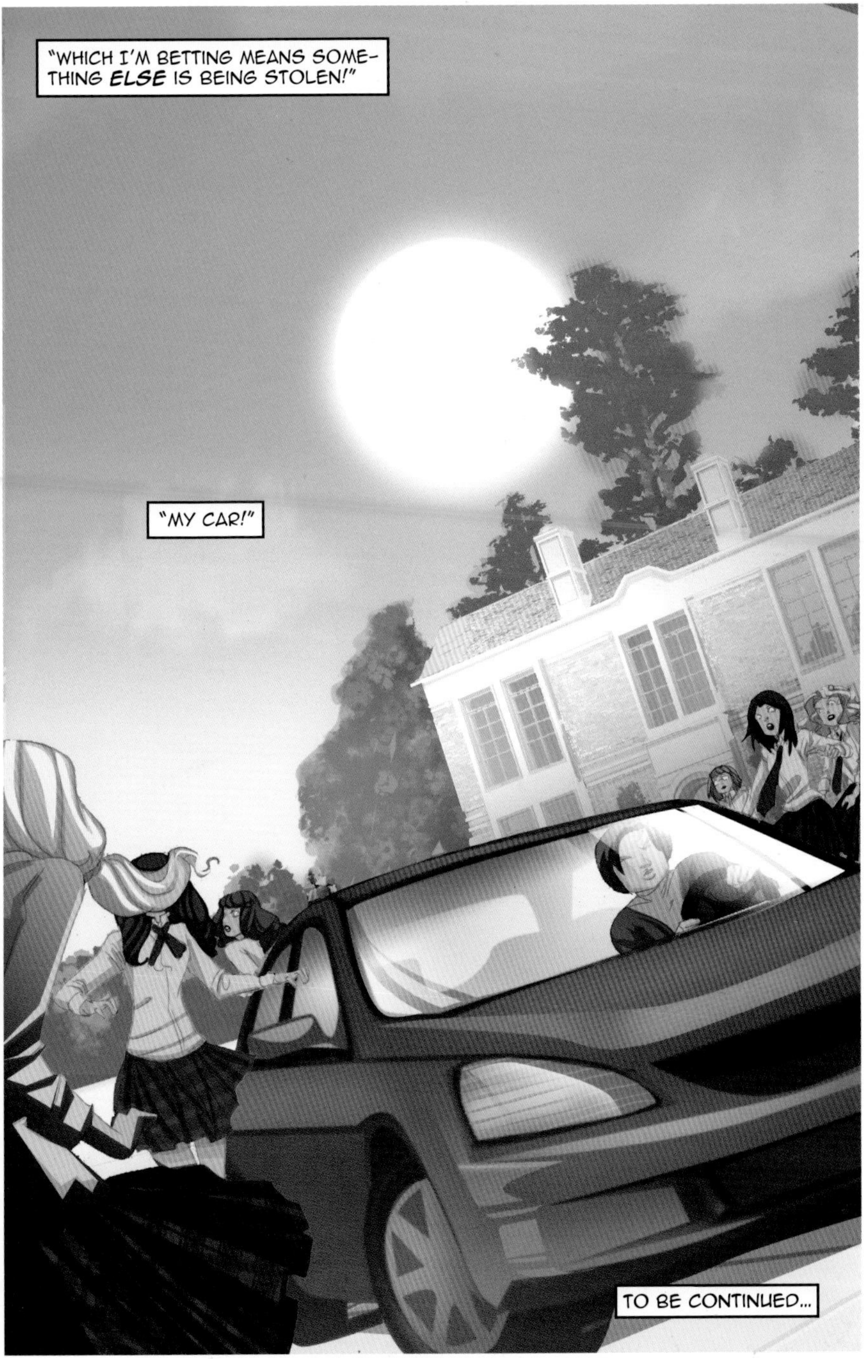
"WHICH I'M BETTING MEANS SOME-THING ELSE IS BEING STOLEN!"
"MY CAR!"
TO BE CONTINUED...

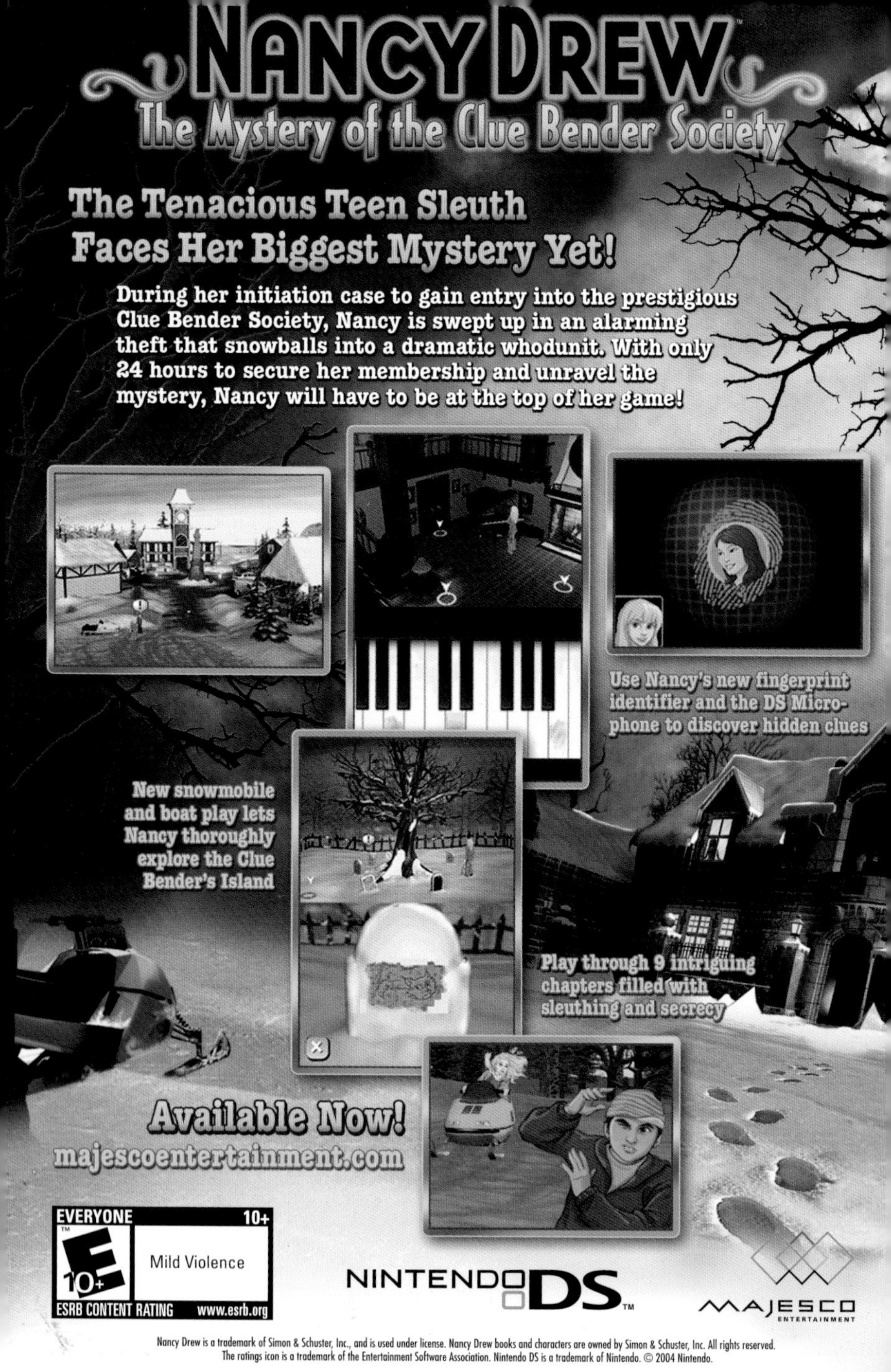
NANCY DREW™
The Mystery of the Clue Bender Society
The Tenacious Teen Sleuth Faces Her Biggest Mystery Yet!
During her initiation case to gain entry into the prestigious Clue Bender Society, Nancy is swept up in an alarming theft that snowballs into a dramatic whodunit. With only 24 hours to secure her membership and unravel the mystery, Nancy will have to be at the top of her game!
Use Nancy's new fingerprint identifier and the DS Microphone to discover hidden clues
New snowmobile and boat play lets Nancy thoroughly explore the Clue Bender's Island
Play through 9 intriguing chapters filled with sleuthing and secrecy
Available Now!
majescoentertainment.com
EVERYONE 10+
Mild Violence
ESRB CONTENT RATING www.esrb.org
NINTENDO DS™
MAJESCO ENTERTAINMENT
Nancy Drew is a trademark of Simon & Schuster, Inc., and is used under license. Nancy Drew books and characters are owned by Simon & Schuster, Inc. All rights reserved.
The ratings icon is a trademark of the Entertainment Software Association. Nintendo DS is a trademark of Nintendo. © 2004 Nintendo.

SPECIAL PREVIEW OF NANCY DREW GRAPHIC NOVEL #21 – "HIGH SCHOOL MUSICAL MYSTERY PART TWO"

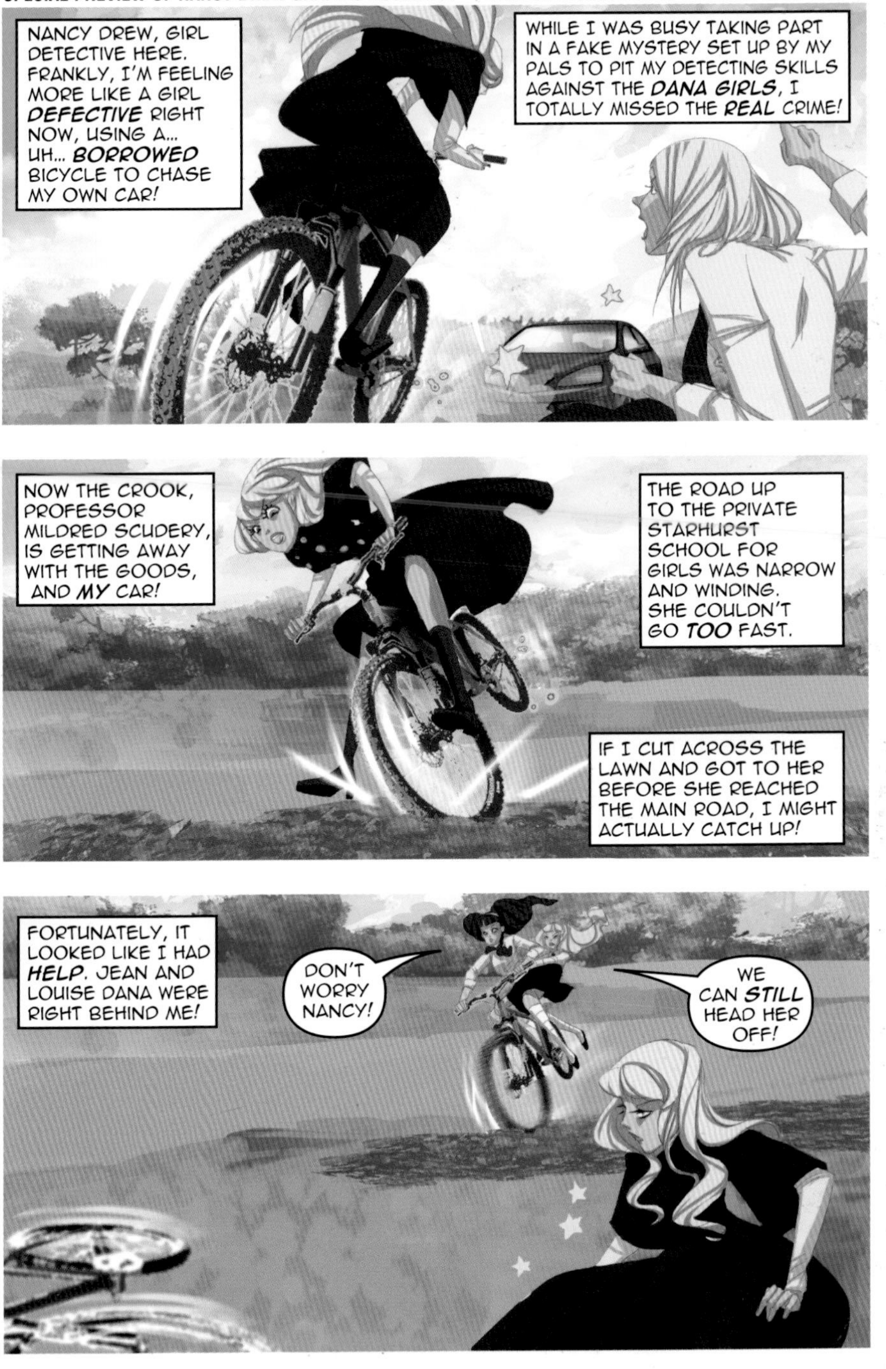
NANCY DREW, GIRL DETECTIVE HERE. FRANKLY, I'M FEELING MORE LIKE A GIRL *DEFECTIVE* RIGHT NOW, USING A... UH... *BORROWED* BICYCLE TO CHASE MY OWN CAR!
WHILE I WAS BUSY TAKING PART IN A FAKE MYSTERY SET UP BY MY PALS TO PIT MY DETECTING SKILLS AGAINST THE *DANA GIRLS*, I TOTALLY MISSED THE *REAL* CRIME!
NOW THE CROOK, PROFESSOR MILDRED SCUDERY, IS GETTING AWAY WITH THE GOODS, AND *MY* CAR!
THE ROAD UP TO THE PRIVATE STARHURST SCHOOL FOR GIRLS WAS NARROW AND WINDING. SHE COULDN'T GO *TOO* FAST.
IF I CUT ACROSS THE LAWN AND GOT TO HER BEFORE SHE REACHED THE MAIN ROAD, I MIGHT ACTUALLY CATCH UP!
FORTUNATELY, IT LOOKED LIKE I HAD *HELP*. JEAN AND LOUISE DANA WERE RIGHT BEHIND ME!
DON'T WORRY NANCY!
WE CAN *STILL* HEAD HER OFF!

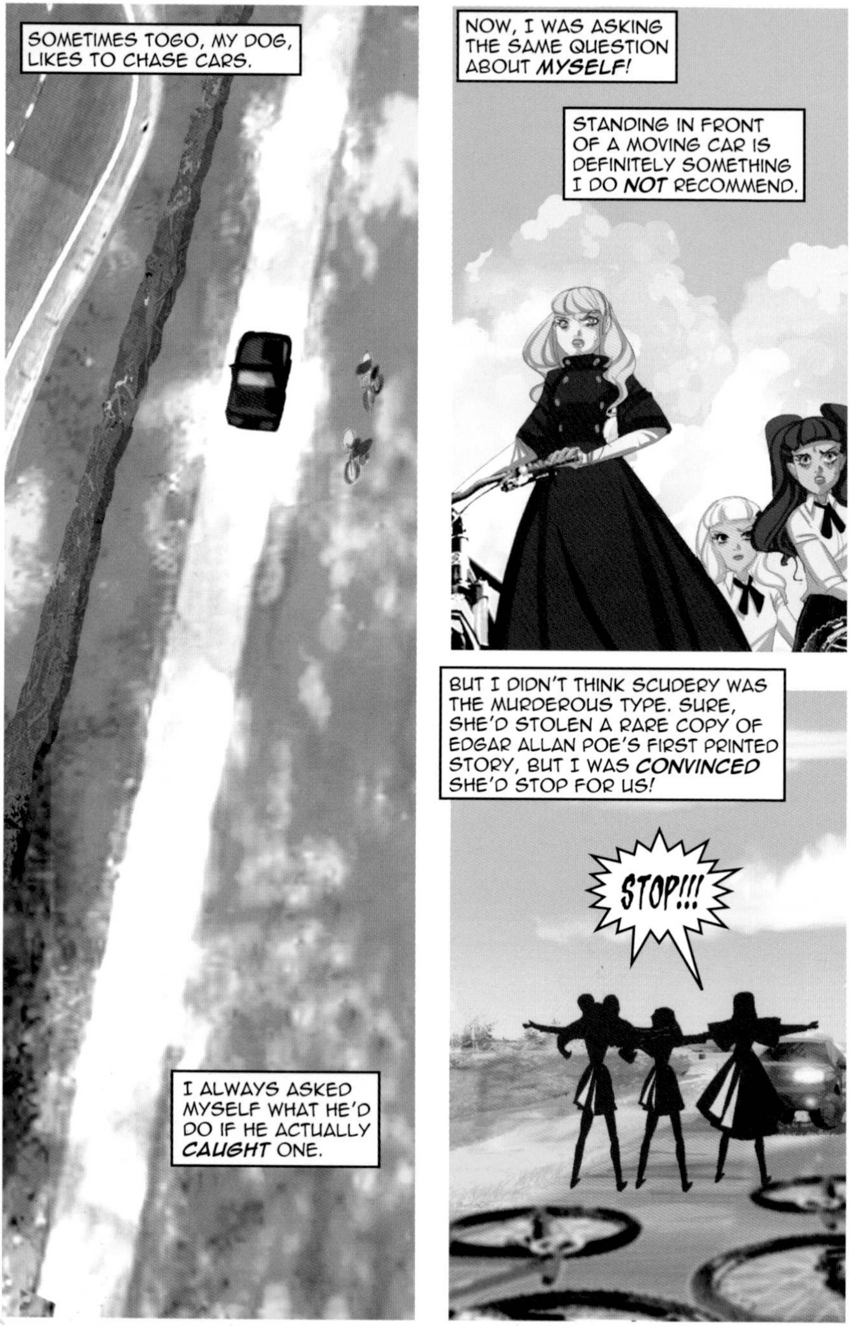
SOMETIMES TOGO, MY DOG, LIKES TO CHASE CARS.
I ALWAYS ASKED MYSELF WHAT HE'D DO IF HE ACTUALLY *CAUGHT* ONE.
NOW, I WAS ASKING THE SAME QUESTION ABOUT *MYSELF!*
STANDING IN FRONT OF A MOVING CAR IS DEFINITELY SOMETHING I DO *NOT* RECOMMEND.
BUT I DIDN'T THINK SCUDERY WAS THE MURDEROUS TYPE. SURE, SHE'D STOLEN A RARE COPY OF EDGAR ALLAN POE'S FIRST PRINTED STORY, BUT I WAS *CONVINCED* SHE'D STOP FOR US!
STOP!!!

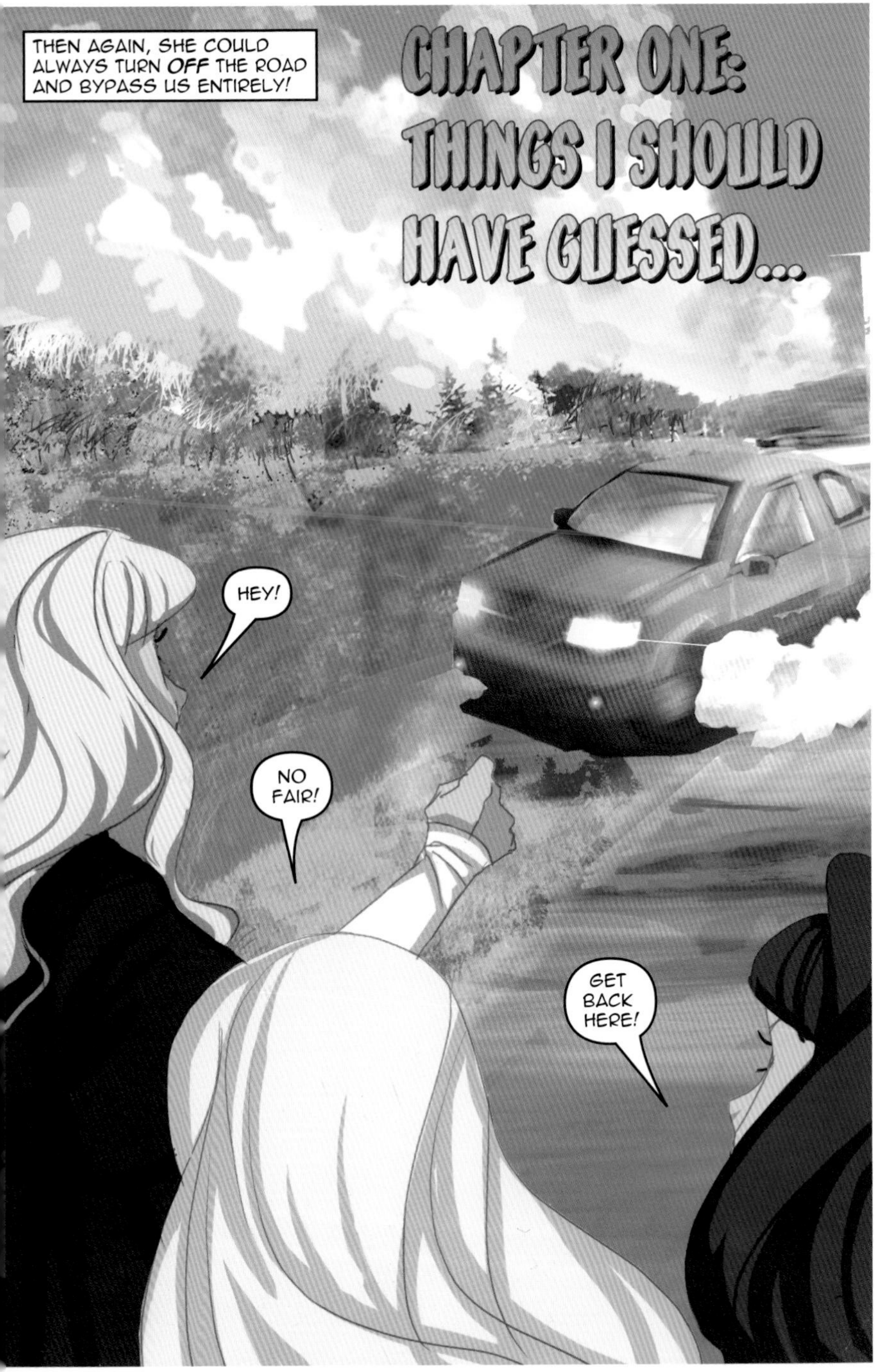
THEN AGAIN, SHE COULD ALWAYS TURN *OFF* THE ROAD AND BYPASS US ENTIRELY!
CHAPTER ONE: THINGS I SHOULD HAVE GUESSED...
HEY!
NO FAIR!
GET BACK HERE!

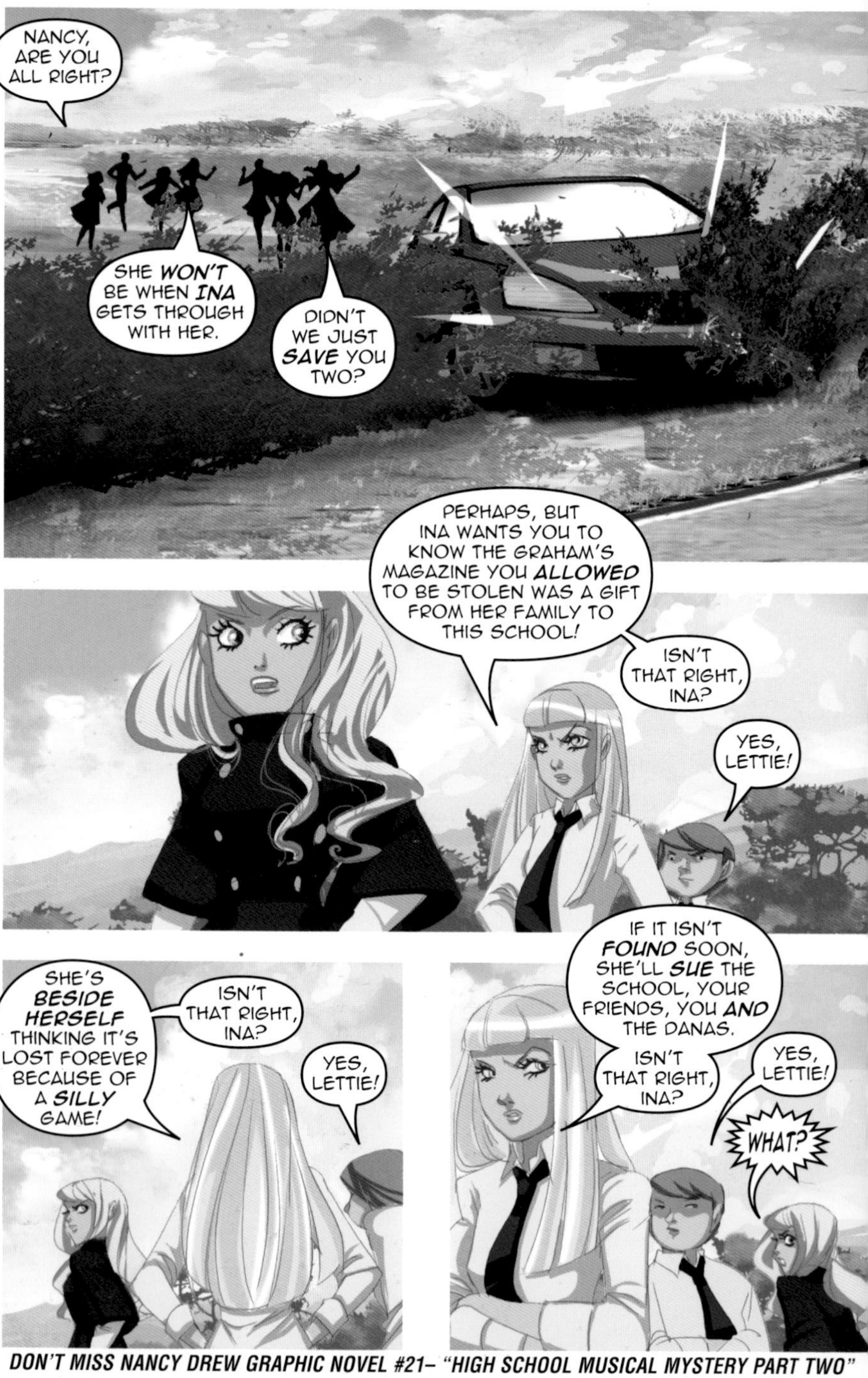
NANCY, ARE YOU ALL RIGHT?
SHE WON'T BE WHEN INA GETS THROUGH WITH HER.
DIDN'T WE JUST SAVE YOU TWO?
PERHAPS, BUT INA WANTS YOU TO KNOW THE GRAHAM'S MAGAZINE YOU ALLOWED TO BE STOLEN WAS A GIFT FROM HER FAMILY TO THIS SCHOOL!
ISN'T THAT RIGHT, INA?
YES, LETTIE!
SHE'S BESIDE HERSELF THINKING IT'S LOST FOREVER BECAUSE OF A SILLY GAME!
ISN'T THAT RIGHT, INA?
YES, LETTIE!
IF IT ISN'T FOUND SOON, SHE'LL SUE THE SCHOOL, YOUR FRIENDS, YOU AND THE DANAS.
ISN'T THAT RIGHT, INA?
YES, LETTIE!
WHAT?

DON'T MISS NANCY DREW GRAPHIC NOVEL #21– "HIGH SCHOOL MUSICAL MYSTERY PART TWO"

THE HARDY BOYS

A NEW GRAPHIC NOVEL EVERY 3 MONTHS!

#15 "Live Free, Die Hardy!"
ISBN – 978-1-59707-123-9
#16 "SHHHHHH!"
ISBN – 978-1-59707-138-3
#17 "Word Up!"
ISBN – 978-1-59707-147-5
#18 "D.A.N.G.E.R. Spells The Hangman!"
ISBN – 978-1-59707-160-4
NEW! #19 "Chaos at 30,000 Feet!"
ISBN - 978-1-59707-169-7

NEW!

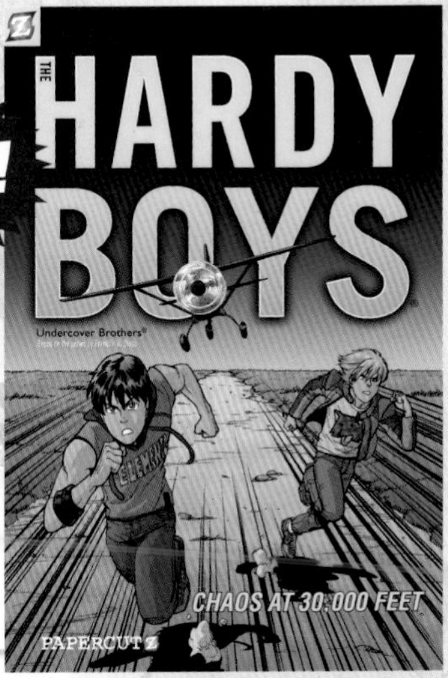
THE HARDY BOYS
Undercover Brothers
CHAOS AT 30,000 FEET
PAPERCUTZ

Also available – Hardy Boys #1-14
All: Pocket sized, 96-112 pp., full-color, $7.95
Also available in hardcover! $12.95

THE HARDY BOYS BOXED SETS

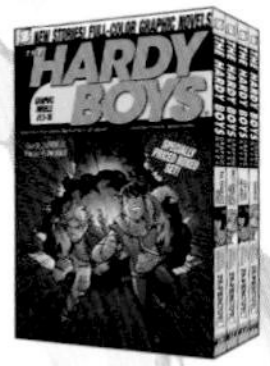
HARDY BOYS

#1-4 ISBN – 978-1-59707-040-9
#5-8 ISBN – 978-1-59707-075-1
#9-12 ISBN – 978-1-59707-125-3
#13-16 ISBN – 978-1-59707-173-4
All: Full-color, $29.95

CLASSICS Illustrated

Featuring Stories by the World's Greatest Authors

#4 "The Raven and Other Poems"
ISBN - 978-1-59707-140-6
#5 "Hamlet"
ISBN - 978-1-59707-149-9
#6 "The Scarlet Letter"
ISBN - 978-1-59707-162-8
#7 "Dr Jekyll & Mr. Hyde"
ISBN - 978-1-59707-171-0
NEW! #8 "The Count of Monte Cristo"
ISBN - 978-1-59707-177-2
Also available – Classics Illustrated #1-3

NEW!

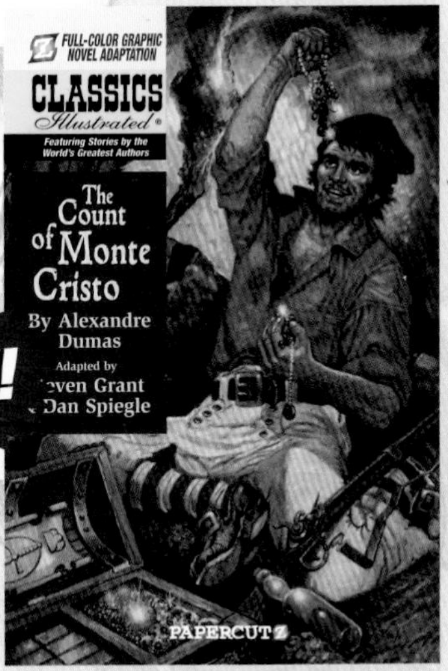
FULL-COLOR GRAPHIC NOVEL ADAPTATION
CLASSICS Illustrated
Featuring Stories by the World's Greatest Authors
The Count of Monte Cristo
By Alexandre Dumas
Adapted by
PAPERCUTZ

All: 6 1/2 x 9, 56 pp., full-color, $9.95, (except #8, $9.99), hardcover only

ON SALE AT BOOKSTORES EVERYWHERE!

Please add $4.00 postage and handling. Add $1.00 for each additional item.
Make check payable to NBM publishing. Send To:
Papercutz, 40 Exchange Place, Suite 1308,
New York, New York 10005, 1-800-886-1223
www.papercutz.com

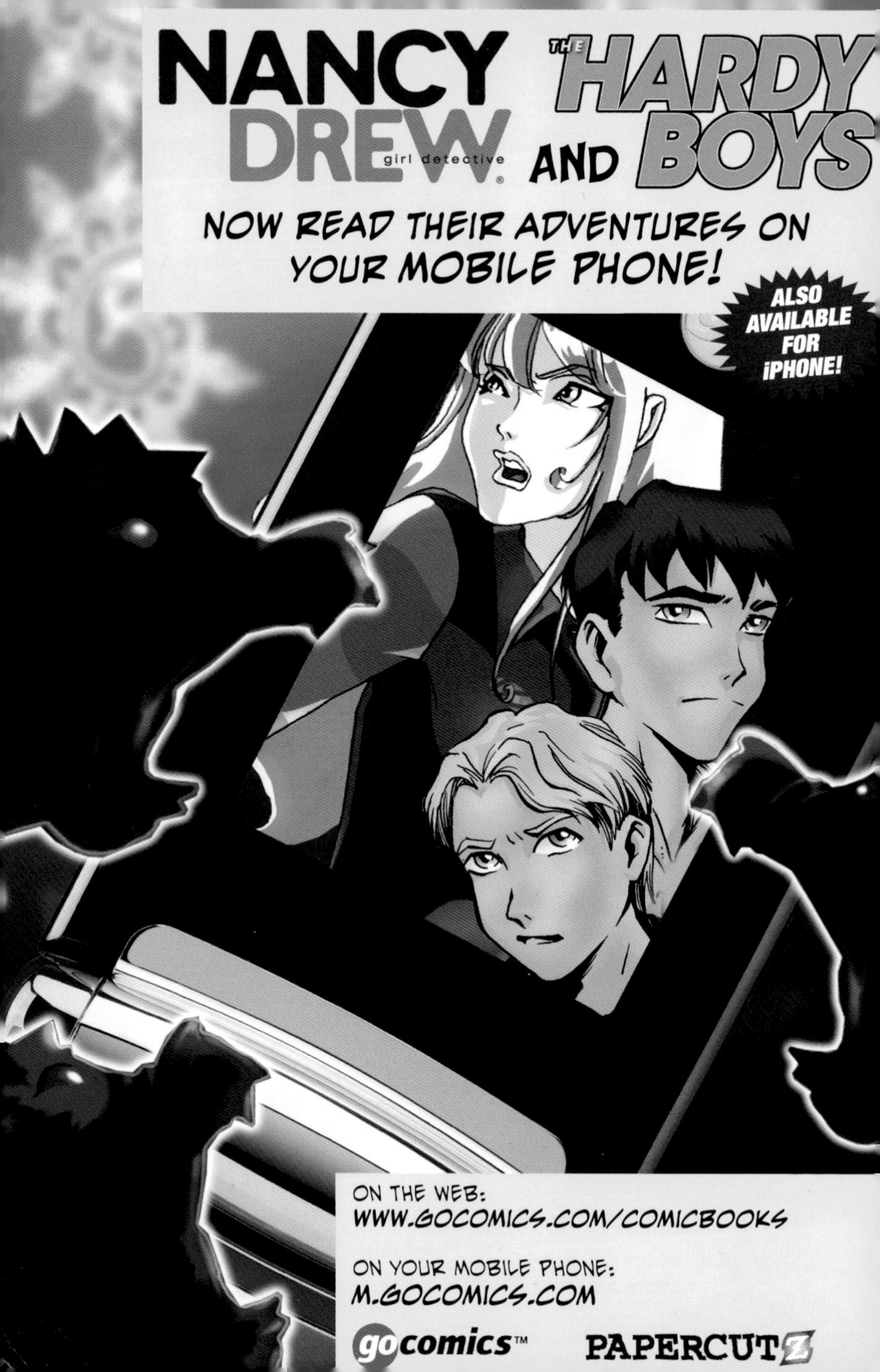
NANCY DREW girl detective AND THE HARDY BOYS
NOW READ THEIR ADVENTURES ON YOUR MOBILE PHONE!
ALSO AVAILABLE FOR iPHONE!
ON THE WEB:
WWW.GOCOMICS.COM/COMICBOOKS
ON YOUR MOBILE PHONE:
M.GOCOMICS.COM
gocomics™
PAPERCUTZ

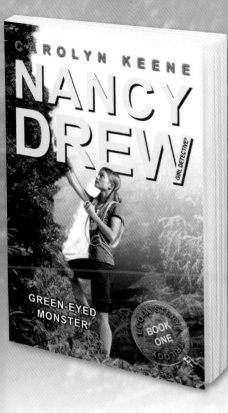
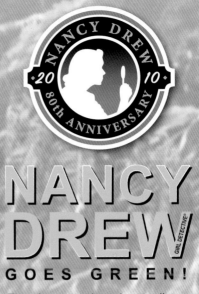
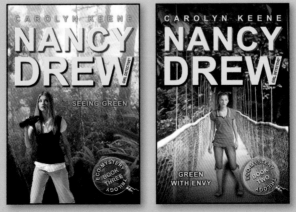

New from Papercutz

Geronimo Stilton

Graphic Novels

6 1/2 x 9, 56 pages full-color
Hardcover only: $9.99/$11.99 Canada

All-new, full-color Graphic Novel
Geronimo Stilton
THE DISCOVERY OF AMERICA
PAPERCUTZ

#1 "The Discovery of America"
ISBN - 978-1-59707-158-1

All-new, full-color Graphic Novel
Geronimo Stilton
THE SECRET OF THE SPHINX
PAPERCUTZ

#2 "The Secret of the Sphinx"
ISBN - 978-1-59707-159-8

All-new, full-color Graphic Novel
Geronimo Stilton
THE COLISEUM CON
PAPERCUTZ

#3 "The Coliseum Con"
ISBN - 978-1-59707-172-7

All-new, full-color Graphic Novel
Geronimo Stilton
FOLLOWING THE TRAIL OF MARCO POLO
PAPERCUTZ

#4 "Following the Trail of Marco Polo"
ISBN - 978-1-59707-188-8

Saving the future, by protecting the past!

Geronimo Stilton is the editor of the Rodent's Gazette, the most famous paper on Mouse Island. In his free time he loves to tell fun, happy stories. In these adventures, Geronimo has to face his worst enemies, The Pirate Cats, who have discovered a way to travel back in time and change history...

Available Now at Booksellers Everywhere. Or order from Papercutz:
Please add $4.00 postage and handling, $1.00 for each additional item. Make check payable to NBM publishing.
Send To: Papercutz, 40 Exchange Place, Suite 1308, New York, New York 10005
Or call 1-800-886-1223. MC, VISA, and AMEX accepted.

www.papercutz.com

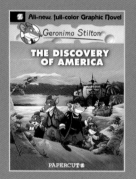

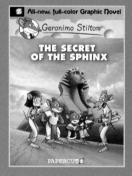

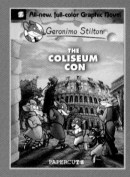

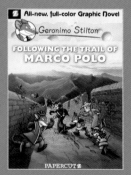

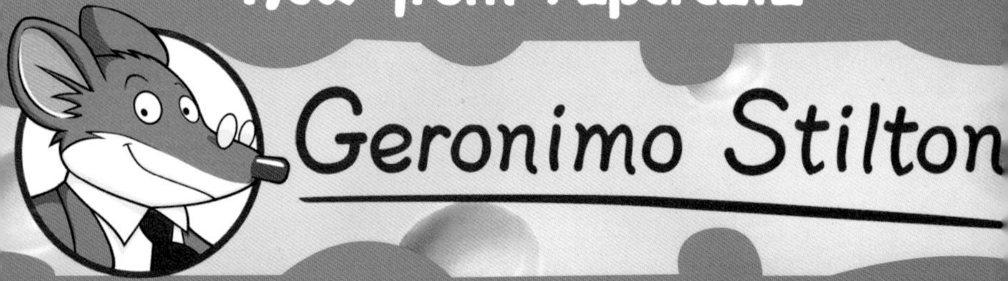

WATCH OUT FOR PAPERCUTℤ™

Welcome to the bouncy Backpages – or should that be Backbeat?—of NANCY DREW Graphic Novel #20 "High School Musical Mystery Part One." And although I may not be able to carry a tune, I'm still Jim Salicrup, Editor-in-Chief or the Maestro of Papercutz, conducting the creation of such musical graphic novels as BIONICLE, CLASSICS ILLUSTRATED, DISNEY FAIRIES, GERONIMO STILTON, THE HARDY BOYS, and TALES FROM THE CRYPT! In case you're wondering why we're in such a musical mood, we've got plenty of reasons to celebrate…

The biggest reason is that 2010 marks the 80th Anniversary of our favorite Girl Detective, Nancy Drew! Yes, it was back in 1930 when the very first Nancy Drew Mystery – "The Mystery of the Old Clock" by Carolyn Keene – was originally published. And Nancy still doesn't look a day over 18! We wanted to do something special to commemorate this truly historic literary milestone, and we thought it might be fun to finally have Nancy meet sister-sleuths the Dana Girls, who were also created by Carolyn Keene. Hard to believe they never met before!

But once Stefan Petrucha and Sarah Kinney started putting the story together, it became clear that this event was just too big to be contained in one graphic novel (Just ask Sho Murase! She's still pulling her hair out trying to squeeze in our colossal cast of characters into Part Two!), so it's also our first official two-part story. It's true! While Graphic Novels #9-11 combine to tell one awesome adventure—"The High Miles Mystery" – #9 told a complete story, and #10 and #11 were more like sequels. Likewise, with #17 and #18. And even Graphic Novel #19, ironically titled "Cliffhanger" was a complete-in-one tale.

Gee, it seems like only yesterday that we celebrated Nancy's 75th anniversary with Graphic Novel #3 "The Haunted Dollhouse"! And now that we think of it, this graphic novel also marks Nancy Drew's 5th anniversary as the star of her graphic novel series. Now, that may not be as impressive as an 80th anniversary, but we like to think we're just getting started and the best is still to come!

Before we run out of room, sharp-eyed Nancy Drew fans will have noticed that the story also features a shout out to Edgar Allan Poe's "The Murders in the Rue Morgue," which has often been called the very first detective story. To keep the celebration going, we offer a small sample of CLASSICS ILLUSTRATED #4 "The Raven and Other Poems" by Edgar Allan Poe, illustrated by Gahan Wilson. While some may find "Annabel Lee" a bit of a downer (hey, it's all about love!), "Lines on Ale" wraps our party up with a final toast—from Mr. Poe himself!

But hey, the party's not over yet! Don't miss NANCY DREW Graphic Novel #21 "The High School Musical Mystery Part Two"! Consider this your personal invitation!

Thanks,

JiM

Special excerpt from CLASSICS ILLUSTRATED Graphic Novel #4
"The Raven and Other Poems" By Edgar Allan Poe

ANNABEL LEE

It was many and many a year ago,
In a kingdom by the sea,
That a maiden there lived whom you may know
By the name of Annabel Lee
And this maiden she lived with no other thought
Than to love and be loved by me.

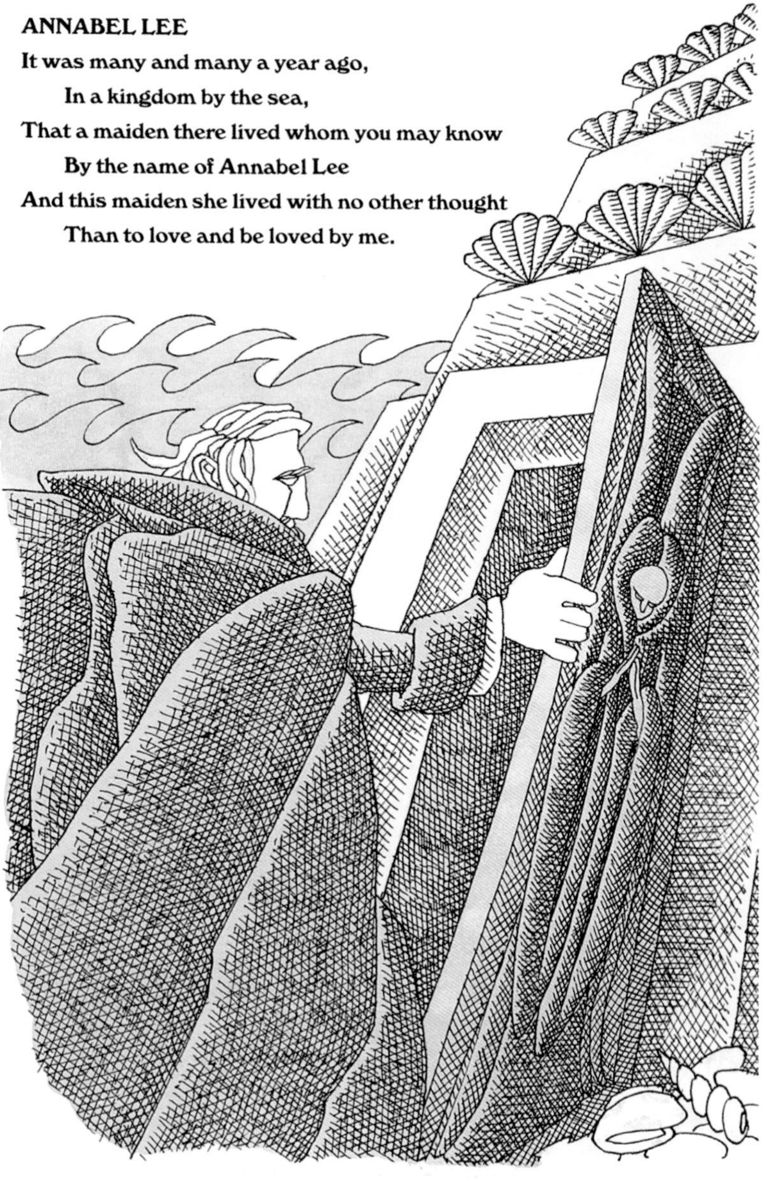

I was a child and she was a child,
    In this kingdom by the sea;
But we loved with a love that was more than love—
    I and my Annabel Lee;
With a love that the wingèd seraphs of heaven
    Coveted her and me.

And this was the reason that, long ago,
    In this kingdom by the sea,
A wind blew out of a cloud, chilling
    My beautiful Annabel Lee;
So that her highborn kinsman came
    And bore her away from me,
To shut her up in a sepulchre
    In this kingdom by the sea.

The angels, not half so happy in heaven,
    Went envying her and me—
Yes!— that was the reason (as all men know,
    In this kingdom by the sea)
That the wind came out of the cloud by night,
    Chilling and killing my Annabel Lee.

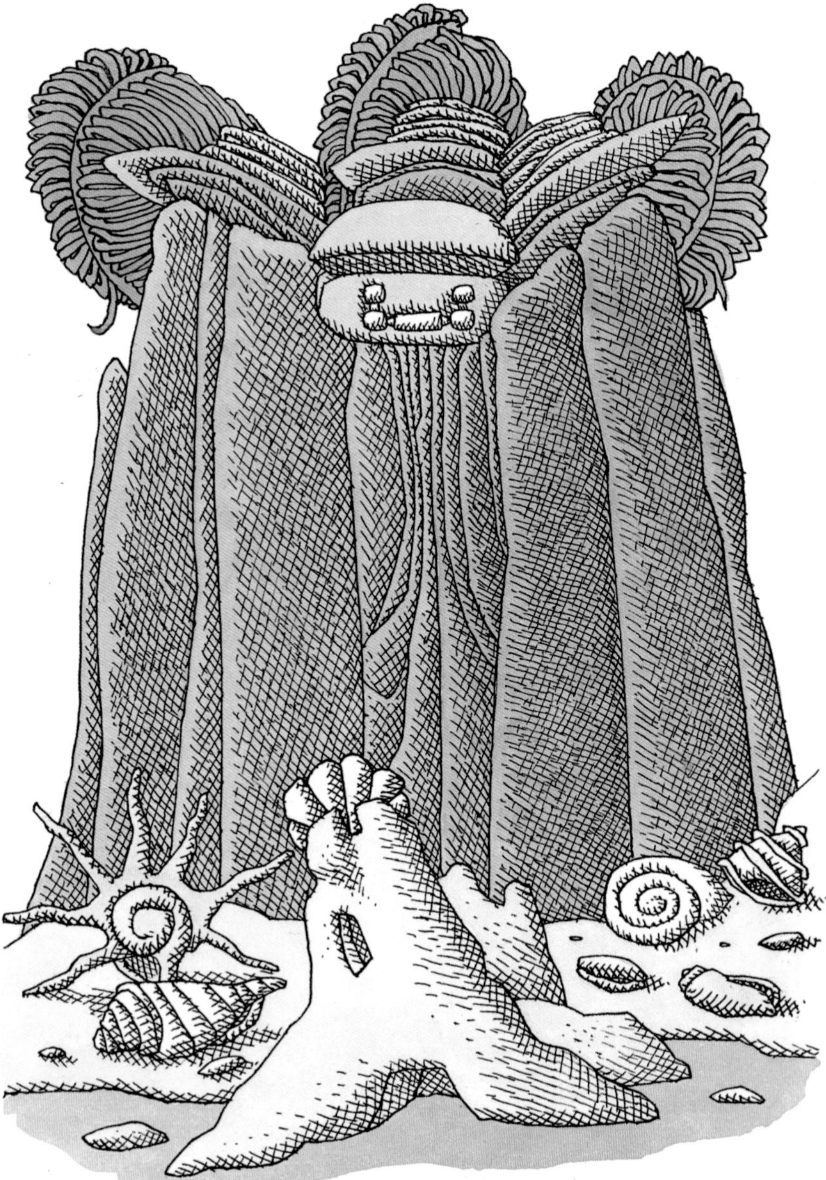

But our love it was stronger by far than the love
Of those who were older than we—
Of many far wiser than we—
And neither the angels in heaven above,
Nor the demons down under the sea,
Can ever dissever my soul from the soul
Of the beautiful Annabel Lee.
For the moon never beams
without bringing me dreams
Of the beautiful Annabel Lee;
And the stars never rise but I feel the bright eyes
Of the beautiful Annabel Lee;

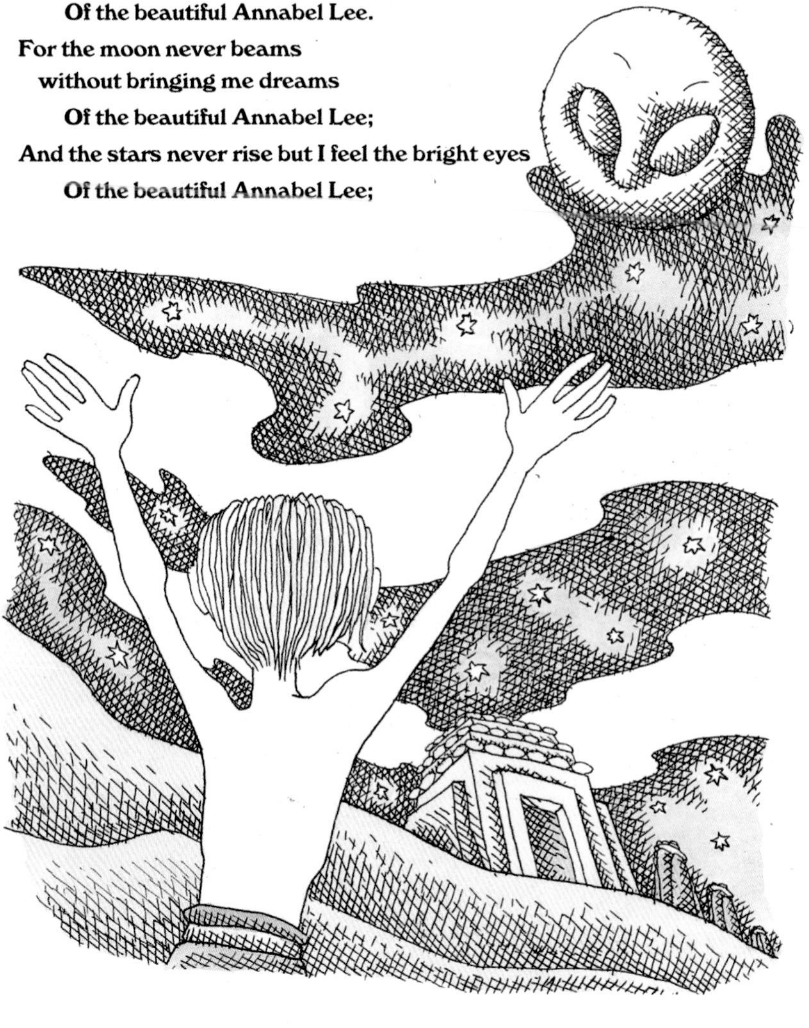

And so, all the night-tide, I lie down by the side
Of my darling— my darling— my life and my bride,
In the sepulchre there by the sea,
In her tomb by the sounding sea.

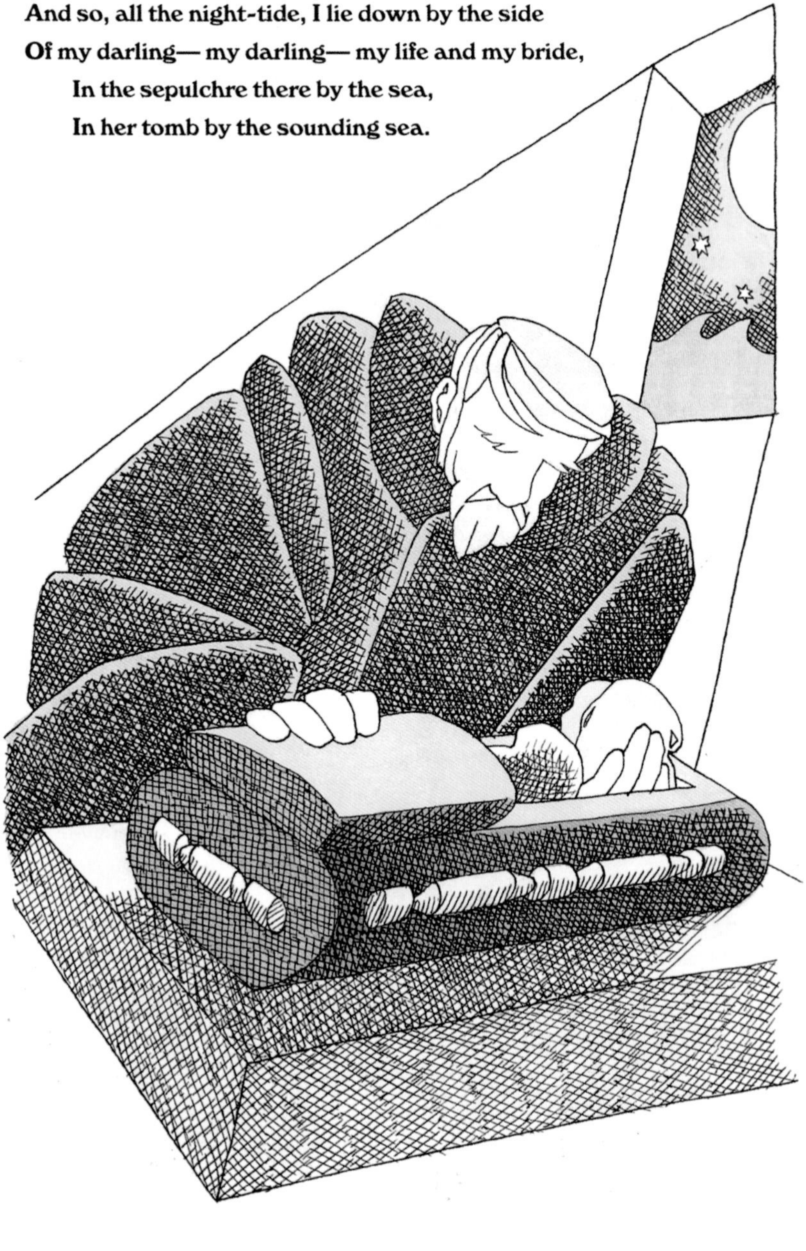

LINES ON ALE

Fill with mingled cream and amber,
I will drain that glass again.
Such hilarious visions clamber
Through the chamber of my brain—
Quaintest thoughts— queerest fancies
Come to life and fade away;
What care I how time advances?
I am drinking ale today.

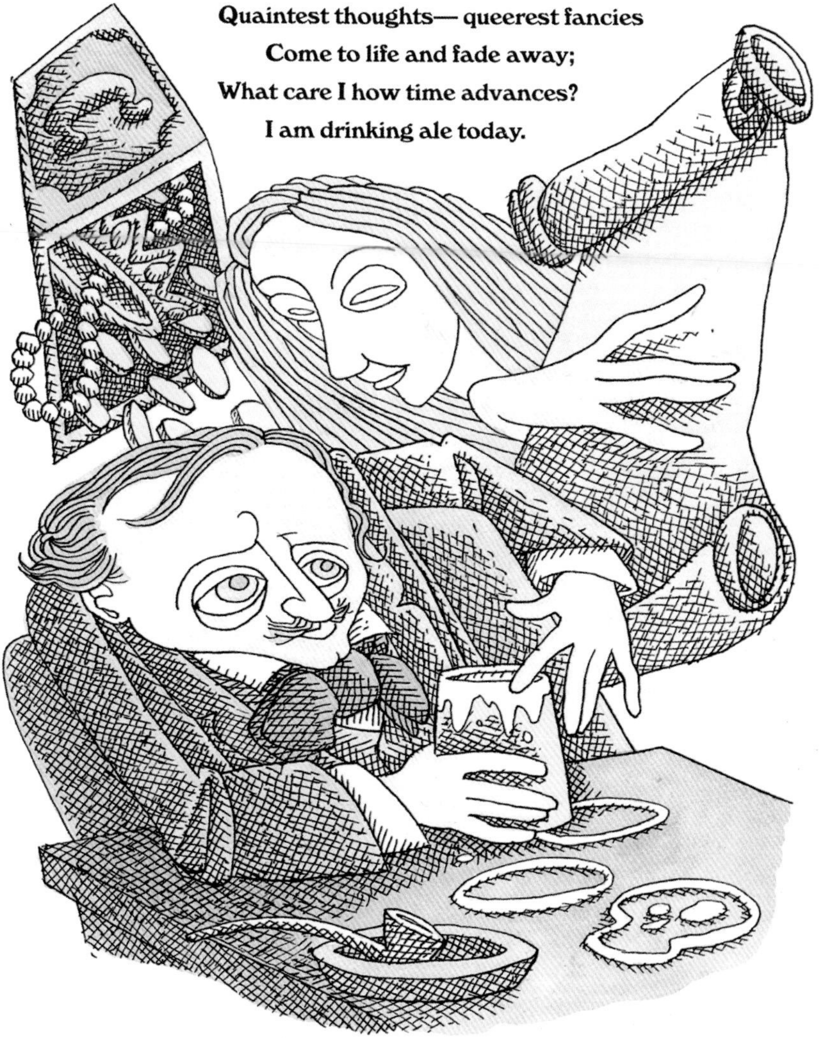

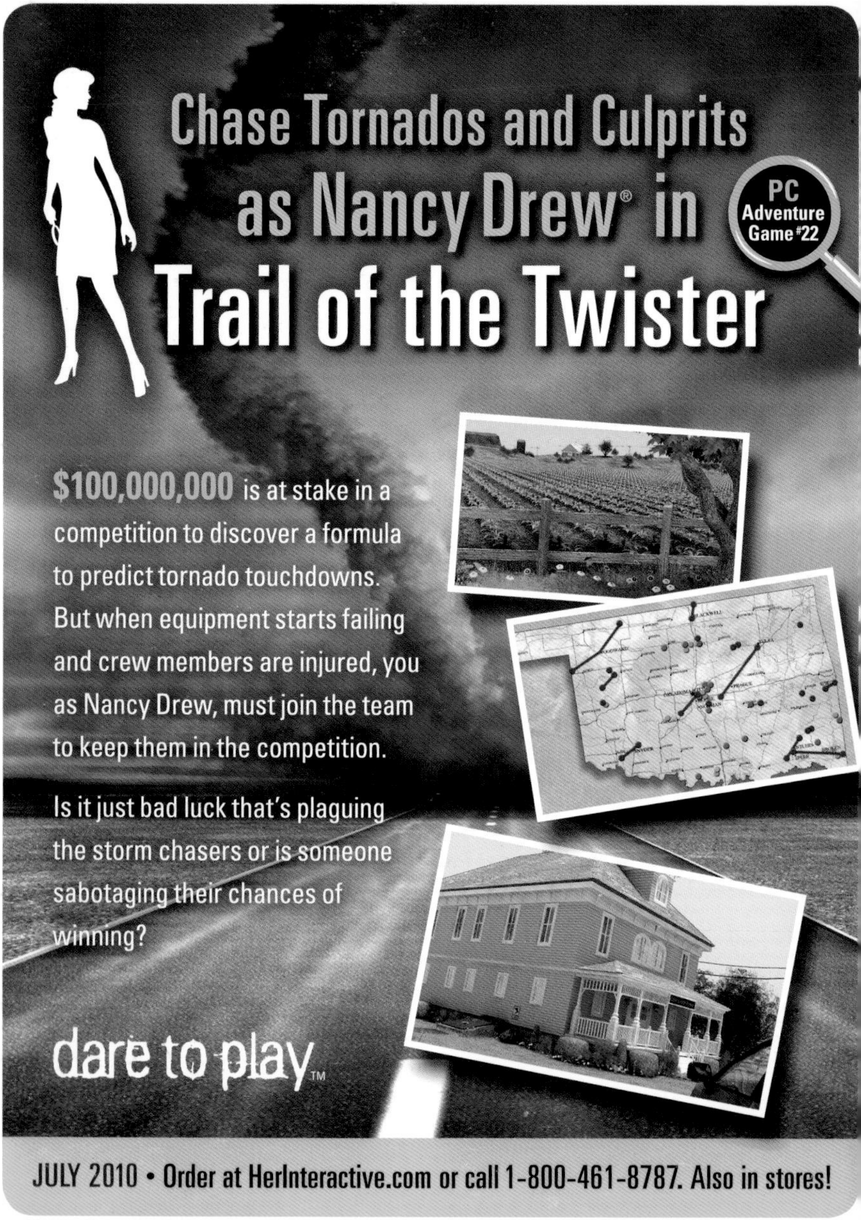
Chase Tornados and Culprits
as Nancy Drew® in
Trail of the Twister
PC Adventure Game #22
$100,000,000 is at stake in a competition to discover a formula to predict tornado touchdowns. But when equipment starts failing and crew members are injured, you as Nancy Drew, must join the team to keep them in the competition.
Is it just bad luck that's plaguing the storm chasers or is someone sabotaging their chances of winning?
dare to play™
JULY 2010 • Order at HerInteractive.com or call 1-800-461-8787. Also in stores!

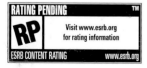